'Tough, genuine, racy – serving up London hard-boiled.' Andrew Klavan

'Refreshingly assured . . . I can't wait for her next book.' Simon Brett

'A light touch and sparkling dialogue make this the most promising first for some time.' *Irish Independent*

'Sharp and funny portrait of life in a low-rent radio station.' *Daily Mail*

'An excellent debut, with hopefully more in a similar vein to follow.' *Crime Time*

'A good, engrossing tale which should keep its readers turning the pages.' *Oxford Mail*

'A slick and cheeky debut.' Val McDermid, *Manchester Evening News*

'An excellent first novel . . . Stylish, witty and making convincing use of its West London locations, this is a highly accomplished debut.' *The Hill*

'No airport reading would be complete without a terrific thriller, and *Run Time* is just that . . . The thrill factor doesn't slacken for a second.'
Cosmopolitan

'Chris Niles' novel is brilliant.' *Eva*

'*Spike It* was one of the most refreshing novels to hit the crime fiction shelves last year . . . Fast, furious and fun . . . *Run Time* shows that Sam Ridley is a memorable addition to the ranks of crime fiction heroes.' *Sunderland Echo*

'I raved about her debut novel *Spike It* and Chris Niles has followed up with a second that is every bit as good . . . A book that is difficult to put down and I cannot wait for the next.' *Shropshire Star*

'Chris Niles could be on the verge of becoming one of the all-time great crime writers with the release of these excellent novels.' *Luton and Dunstable Herald*

Crossing Live

Chris Niles was born in New Zealand. She has worked as a TV and radio journalist in New Zealand, Australia, Britain and Eastern Europe. She currently lives on the Upper East Side in Manhattan.

Crossing Live is her third novel, following *Spike It* and *Run Time*, which also feature Sam Ridley.

Her new novel, *Hell's Kitchen*, is a wonderful comedy of murder, money and Manhattan madness. It is available in Pan paperback in February 2001.

By the same author

Spike It
Run Time

Chris Niles

Crossing Live

PAN BOOKS

First published 1999 by Macmillan

This edition published 2000 by Pan Books
an imprint of Macmillan Publishers Ltd
25 Eccleston Place, London SW1W 9NF
Basingstoke and Oxford
Associated companies throughout the world
www.macmillan.co.uk

ISBN 0 330 37599 7

Copyright © Chris Niles 1999

The right of Chris Niles to be identified as the
author of this work has been asserted by her in accordance
with the Copyright, Designs and Patents Act 1988.

All rights reserved. No part of this publication may be
reproduced, stored in or introduced into a retrieval system, or
transmitted, in any form, or by any means (electronic, mechanical,
photocopying, recording or otherwise) without the prior written
permission of the publisher. Any person who does any unauthorized
act in relation to this publication may be liable to criminal
prosecution and civil claims for damages.

1 3 5 7 9 8 6 4 2

A CIP catalogue record for this book is available from
the British Library.

Phototypeset by Intype London Ltd
Printed and bound in Great Britain by
Mackays of Chatham plc, Chatham, Kent

This book is sold subject to the condition that it shall not,
by way of trade or otherwise, be lent, re-sold, hired out,
or otherwise circulated without the publisher's prior consent
in any form of binding or cover other than that in which
it is published and without a similar condition including this
condition being imposed on the subsequent purchaser.

Visit our website at www.panmacmillan.com

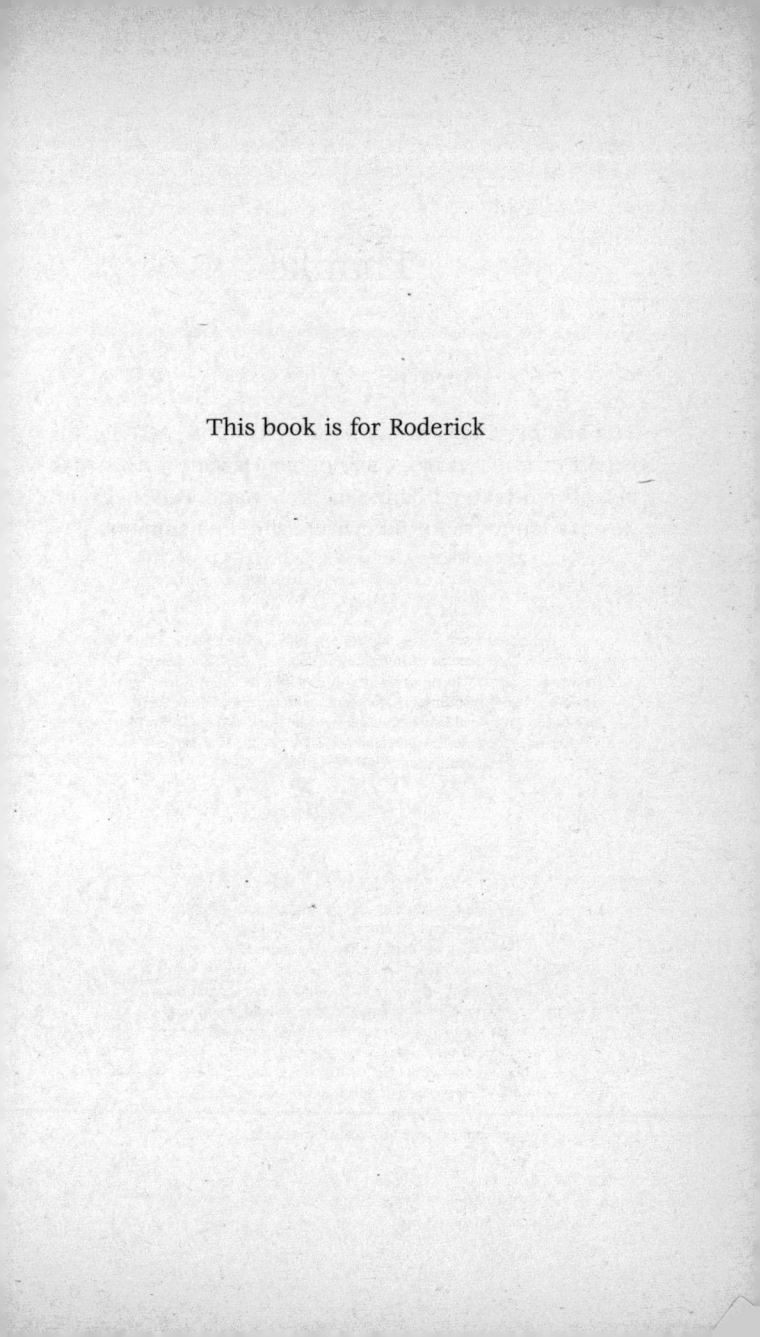

This book is for Roderick

Thanks

The author wishes to thank Reg Dixon of FACT for his expert criminal mind. Christopher Haskett for his rock 'n' roll stories and Jamie Lehrer, Carla Petschek and Beverly Huntress for their friendship and support.

Prologue

It was a typical Saturday morning. Or would have been, except for the phone call.

I left my breakfast immediately. Took a fast taxi to Shepherd's Bush. The driver dropped me at the end of the street because it was one-way. I sprinted the last heart-pounding hundred yards.

I knew the number of the house. The door flung open as I ran up the steps. My colleague Felicia Randall stood on the other side. Last time I'd seen her she'd been decked out in a red dress and high-heeled sandals. That was the night before. Now she had on jeans, a sweatshirt and boots. She was pale.

'Thank God,' she said, her voice shuddering with emotion. 'Thank God you're here.' She grabbed my hand so tight I thought it would fold in half.

'It's okay,' I said. I patted her on the back like you would a young kid.

'No. No, it's not.'

She led me into the living room. The place smelt party-stale. It was cluttered with empty bottles, scattered bowls of half-eaten party snacks. Dirty glasses doubled as ashtrays.

I eased my hand out of Felicia's and took her elbow. She wasn't steady on her feet.

'Where's Bruce?' I asked.

She led me mutely to the other end of the room. The chaise longue faced out on to the garden.

Bruce McCarthy was lying on it, on his back, one hand trailing on the ground. His handsome face still and quite calm. There was a syringe sticking out of his left arm and the crook of his elbow was a mess of blood. Blood vessels in his eyes had burst and blood dried like tears on his cheeks.

'I found him like this,' Felicia said. 'He's not breathing.'

Chapter One

I would never have met Bruce McCarthy if it hadn't been for my new neighbours. A dozy Trustafarian and her equally brain-dead boyfriend had moved in upstairs and brought with them a sound system you normally only see on the back of a truck at the Notting Hill Carnival.

They played it all the time. And they played it loud.

Most nights I lay awake listening to the distinctive thump of the upstairs party and wondered if they were vampires who'd done a tricky trade with the devil so they didn't need to sleep.

I was weary from it all. I'd nodded off at my desk a couple of times but apart from that, hadn't slept a full night since the socialites moved in. Their routine was as precise as a military establishment except that it revolved around drugs and nightclubs that played techno thrash. Most nights they'd have a pre-club party. They'd club. They'd come back and have a post-club get-together. These generally went from about three in the morning until around eight. They'd take a light nap and be up and about, leading the busy lives of the idle rich, at about ten.

That night I toyed with the idea of putting my clothes on and going up there to join the crowd who danced, drank and swallowed tiny pills. But I didn't. They were all twenty-two. If they had anything to say, I didn't want to hear it. Besides, I didn't really want to know them. I preferred hating them from a distance.

Instead I got up, poured myself a whisky, sat in my living room in the half darkness and admired my domain. It looked almost presentable, my rundown, grubby flat, softened by the outside street light. Some traffic moved by on Ladbroke Grove, the streets shiny with night rain. I thought about calling my son, Simon, in Australia but decided against it. I'd only returned from seeing him in Sydney a month ago, and I still had to face the credit-card bills. Better to write. Cheaper too. I found pen and paper and sat at the dining table.

Thump, thump, thump. Thump-thump, ker-thump.

The vibration echoed in my chest. I poised the pen over the pad. Composing the most difficult part of any letter – the opening salutation.

Thump.

Somebody fell over. The crash sounded like the ceiling was about to fall in. Voices were raised, the scuffle of a thousand rats. Then they were laughing. Then they were singing. More dancing.

Thumpety thump. Thump, thump.

The melody, if there was one, was softened by my ceiling boards and plaster so it seemed like they were playing the same song over and over again, just to taunt me.

I put the pen down, stared at my drink and cursed the style gods who'd decreed Ladbroke Grove trendy. Now every freelance PR and fashion stylist with a fat trust fund had laced up their fluorescent Nikes, moved out of mummy's place in Knightsbridge and driven across Hyde Park in their Volkswagen Golfs in search of life on the edge. Organic juice bars and neo-peasant restaurants followed in their wake. Perfectly respectable pubs had swiftly transformed themselves into palaces of neon and distressed paintwork, the old clientele forgotten as the owners fell over themselves to soak up the cash of those who didn't flinch at paying four quid for a beer. And the kiddies, unencumbered by the need to work for a living, played their little hearts out. Night and day. Especially night.

My old neighbourhood had turned into a giant college dormitory and I was starting to resent it.

I had another drink.

Thump, thump. Thump.

'Go away. You're not supposed to start till eight,' said Lyall Wilson, City Radio's chief sub-editor.

It was six in the morning. I flopped down in the chair in front of his desk and placed a cup of coffee beside his computer terminal. Lyall believes caffeine is included in the major food groups.

'The parties, the girls. I couldn't sleep.'

'Then go and nap on Alan's executive couch.' Alan Delaney, the newsroom boss, has not stinted on his furniture budget. The rest of us have to put up with chairs that wobble and desks that look like they've survived a nuclear attack but we're always perfectly comfortable when we're called to Alan's office for his little chats.

I headed for the couch. I slept.

'Sam, old-timer. Finding the pace a bit rough?' I felt a firm hand on my shoulder. I opened my eyes and saw the face of Rick Brittan, City Radio's resident pain in the arse.

'Rick,' I said, smiling just as smoothly and removing his hand. I didn't want to get oil stains on my jacket. 'Fancy seeing you here.'

For one glorious moment about four months back we thought we were to be rid of Rick. He had landed a job as a weather presenter on a local TV station. It was *the* job for Rick: he got to collect a clothing allowance and smile brightly while reading clichés from an autocue.

But it was not to be: the TV station was bought out and the new proprietors showed a startling amount of insight in deciding they didn't want Rick. The really clever part was, that instead of being jobless, he managed to worm his way back into the bosom of his former employer. In matters of staffing policy, the management of City Radio is a bit like an ageing businessman visiting a prostitute renowned for her dexterity with whips and chains: the worse you treat them, the more eagerly they return.

'It's so good to be home, amongst old friends. TV's

okay. But it doesn't have the vitality... the immediacy of radio.' He showed me his teeth, a simulacrum of a smile.

'We're so thrilled to have you,' I said. 'And I mean that sincerely,' I smiled insincerely. Rick and I have never got on. He thinks I'm a quaint relic in the flash new world of tabloid journalism. I think he's a prat.

Lyall appeared with a cup of coffee.

Rick laughed and tapped my cheek with the back of his hand. He chuckled some more, pointed his finger at Lyall and made like he was firing a pistol at him before wandering off to reacquaint himself with the rest of the newsroom.

'One of these days, I'm going to kill him,' Lyall said, handing me the coffee. 'And you're going to give me an alibi.'

I drank my coffee wandering round the newsroom. Imbibing the smell of the place, the atmosphere. The place smells of coffee. The atmosphere is what you'd expect from the last voyage on the ship of the damned. City Radio is one of the few independent radio stations in London. Grossly underfunded and understaffed we bumble along doing the best we can, keeping our spirits up by ignoring the formidable networked resources lined up against us, pretending we don't care about the ratings which show fewer and fewer Londoners give a damn about City Radio.

'Sam! I want to speak to you.' Felicia Randall waved at me from her desk on the other side of the room. I flinched. Her American accent has softened from years of living in London but she can still do the bray if she wants to. Felicia and I have a history of antagonism that makes the Cold War look like a silly playground spat, but we're edging towards détente.

As usual, Felicia was conducting three different conversations on the phone as well as writing something in a notebook. She looked up from the phone, smiled at me and then grimaced at the receiver.

'Is that right?' she said. 'How interesting.' As she said 'interesting', she rolled her eyes.

Felicia mimed extravagant boredom as the voice on the phone rattled on.

'Yes, I see. Well why don't I . . .' the other person was talking loud and fast.

'Why don't I . . .' Felicia attempted to finish what she was saying. The caller interrupted her again.

'Look. I'll . . . okay . . . why don't you fax me the details.' She replaced one receiver, although she still had another pasted to her ear . . .

'. . . no, I don't mind holding . . . that's all I ever do . . . hold . .'

She smiled at me again, drumming her fingers. A genuine, bright, pleased-to-see-you smile. This jovial creature was definitely not the Felicia I knew. I began to wonder if what I was seeing was a clever imitation and the real Felicia Randall was lying in a pod in her basement.

'Are you free for lunch today?' she asked me. 'I've got something I want to . . .'

Another phone rang. Felicia's red-painted fingers shot out, scooped it up.

'She's here already? Okay. Bring her up.' She turned back to me. 'Twelve-thirty . . . the French place on Greek Street.'

'Lunch?' I said rather stupidly. Although we were making a positive effort to be nice to one another, it hadn't yet included shared meals.

'Lunch. You know, the midday meal. Whatsamatter? You don't do lunch?'

'No . . . lunch is fine.'

'Great. You look terrible, Ridley. You should get some sleep.'

I was mustering a biting reply when a voice rang out across the newsroom. People looked up from their computer terminals.

'Darling!'

'Darling!' came the response from *Female A.M.*'s presenter, Crosbie Shaw, as she walked out of her office.

The person she greeted so conspicuously stood at the door poised like a model about to roll down a catwalk. She was a dizzy combination of tight curves and tight suit. There was enough cleavage on display to lift the spirits of all the men present. Her hair was coaxed into a feathery, modern style that didn't suit her. But nobody was looking at her hair.

Crosbie Shaw crossed the newsroom, arms outstretched. The two embraced as though they were a pair of particularly delicate china cups. There was much noisy air kissing and bandying about of 'darling'.

'Darling.' I leant closer to Felicia, lowering my voice. 'Who is that?'

'Stacy Taylor.' She pushed a thick paperback book across the desk. 'Just wrote this. Got paid a squillion for it. She's on the show this morning. Crosbie used to work with her.'

The book was called *Cut and Thrust*. The title was printed in embossed gold in letters about two inches tall. According to the back cover it told the story of an enterprising reporter who, by use of guts and talent plus the willingness to sleep with any man she met, rose to the very peak of her profession.

'Crosbie hates it,' Felicia said, wickedness in her eyes. 'Stacy Taylor was a newsroom secretary when she knew her. Now she's got a six-figure advance on the book and is married to some hotshot documentary film director.'

You wouldn't have known that Crosbie hated her. The two were chatting as though they'd been forcibly separated at birth. Crosbie had one arm draped across the younger woman's shoulders. *Female A.M.*'s brittle, work-shy presenter was known for her ability to seamlessly replicate any emotion.

Felicia gathered up her papers. Her show was about to start. I went back to my desk meaning to put in some calls. Instead I sat rather vacantly. The lack of sleep was teasing out the edges of my brain. I would get an idea in my head but couldn't persuade it to stay there. It'd sit for a few seconds then get up and wander off like a bored child. I needed something mindless and soothing, so I turned up the monitor to listen to Crosbie interviewing Stacy Taylor on *Female A.M.*

'Stacy,' Crosbie began, 'before we get on to *Cut and*

Thrust let's talk a little bit about you. This book came out of your own experiences in broadcasting?' Crosbie was sounding sweeter than normal. I wondered if she had something up her sleeve.

'That's right, Crosbie. I worked at the BBC for a number of years.'

'But only as a secretary. You've never actually been a journalist, have you? Yet your heroine is a reporter. Wasn't it difficult writing about something you have no experience of?'

If Stacy noticed the barb, she rolled with it. 'No. I found it extremely easy. *Cut and Thrust* is more of a love story, anyway... well, when I say love story, it's a love story with loads of sex. And that's something I have plenty of experience of.'

Crosbie laughed politely. A we're-all-grown-ups kind of laugh.

'Now, your husband, Nick Taylor, I think most of our audience would know who he is... his films are pretty well known... he must have helped you... with the technical aspects of television... since you've never actually worked in the field.'

'Oh, yes. Nick helped me. But with the sex part mostly. Nick was a *huge* help with that, if you know what I mean.' Stacy gurgled.

I leant closer to the monitor. Crosbie didn't seem inclined to leap in with a question.

'We did all sorts of interesting things in the name of research. Tried all sorts of interesting positions... locations. I think the book really benefited from my husband's input... as it were.' Stacy laughed a dirty laugh. Or was it a vengeful laugh? I couldn't tell.

'Er—' a dry strangled sound came from Crosbie's throat. She's not used to thinking on her feet. She's not used to thinking about anything much. She has producers to do that for her.

'For instance, Nick once came to my office,' Stacy said, 'out of the blue. He suggested we should – you know – *do it* in an edit suite. When I say suggested, he grabbed me and hustled me inside. Said we should be a bit dangerous – a bit adventurous – all in the interest of research, of course. It's the kind of thing my heroine, Chastity, would do.'

'Research?' Crosbie repeated rather dully. I would have given a week's salary to see the mayhem that was almost certainly ensuing in the control room.

'Yes, darling. For my books, sex is research,' Stacy purred. 'Anyway, so we bonked like bunnies . . . it was rather delicious. I went off and wrote up the scene right after that, while it was still fresh in my mind.'

Across the newsroom there was a mob scene as fifteen people scrambled to get their hands on the office copy of *Cut and Thrust*.

'It was very thrilling,' Stacy went on. 'Have you ever tried anything like that, Crosbie?'

'Well,' Crosbie sounded prim and shocked. 'I don't think this is . . .'

'I recommend it,' Stacy interrupted smoothly. 'But then you can always read my book and find out what it's like. If you don't have a spare man hanging around.' The words 'spare man' were subtly emphasized.

'I'm sure there's, er, lots of people out there who

want to become writers. How, er . . . how did you go about getting a publisher?' Crosbie stammered. She did not yet recognize she'd been outclassed.

'It wasn't difficult,' Stacy said. 'Everybody's interested in sex. And I like writing about sex. Not as much as doing it, of course. But writing about it . . . and getting paid – handsomely paid – for it, is the next best thing.'

My colleagues had settled the problem of who was going to get to the titillating parts first. Lyall, appealing for calm, had ripped the book into sections and was handing them out to eager journalists. You'd have thought it was fifty-quid notes the way they grabbed them. For a moment there was quiet while people scanned their sheets.

'Got one!' Rick Brittan held up his hand. The feverish crowd clustered about him, trying to read over his shoulder. He pushed them away, got up on a desk, cleared his throat and began to read.

' "Outside, the war-shattered city lay smouldering. Inside the armoured car Chastity felt safe from bullets . . . but not from the magnetic effect of the man sitting next to her. His strong, brown hands gripped the wheel of the vehicle, knuckles white from the strain of the previous few hours.

' "Chastity felt a hand, fingers slick with the sweat of fear and adrenaline, slide up her thigh. It was the first time he had touched her. A moment she had imagined many times. The feelings she had struggled to control for so long threatened to overwhelm her fragile defences. She knew she should say no. She knew she should say stop. But her voice and her will had been sucked out of her by the smell of Lance Harding's masculinity." '

There was groaning and gagging from my peers. Rick smoothed his hair, looked lazily at his fellow hacks as he drew the moment out.

' "Chastity shivered as Lance Harding's fingers proved as assured in negotiating her bulletproof vest as they were at punching out a lead story on his battered Olympia. His touch burnt her, her body responding involuntarily to the" ' . . . Rick paused for emphasis.

'Don't stop, darling,' came a droll reporter's voice. 'Please don't stop.'

Listening to the monitor, I could tell that Stacy Taylor's interview had finished rather abruptly. Crosbie had rather waspishly thanked Stacy for sharing, which meant she would be coming back any minute.

'Chaps,' I called out. But they weren't listening to me. They were listening to Rick.

' " 'You're a difficult woman to get to know,' said Lance Harding, his rich baritone voice, usually heard on the evening news by thousands, was coarse with desire. 'How many war zones do I have to crawl through before I can convince you that I want you more than any other woman alive?' " '

I didn't get to hear Chastity's answer. Stacy couldn't be far away. I tried to catch Lyall's eye. He wasn't looking. I got up and elbowed my way through the crowd. Rick was warming up to it now:

' "One hand deftly steering the heavy armoured car, Lance used the other to delve further. Chastity felt a pulsating tide of pleasure beginning at her feet. It surged slowly up towards her . . ."'

I got up on a chair beside Rick and nipped the paper out of his hands just as Stacy came through the door. There was a pause. She looked at me. She looked at Rick. She looked at the crowd.

'That's all I have to say for the moment.' I held up one hand in a gesture of admonition, stuffed the pages from the book in my jacket. 'But don't forget, it's your pension plan too and you only get out what you put in. Now we've sorted out those little problems with the fund manager – they've extradited him from Costa Rica and I can assure you he will be going to prison for a very long time – let's see those contributions rolling in.'

Stacy walked through the newsroom. The crowd melted away. I leapt nimbly to the ground. My knees sent an ambassadorial message of agony to my brain.

'Sam,' Rick did a boxing feint in front of my face, 'nice move, old boy.'

'It's called thinking on your feet, Rick. I'll tell you about it some day.' I wanted a cigarette. I wanted a whole night's sleep. I should have at least one of those things, I decided.

Stacy Taylor was smoking on the front steps when I got there. I introduced myself and asked her if she needed a cab.

'On its way,' she said. 'I don't mind waiting. I need a fag, anyway.' She offered me the packet.

I thought of accepting, then remembered Simon. He'd asked me to quit, I would quit. After all, how hard could it be? I shook my head.

'I've quit. I promised my son.'

'There's no way I'm going to quit. I don't drink and a vice-free life is not worth living, wouldn't you say?'

Just my luck, I finally meet a woman who shares my outlook on life and she's already married.

Stacy smoked for a bit and I stood as close as was decent, willing smoke my way. When her taxi drew up, I held the door open for her.

'Pension plan,' she said before I shut the door. 'I like it.'

Chapter Two

The café was crowded but I managed to grab a table from a couple who were leaving. I sat amongst the untidy clutter of used ashtrays, food-smeared plates and milky puddles of spilled cappuccino waiting for someone whose job it was to clear it off. I desperately wanted a cigarette but I ignored the voice in my head that was cooing nicotine's delights. I hadn't had a fag for a day. The worst part was surely over.

I waited ten minutes. Neither Felicia nor a single member of the restaurant's serving staff arrived at my table. The used ashtray began to smell better and better. Again I felt in my pocket for cigarettes. There still weren't any there. If I couldn't have nicotine then alcohol was the next best thing. I signalled for a waitress, but the lithe young thing in designer black had taken a degree in keeping people in their place. She swept by me, eyes firmly averted. I slumped back in my chair, drumming my fingers in a nicotine-deprived tattoo.

'Sorry I'm late.' Felicia slid into her chair and slipped off her coat in one fluid movement. 'Crosbie wanted a post-mortem. I had to put her ego back together. It's not an easy job – there's so much of it.'

She wiggled her fingers at Designer Black who appeared immediately and began clearing plates and wiping surfaces. Felicia had an authoritative discussion with the waitress about the specials of the day and ordered us both something with a French name. I didn't mind. Unless it was slathered with nicotine I probably wasn't going to taste it anyway. Two glasses of wine were ordered and appeared microseconds later.

Felicia clasped her hands together and leant over the table. She smiled broadly. Something was definitely up. Felicia has what you'd call a melancholic personality. She never smiles when a snarl will do.

'You look good,' I said. It was true. She appeared to have put on a little weight but was in good shape. Her blonde hair shone. Her green eyes sparkled. Her brightly coloured clothes and make-up were as immaculate as ever.

'Radiant is the word, Ridley,' she said smugly, taking a very small sip from her glass.

'Radiant?'

'You're supposed to say I look radiant.'

'Really?'

'Yes.'

'Oh. Why?'

Felicia sighed. 'God, Ridley, you can be dense sometimes.'

'I'm nicotine deprived.'

'I'm pregnant,' Felicia said. She reached over and grabbed my arm. 'Can you believe it? Isn't it fantastic?'

Felicia's personal life, by her own admission, is

complicated. I wasn't sure which question to ask next, so I blundered on in.

'What about the, er, boyfriend?' Last I heard, Felicia had been seeing a married man. A Frenchman who'd given her the old line about his wife not understanding him. The misunderstanding, however, wasn't sufficiently deep for him to leave his wife and take up with Felicia. The situation had been going on for a couple of years and showed no sign of resolving itself to Felicia's satisfaction.

'He's history,' she said, beaming. 'I finally told him it was over and then a couple of weeks later discovered I was pregnant. It's too perfect.'

'So what does he think?'

'He doesn't know.'

'Aren't you going to tell him?'

'Why should I? It's none of his business.'

'Except he's the father.'

'It's completely over, Ridley. I don't want him near me or my child.' She rolled the last two words – an unfamiliar conjunction – around, savouring their novelty.

'What about money? Kids need money.'

'I can do that,' she said defiantly.

Modern women. Sometimes I don't understand them, but I had no doubt Felicia would achieve whatever she set her mind to.

'There's just one problem,' she said. 'I'm homeless. The apartment belongs to Claude. I can't stay in it.'

Felicia's flat was a spacious, architecturally designed place in South Kensington. I'd always wondered how she'd been able to afford it on the risible salaries City Radio paid. A rich French lover was apparently the answer to that question.

'Has Claude got any rich sisters?'

'Sam, please.'

'I'm not fussy – fat, thin.'

'I'm trying to discuss my future.'

I took a sip of wine, thought about nicotine-flavoured alcohol and why someone hadn't come up with the idea before.

'So discuss.'

'I was wondering,' Felicia halted, embarrassed. She twirled the stem of her glass. 'I was wondering... It'll be temporary.'

'What will be temporary?'

'Can I move in with you?'

I tried to picture Felicia in my flat.

'I don't think . . .'

'A couple of weeks at most. Please, Ridley. I'll cook.'

I had my doubts about Felicia and me in such close proximity, but I had no doubts about her cooking. She loved to cook. I loved to eat her food. I'd tried it once and it was heaven on a plate. With this in mind I reasoned that it would be heartless to refuse a pregnant woman shelter. Sure we'd had our problems, but that was all in the past. We could get on for a couple of weeks. Not a problem, as my son would say.

'Okay. When?'

She squeezed my hand. 'How about tonight?'

*

Felicia arrived at seven-thirty. I heard honking on the street outside. Her red Saab pulled up and she was struggling with suitcases and boxes. I went down to help her.

'This is two weeks' worth?' I asked as I peered into the car. Every inch was jammed with possessions.

'Ridley, can we talk about this later?'

I staggered into the building with my load, Felicia hopping along at my side, issuing instructions.

Three or four more journeys and we had transferred the contents of the car into my flat, which seemed to shrink during the process.

'Got to get one more thing,' Felicia said.

She was gone for much longer than a trip to the car should have taken. I looked out the window. Her car was there, closed and empty. I decided to check whether she was okay. In my neighbourhood you can never take these things for granted.

'Sam!' Felicia gestured to me as I went down the stairs. She was standing outside the door of my neighbour Everard Montgomery's flat. She had one hand on his plump arm and – this was the strangest part of all – he was smiling. Everard's face, in my experience, has only one expression and that's pinched, suffering outrage. With Felicia on his arm he looked as though he'd been given an immoderate dose of nitrous oxide and would burst into loose laughter at the feeblest witticism.

'I was just telling Everard that I'm gonna be staying with y'all over the next couple of weeks,' she cooed. Felicia, who I know for a fact is from Surf City, New Jersey, had magically acquired a southern accent. She sounded like she'd strayed off the set of *Gone with the Wind*. 'And he has very kindly agreed to let me store some of my things in his li'l ole basement.'

'My dear, that's no problem at all,' Everard said, patting the hand that lay on his arm. 'You just bring down whatever you like and we'll *pop it away*.' He giggled. That was too much for me. I turned to go back upstairs. But not before I heard Everard asking Felicia if she'd care to join him for a glass of sherry.

I woke early the next morning with my usual ration of about ninety minutes' sleep thanks to the folks upstairs. I could hear the radio – City Radio – and the sound of the shower running. I turned over, hoping that my body would be tempted back to unconsciousness. But there's a peculiarity about the plumbing that makes this impossible. About ten minutes into a shower, the pipes clank loudly and become more urgent the longer the tap is on. I'd always meant to get it fixed, but since my showers rarely last longer than ten minutes, it hadn't been a priority.

There was nothing to do but get up. I struggled into some clothes, padded into the bathroom. It was filled with steam and smelt as close to a Swedish pine forest as the cosmetics industry is ever likely to get. Bottles, brushes and bags crowded previously uncluttered surfaces. A stack of thick, green towels which weren't mine hunched on the towel rail. I showered. The water was cold. I dressed and went to the kitchen. Warm, food-associated smells wafted around the flat.

'Nice neighbours,' Felicia said, busy with the coffee machine. 'I won't even ask if you slept.'

'They used to torture prisoners of war by depriving them of sleep. After a few days they'd start hallucinating.'

'I thought they finally turned the music down,' she said. 'But maybe I just passed out. I'm going to give them a piece of my mind.'

'I tried that. Didn't work.'

'What'd you say?'

'I asked if she could keep it down. Between, for example, the morning hours of three and seven.'

'And what'd they say?'

'She. She said, "Gotta live my life." '

'What'd you say?'

'At the volume you play your stereo, I've got to live your life, too.'

'What'd she say?'

'She grunted. Then went inside and turned the stereo up.'

'You obviously took the wrong approach,' Felicia said. 'I'm thinking violence. Want some coffee? It's Italian organic . . .'

'Pour it over my head, I'll take anything that's hot.'

Heedless of what the gossips would say, we went to work together. My head was buzzing from lack of sleep and the too much Italian organic that I took to compensate.

Crosbie was waiting for Felicia when she came in. This was an unusual event. Crosbie is always late. She's based her career around it. There was another odd thing, she had no make-up on. Her forty-something face looked blotchy and showed thread veins that didn't normally get an outing. Her usual smart outfit was replaced by frayed jeans and a sloppy jumper.

'Felicia, I need to talk to you.' Crosbie's thin hand raked at Felicia's sleeve.

'What's the matter? Aren't you well?' Felicia sounded genuinely concerned. Even though she often fantasized about having a hit taken out on Crosbie so she could replace her with someone who understood the concept of work, Felicia does have a good heart.

'No, no. Nothing like that. We have to talk. In my office. I need you to help me, I don't know what to do.'

I wanted to tag along and hear about the cataclysmic event that had caused Crosbie to leave the house without make-up. But I was cornered by the newsroom manager, Alan Delaney. His professional salesman's smile tacked on to a face that I'm sure would make even his mother feel uneasy.

'Sam. I've got a proposal that might interest you.'

A proposal, to Alan's mind, is usually nothing to do with news or City Radio. Alan Delaney is a man of many parts. Actually, it's more correct to say angles. He's sleazy New Age. He's taken all the self-improvement techniques and set them to work making money for him. Usually, this takes the form of pyramid selling schemes. A few months ago it was water filters. When he found he didn't have enough friends to offload them in ways that would make any serious amounts of cash, he switched to a product called Super Enzyme. It's a primeval pond sediment that some clever person dredged up from a dank place in Norfolk, invested with magical qualities and sold off to gullible city folk too stressed and exhausted to realize they've been conned into drinking dehydrated farm mud.

Alan often tries to woo his colleagues into joining his sales force, tempting us with tales of the money we can make. Every last one of us has turned him down. Journalists may languish on the social scale somewhere between child molesters and serial killers, but we can hold our heads up because at least we're not salesmen.

Alan was drinking a cup of his miracle product from a delicate china cup. It was dark brown and a tiny bit of it had wedged itself traitorously between his front teeth.

'Sam,' he said, waving me to his couch. I sank into it, thinking about the refreshing nap I'd had there the morning before. 'You look tired. Like to try some?' He pointed a finger at it, like a 1950s advertisement. 'I've found it really does boost the energy levels,' he chuckled as he held the cup up and tried to look as though he was more concerned with my well-being than his sales figures. 'If you're not getting a balanced diet . . .'

'I heard the DTI's about to outlaw that stuff,' I said. Just to shut him up.

It did. For a good, blissful few seconds. Then: 'Where'd you hear that?' he looked shifty.

I tapped the side of my nose. Made it appear as though I was connected to the official grapevine. Being police reporter has some advantages.

Panic wiped the smile from his face. Then he relaxed and laughed weakly so I'd know he was one of the boys who could take a joke. He remembered the business, he straightened himself up in his executive chair, drew a deep breath and assumed his I'm-a-person-with-authority look.

I knew that look. I've seen it before. It meant he was going to make a proposition that would be deeply unsatisfactory to me.

Chapter Three

'We're setting up this new show ... it's called *Lively London*. Andie Turner's going to produce it. We want to blast away the old myth that London isn't as happening at night as New York.'

I thought of the New Yorkers who'd be quaking with mirth when they heard the news.

'Happening,' I said. Delaney's slang repertoire is sadly out of date.

'We need someone with experience to help start it. We need you, Sam.'

I regarded him levelly.

'It'll only be for a week or two – till the new person arrives. You can work overnights,' Delaney rushed through that bit, 'and you can still do your police rounds in the morning.' He ended with a flourish and a beam, as though he'd just handed me a pearl of great price.

'Overnights?'

Delaney flexed his arms against his executive chair. He'd expected me to flatly refuse and he was marshalling his arguments, rehearsing what he'd say to his boss, John Marlowe, who'd then have to come down and rough me up a bit because Delaney didn't have the guts for it.

But I wasn't thinking about saying no. I was thinking about sleep. Working nights was the answer to my problems. I could sleep during the day and be out of the house when the hyperactive neighbours were dancing on my ceiling. And I'd avoid Felicia. I could have hot showers. I could have peace. I could have an approximation of my old life back.

The mere thought of it brought a smile to my face.

'I'll do it.'

'You will?' Alan looked stunned. I don't usually do anything he wants without a fight.

'Sure. When do you want me to start?'

'Tonight?'

'Great,' I said. 'By the way, Alan, you've got slime between your teeth.'

He laughed again, like I was kidding.

I went home and slept.

I woke at six and the urge to smoke a cigarette was strong. The Urge, which was a big green monster, a bit like the Incredible Hulk, was beating up my puny Will, a pathetic fellow in spectacles. Somehow I didn't think Will was going to get past the second round.

Felicia was on her hands and knees scrubbing the kitchen floor.

'What are you doing?'

She sat up, wiped her forehead with her sleeve. 'Chairing a meeting of the Security Council. What does it look like?'

'Why?'

'Why? This place is filthy, Sam. I can't cook in this kitchen. When was the last time you did anything around here? Not since the Dodgers left Brooklyn by the looks of things.'

'I happen to like it this way. I didn't invite you here to lecture me about how to run my life. In fact, come to think of it, I didn't invite you here at all.' It was the lack of nicotine talking. I couldn't smoke so I had to indulge in some other form of destructive activity.

Felicia threw down her sponge. 'Lecturing you? I'm doing you a favour. Well, slop around in your own slime. I'm going out.'

After she left, I settled down to feeling bad. Felicia had just been trying to help. And she was right, the place was a pit. I walked about a bit, noticing the grimy walls, the dingy curtains, the colourless smudges around the light switches. I made up my mind. I selected a Jimi Hendrix album, put it on the stereo and took up where Felicia had left off with a sponge and a bucket of soapy water.

A few minutes later there was a knock at the door. It was my downstairs neighbour, Everard. Everard often visits me at home. Usually it's to complain about the noise I make or the hours I keep, or the fact that there aren't any cheerful plants in my window boxes. I like to think that I give Everard's life some texture.

He'd rather not be living at the newly hip northern end of Ladbroke Grove. He'd rather be secure in old-and-stuffy Belgravia or Hampstead, but he's fallen on hard times. So he's here among the common folk, making the best of it.

'Sorry about the racket, Everard,' I said as I opened the door. 'As you can see,' I gestured with my rubber gloves, 'I'm spring cleaning.'

But Everard, for once, had not come to complain. He was carrying a large bunch of white lilies and wearing that unfamiliar smile I'd seen when Felicia moved in.

'These for me?' I put a hand out for the flowers. 'What a sweet thought. And my favourite kind, too.'

The flowers moved back out of my reach but Everard kept his smile. 'Is Felicia in?'

'No. Can I help?' I said cheerily, knowing full well I couldn't.

'I wanted to ask her whether she'd care to join me for a spot of luncheon this weekend?'

Luncheon? I thought. Do people actually still say that?

'I'm sure she'd be thrilled.'

'Really?' Everard was clearly smitten. I'd told him exactly what he wanted to hear.

'Absolutely. In fact, she was saying to me only this morning what a charming and cultured person you were. You've made a real impact, Evvie,' I said, slapping him on the shoulder.

He held out the flowers. 'Would you give these to her?'

'Sure. And I'll have her contact you the minute she gets in.'

I returned to my cleaning with renewed vigour.

Felicia hadn't returned before I left for work. I left her a note explaining about the flowers which now held pride of place on the dining table.

Although City Radio is a twenty-four-hour operation, not much really goes on at night. There's Ted Franklin, the night editor, whose brains were so mashed by a bad LSD trip in 1973 that he believes his declining mental capacity to be a side effect of all kinds of accoutrements of the modern age, things like fluorescent lights and PVC plastic. Ted runs the show with the minimum of fuss, assembling all the bulletins in the first hour, placing them in very neat piles and then settling back to internally debate important issues such as what 'Midnight Train to Georgia' would sound like if The Pips did it without Gladys Knight. A freelance newsreader lurches in from time to time, thought processes hazy from whatever chemical crutch has forced them to take this the ultimate no-hoper job, grabs the relevant stack and meanders off to broadcast to a largely uninterested metropolis. City Radio's ratings, never that impressive, whittle away to insignificance after nine at night. The strive for perfection is hard to maintain in the face of such implacable reality.

But the station likes to make periodic attempts to improve its fortunes. Hence the new show, *Lively London*.

News managers, when in doubt, tend to fall back on alliteration to create the illusion of sparkling thought.

The *Lively London* corner of the newsroom, as far away from Ted as he could make it, was buzzing with the desperation of the uncertain, underfunded and inexperienced.

'Sam. What do you know about ghosts?' Andie Turner, who used to be a production assistant on Felicia's show, had been offered the job of producer and had jumped at any opportunity to convince herself that her career hadn't stalled. Andie's bright and competent, two very good reasons why she'll never get anywhere at City Radio, which prefers to nurture the inept and the talent-free.

'Nothing. But it's never stopped me in the past.' I grinned. Andie is a fine-looking girl with the best pair of legs a lecherous satyr like me could wish for. Short skirts were in again this year and Andie is a slave to fashion. I mentally thanked the Style Politburo that had dictated there be more of Andie on show.

'Stop smirking, Sam. You can't have sex with me.' Andie had gained an attitude along with her promotion. 'Call this guy. He's got ghosts. Can you do something spooky?'

'Whatever you desire, madam.'

'Spooky and witty?'

'That costs extra.' I waggled my eyebrows.

'For a response to that, refer to my previous excoriating put down.' Andie handed over a file. I took it. Shuffled off. Mumbled something about her living to regret the day she said those harsh words. Andie just laughed.

'Do it like it's a live cross,' she shouted at me across the newsroom. 'Make it sound more immediate. Nobody will know.'

Bruce McCarthy, the lucky guy with the ghost, lived in Shepherd's Bush. I drove the radio car through heavy traffic on Holland Park Avenue, reading the file in the lengthy stops for traffic lights. McCarthy, a builder, had bought a Victorian house to do up and sell on and had discovered it came with the ghost. Big deal, I would have said under normal circumstances. But I wasn't saying it this time. For a decent eight hours' sleep I was prepared to do anything. Even interview ghosts.

Besides, London is peaceful at night. You can reclaim a sense of ownership when there are fewer people engaged in the Darwinian struggle. It feels liveable instead of overcrowded and tense.

That's what I told myself.

Bruce's place was a short distance from the Shepherd's Bush Green. It was a terraced street, identical houses all in a row.

His door had no paint on it. I knocked loudly. Music throbbed. I knocked again. Saw the doorbell and lent on that for a few minutes. Finally the music subsided and the door opened.

'The guy from the radio! Come in.'

It was a cold March night but Bruce McCarthy wore only a grey T-shirt, jeans and plimsolls. Grasping a bottle of beer in one hand and a paintbrush in the other, he had dark good looks that you see on male models in women's magazines. Firm, even features. Wide-spaced blue eyes that crinkled round the edges when he laughed. Broad shoulders and narrow hips.

He balanced the paintbrush on a can of open paint, wiped a perfectly shaped hand on his jeans and shook mine.

'Get you a beer?'

'Sure.'

He disappeared and I looked around for something to sit on.

The house, stripped back to its shell, was more roomy than it looked from the outside. The living area spread from the front of the house to the back. One end looked out on to a large garden. The other faced the street. The staircase, which didn't have a banister, clung to one wall.

'Faces due south. It'll be good in the summer. If I'm still here.' Bruce handed me a bottle. The room had one piece of furniture, a chaise longue, and it was covered in a painter's drop cloth. There was a large stereo, sitting on boxes. It had plastic draped over it. Bruce closed a couple of paint cans before using one as a seat.

'Nice place,' I said to get the conversation barrelling along. Bruce was painting broad strokes of bright blue paint on the walls in a very haphazard fashion. Like his mind wasn't on the job.

'Yeah. Would be. If I didn't have the unauthorized flatmate. Phil Spectre.' He laughed too loudly at the weak joke. I smiled, swallowed some beer. The place was cold. There was a draught coming from somewhere and it cooled my back.

Bruce stretched out his long legs and examined his shoes. They were spattered with the paint he was putting on the walls.

'Do you believe in ghosts?' He looked hard at me. There were stress lines around his eyes. Too many for a guy who was probably in his early thirties.

I shrugged. 'I've never seen one.'

'Stick around. You will.' He was obviously unfamiliar with the requirements of radio news. Faced with the gaping maw of twenty-four hours of airtime to fill, we don't have time to loiter on stories. I planned to do the interview live and get out. If the ghost could slot into my schedule, fine. If not, I couldn't afford to wait around. There was a chunk of silence while I tried to assess the situation. Bruce's foot tapped lightly. His hands gripped the beer bottle firmly.

I turned on the tape-recorder. Angled the microphone his way. Said a few words that would fool all of the three listeners into thinking we were crossing live from the studio.

'Bruce, how do you know you're living with a ghost?'

'You'll see. He usually starts about now.'

'Doing what?'

'Ghost stuff. Creaking about. Rattling his chains.' Bruce grinned, but he seemed tense. 'God, where'd I put my glasses.' He groped around a bit. I spotted them sitting on a box. 'Thanks,' Bruce said. 'Blind as a bat.'

'Did you know about the ghost when you bought the place?'

'Let's just say it wasn't included in the real-estate details.'

'And now you want to sell?'

'Hell, no.' Bruce jumped up. He went to the window and stared out, wiping one hand on the leg of his jeans again. Then he turned back and blinked at me. 'He's done me a favour. I have a lot to thank him for.'

That wasn't what his body language was saying but I let it pass. I wondered how much he'd had to drink.

'Such as?'

Bruce turned. 'Hear that?' He grabbed my arm. 'Hear it?'

I couldn't hear anything.

'He's upstairs.' He pulled me with him. 'I know where he is. Let's go and find him.'

Chapter Four

Bruce dragged me up the half-finished stairs and I kept as close to the wall as possible because of the lack of banister. Irrationally, I kept my Marantz tape-recorder hugged tight to my chest. It's a clunky old bird but we've been through a lot together and not much harm has come to me so far. Superstitiously I imagined the tighter I held it, the less likely I was to face a bad end with a lunatic entertaining visions of the supernatural.

'He's regular like clockwork.' Bruce strained ahead of me. He cleared the steps and turned right on the landing. There was less light here and I groped along behind him.

'No, not there.' Bruce came out of the first room and went into the second. 'Not in my room. *Where are you now? You cunning sod. Come to daddy. Don't play hard to get!*' He crept like a cat, his voice high and crooning. I began composing the story I'd tell Andie to explain why seven minutes of programme time would need to be filled by somebody with a firmer grip on reality.

'Here we go.' Bruce slunk out of the second room. 'He's bound to be in here.' Bruce beckoned me to follow him. The room was maybe ten feet by ten and had a desk and a filing cabinet. There was light from a small lamp which sat on top of a desk. Bruce switched it off.

'Your eyes'll get used to the dark,' he said. 'Then we'll see him.'

I couldn't see or hear anything.

'When did this start?'

'A month ago.' Bruce was distracted. He prowled the room, picking things up and putting them down again. 'He takes things and moves them. He especially likes the study.'

He became excited. 'He's gone. Come on, we'll trap him in the bedroom.' He dashed out, I followed him blindly. After blundering around in the dark, I found the second bedroom. Bruce was in there, still in the dark.

'He's gone,' he said. He turned on the light.

'Okay. Well, I'll be going—'

'Don't you want to ask me some more questions?' Bruce grasped my arm, held it tightly.

'I—'

'You don't believe me.'

'Well, I—'

'He's in my house. Every night he's in my house. He walks around, moves things. In the hallway, on the landing. Going through my papers. It's a sign.'

'A sign of what?'

Bruce didn't reply for a while, as though he was debating what to tell me. But he seemed to calm down. We went downstairs. Bruce picked up his beer bottle where he'd left it.

'Have you ever seen this, er, ghost?'

'I hear him. Isn't that enough?' His eyes searched my face, desperate for understanding of some sort.

'Well, I—'

'I'm being punished. I'm being punished,' he said. 'That's what happens, that's what they say, isn't it? It's karma, the law of the universe.'

'What are you being punished for?'

'Things, bad things. All the shitty stuff I've done and got away with. I've got clean away with it, you know that? I've been a lucky guy, I've never had to pay. But now.' Bruce's face was shining with the look of the recently converted who's muddled his belief systems. 'But now I have this feeling the ghost is telling me to put things right. I've sinned and now I should bloody well put things right. You ever get that feeling?'

'Sure,' I lied. 'All the time.'

'What goes around, comes around,' he said, 'and I can't escape. I know that now. There's no escape.'

Andie wasn't happy to hear Bruce was a non-starter. 'I don't care if he's insane,' she said. 'Who's listening at this hour who'd be able to tell the difference?' It was three-thirty in the morning and the first flush of enthusiasm for the show had faded.

'He thinks he's the next Saul of Tarsus.' I played her part of the tape to make my point.

Andie groaned, put her head in her arms. 'All right, you win.'

I spent the rest of the evening interviewing

nightclubbers about their attitude to drugs. As most of the people I spoke to were high on whatever they'd taken to make their evening go with a swing, their responses were probably not of true scientific value. But I did it anyway. I've done crap jobs before, I'll do crap jobs again. I held the picture of myself sleeping soundly to get me through the distasteful experience and tried to ignore the sharp impression that I'd just passed a sign which read: 'New Career Low'.

It didn't get any better over the next few nights but once I got into it, I was able to sleep for a few hours during the day. Crosbie cornered me at the lift one morning, as I was about to slink home. Sleep was so near I could taste it. I longed to take off my shoes and my clothes and lie down for several hours. My body was weak with anticipation.

'Hi, Sam,' she said. She looked pale. 'Can we talk?'

'Sure,' I said, suspicious. Crosbie and I never talk. I wanted to sleep but I'm also nosy. I invited her to join me for coffee at the greasy caff across the road from the office on Tottenham Court Road. She became even paler when she saw what I classed as a balanced meal to start the day.

'Tell me everything,' I said, tucking into eggs, bacon, baked beans and fried bread.

Crosbie toyed with her glass of mineral water. She averted her eyes from my meal. In an attempt to halt the ageing process she only ever eats organically produced tofu and anti-oxidant vitamins.

'I've got a stalker,' she said.

I stopped eating. Crosbie saw that she had my attention. 'He's a horrible, grubby little man,' she said. 'I thought you might know what to do...'

'... being a horrible, grubby little man yourself.' She didn't say it but the implication was clear. Crosbie has the crass tactlessness of the self-obsessed. I shoved some more food in my mouth to stop me from making a sharp remark.

'He's found out where I live and now he's always outside my house. He's started ringing me. God knows how he got my number, it's unlisted, and when I pick up the phone he just breathes at me.'

'Do you know who it is?'

'Of course not.'

'Has he approached you? Said anything?'

She shook her head.

'How long's he been doing this?'

'About a week.' She looked about to burst into tears. I felt something I recognized as pity. I knew she didn't have a partner or family. And flash designer clothes, which she did have, don't provide much in the way of conversation.

'I can't sleep,' she said. 'Every time I shut my eyes I imagine him standing outside. Waiting for me.'

'Have you spoken to the police?'

'They came round. They've done nothing. They say there's not enough evidence to do anything.'

'What about British Telecom. They can put a bar on your phone.'

'I don't want a bar on my phone,' Crosbie said patiently, as if to a child. 'I want him to stop following me around.'

'Sure you don't have an idea who it is? Most stalkers know their victims.'

It was the wrong thing to say. Crosbie stood up, angry. 'Not celebrities. We're wide open to every nutcase with a dirty mac. You sad little loser, you have no idea of the pressure I'm under. Always in the public eye... always expected to look good... I expected something more constructive from you, Ridley.'

'What would you like me to do?'

'Nothing. Just do nothing. You're as useless as all the rest,' she said, pushing her chair in with a clatter. Everyone turned to stare. 'I don't know why I even bothered.'

She stomped off, leaving me wondering exactly what had happened.

I ordered a second helping of bacon.

The flat was quiet when I got home. I pulled off my shoes and outer clothes and flopped into bed.

The doorbell woke me up. I rolled out of bed and felt my way to the answerphone and growled into it with bad grace.

'Felicia?'

'She's not here.'

'I want to speak to her.'

'You can't.'

'Who is this?'

'Sam Ridley. Who's this?'

'It is Claude.' I could detect a trace of a French

accent, which meant there was a good chance this was Felicia's ex-amour.

'Why don't you come up?' I didn't much like the idea of having a conversation over an intercom. I buzzed him in and dashed to get my clothes.

I was patting my unruly hair down as he stepped over my threshold. He looked me over more searchingly than an English person would have considered polite. He took in the ragged jeans, the creased shirt, the dark rings under my eyes and he smiled. We could be friends because patently I was not competition.

I noticed his thin hair, the nose two sizes too large for the face it sat on, and the height. Claude must have only reached Felicia's armpit. I shrugged and smiled. No time to be petty about poor old Claude, who looked most miserable.

'Felicia won't see me. She moved out of the flat. I have been worried.'

'That's what happens when couples break up. One party usually moves out.'

'Yes . . . but.' He made a gesture which seemed to imply that he thought Felicia was holding out for an expensive bauble. He looked around the flat in faint surprise. It was true it didn't measure up to what he'd laid on in Kensington.

'It's hip, this area,' I said. 'The place to be in London. You should see the restaurants around here.'

'Felicia? She is fine?'

'Yep. Very fine.' I was tempted to add 'better than I've ever seen her,' but I didn't. I've been where Claude was and it's not much fun. But then again, he was married. I steeled myself to feel no pity. This man had a life, a family, cosseted in some grand arrondissement in Paris. He had no need of anything else, especially not a single young woman who wanted a man of her very own.

'Oh.' He sank into the couch, but not before checking the seat for dust and hitching up his precisely creased trousers. Claude, like many Frenchmen of his class, was dressed in the style they imagine emulates the English country gentleman, not realizing that the only time the English wear blue and green together is on the football pitch.

He sat there for the longest time, not saying anything, looking at his shiny brogues.

'Coffee?' I enquired brightly after he showed no inclination to break the uncomfortable silence. 'It's Italian organic.'

'Her favourite kind.' His face crumpled and looked as though he might break into tears. I went to the kitchen. At least wrestling with the coffee machine would stop me from having to console him or whatever the French expect in these circumstances.

Felicia had brought with her a little Italian espresso maker which I attempted to make sense of. I was rattling it around so I didn't hear the door open and Felicia arrive.

She looked at Claude, hunched on my sofa. She looked at me, coffee cups in hand.

'You are in big trouble,' she said to me.

'Me?'

'How dare you let him in here?' Felicia dumped her briefcase and the bag of groceries she was carrying on the floor. I thought I heard the splinter of eggs. Claude leapt to his feet, wiping tears from his eyes. He stepped forward, murmuring endearments in French, holding out his arms to her. Felicia ignored him.

'It's my house. I invite who I like.'

'Thanks a lot, Ridley. That's exactly what I expect from you, you insensitive moron,' she hissed before turning to Claude and switching to French.

French is just one of the many languages I don't speak, so I wasn't able to follow their conversation closely. However, I could imagine the gist of it: she told him to bugger off, they'd been through all this. He said he couldn't live without her. She said well leave your wife then. He said these things take time, I can't do it right now, she's recovering from liposuction. She said I haven't got time, so piss off.

Or something like that.

He got the message. But as he was leaving he turned back and held some keys out. Said in English: 'Please take the flat. It's yours. I want you to have it. I can't go there any more. It would break my heart.'

Felicia looked like she was about to explode. 'Do you think I'd fall for a cheap trick like that?'

'Not cheap,' I said. 'It's probably worth half a million that place.'

'Sam. Will you stay out of this?' Felicia rounded on me.

'Please take it,' Claude was pleading now. 'I want you to be comfortable . . . not like this.' His eyes slid around the room.

'We're perfectly comfortable here,' I said, offended.

Just then the upstairs stereo began its familiar, a-rhythmic tattoo. Jungle drums cranked up so loud I could feel the beat in my fillings.

Claude shrugged. 'If you change your mind . . .' and he left, his shoulders drooping.

'Satisfied?' Felicia said after she'd shut the door behind him. 'What were you thinking, letting him in Ridley? Did you really imagine I'd appreciate coming home after a helluva day at work, feeling morning sick and coping with a hysterical Crosbie, to find the man I have just broken up with sitting in the living room? You're supposed to be supporting me, Sam.'

'I . . .'

I didn't get any further, which was probably just as well because I didn't know what I was thinking. Felicia broke down in tears. The upstairs stereo was turned up a notch and I could barely hear myself speak. So I mimed the suggestion that we go out.

There are new coffee places opening in Notting Hill every week. It's becoming hard to choose between pub coffee, art-gallery coffee, bookshop coffee or Internet coffee. We chose the old-fashioned, coffee-house coffee. At least I did. Felicia was not in the mood to take decisions. I ordered from a nice young girl who didn't appear inclined to ignore me. I liked the place immediately.

'Claude just turned up. I couldn't leave him out on the street,' I said. 'He was worried about you, that's all.'

Felicia sniffed. Her mascara was running. I handed her a paper napkin.

'I think he cares for you.'

'Fuck off, Ridley. Whose side are you on?'

'Just making an observation.'

'He also cares for Marie-Joseph and little Phillippe and precious Louis. No, I'm on my own now. I should never have moved into his apartment in the first place. That was such a stupid mistake, it put me in his debt. My mother was furious with me. She said it made me no better than an eighteenth-century courtesan.'

I smiled, thinking of Felicia well disciplined in a corset. Or maybe it was a leer because she slapped me on the arm. Then she looked up. And her face broke into a big smile.

'Sam Ridley, the ghost man!' Someone was gesturing at me from the gloomy back of the café. 'Bruce McCarthy, remember? You interviewed me.'

I did remember. Bruce was dressed quite differently from the last time I'd seen him. He had on designer jeans, a spiffy chocolate-coloured suede jacket with button-down shirt and tie. I could see the reason for Felicia's smile. Big-nosed, short-arsed Claude was wiped off the map, blitzed by the indubitable perfection of Bruce McCarthy's face and form.

Chapter Five

'I'm Bruce,' he said, reaching past me to slobber all over Felicia. Gone was the shaking bag of nerves from the other night. Bruce was on form.

'Hello, Bruce,' she said. I could have been imagining it, but her voice seemed to get lower.

'I interviewed Bruce about his ghost in Shepherd's Bush,' I explained, although I didn't think she was listening to me.

'I didn't know there was intelligent life out there.' Felicia wiped her fingers under her eyes to mop up any lingering mascara. She tried out her smile which is all the more dazzling for being rare. Bruce was impressed, I could tell by the way he altered his stance. He placed his hand on the table and bent over to be closer to Felicia.

'Sure is,' he said. 'You should come up and see my spectre.'

I was trapped in the middle of a primitive mating ritual. They giggled like teenagers. Or Bruce did. Felicia smiled an alluring smile that I'd never seen before.

'Felicia and I work together,' I said to slice through the pheromones.

'Lucky old you.' Bruce said it to me but he didn't take his eyes off Felicia. 'You're American.'

'For my sins.'

'I was just there – in LA.' Bruce plucked at his leather jacket. 'Clothes are cheap. I got this for two hundred bucks.'

Felicia nodded. 'Anybody ever said you look like John Kennedy?'

Bruce raised one eyebrow as if to say 'all the time'.

A young blonde woman stuck her head around the door of the café.

'Come on, Bruce,' she said. 'I'm double-parked.'

'Coming, Lindy.'

He turned to Felicia. 'I'm having a party tonight. Sam has the address. You'll come, won't you?'

For some reason Felicia looked at me. Seeking my approval, I wasn't sure why.

'Sam's invited too,' Bruce said. As an afterthought.

'Bruce!' Lindy wailed. 'There's a parking warden one street away.'

'You will come . . . it'll be great. I throw the best parties, ask anyone.'

'Sure,' said Felicia. 'We'll be there.'

'Don't do it,' I said after Felicia had gazed on Bruce's departing backside. I told her about the disastrous interview.

'I can't believe I said that stupid line about JFK.' Felicia thumped her forehead. 'What a moron, what a klutz. He probably gets that all the time.'

'He may look like JKF, but in his own house he acts like Norman Bates.'

Felicia just smiled serenely and patted my hand. 'I think I'm owed a little harmless fun, don't you? Before I get so big that the only males who'll find me attractive will have fins and blowholes?'

I couldn't make the party because I'd devoted my services to *Lively London*. Felicia tried to persuade me to put in an appearance before my shift started at midnight but I declined. A couple of quiet whiskies were what I needed to brace me for the inanities of the night ahead, not a roomful of screaming twenty-somethings.

But avoiding screaming twenty-somethings was an increasing challenge in Ladbroke Grove. The upstairs set began their pre-club gathering at about eight, so my flat was vibrating like a spin dryer. And my local on Ladbroke Grove had been taken over and re-established as part of a chain. It was now painted pink and served nachos and alcohol-flavoured fruit drinks. The regular clientele had left, once the novelty of gaping at young women's pierced navels had worn off.

I decided to strike out and see where fortune would take me.

Everard Montgomery glided out from his flat as I descended the stairs. 'Sam,' he said, rubbing his hands together, 'care to join me for a sherry?'

There was nothing I cared for less.

'I'm on my way out, Ev. Thanks all the same.'

'Wait—' Everard's podgy, pale hand stretched out,

imploring. 'I think I can find some whisky, if you'd prefer that.' He almost winced as he said it.

I knew why. Everard had once told me in a fit of weakness that his father, before the irreversible decline in the family's fortunes, had regularly had a single malt bottled for him at a select distillery in Scotland. When his father had died he left the bottles to his son.

'Maybe I'm not in that much of a hurry,' I said shamelessly.

'Is Felicia—?' Hope gleamed in his little lashless eyes.

'Out, I'm afraid.'

'She hasn't got back to me about luncheon,' Everard said, issuing me inside his gloomy flat.

'She's been busy. She has a terribly important job.'

'Yes, yes. Of course.'

I sat in one of Everard's delicate, antique chairs chosen by one of his ancestors specifically for the degree of discomfort it could inflict upon the sitter. Everard poured me a generous millimetre of whisky into a cut-crystal glass.

'Don't hold back,' I said, jovial as only the person who holds the whip hand can be. Everard wanted something and I had a fair idea what it was.

Everard grimaced as he obeyed my instruction. It seemed to cause him actual physical pain to pour his father's expensive booze out for a person he considered to be an uncultured clod. Teeth clenched, sinews stiffened, he handed the glass over.

'Down the hatch,' I said before I slugged it back.

It was flat-out cruel but I couldn't resist. Everard's jaw got so tight he was going to need a hydraulic winch to open it.

'Not bad,' I said. 'Does Oddbins stock this stuff?' A cool silence met my remarks. Everard looked like a guy who'd just been told the barbarians had not only breached the gates but were running amok with sex toys in the queen's bedroom. I was never, ever going to be invited to drink anything with Everard again, not even if ten Felicia clones moved in upstairs, but what can I say? Sometimes being petty is too much fun to pass up.

The whisky was actually so close to perfect that it was difficult to talk at all. Drinking it, I suddenly understood what inspired poets. But I wasn't going to tell Everard that. He expected me to behave like a plebeian, and I hated to disappoint.

Everard took a sip from his sherry. It slurped through his pursed lips.

'I invited you here to ask you something.'

'Sure,' I said. 'But first, any more of that booze sloshing round?'

Everard got up, took my glass, recharged it. Returned it to me. I had the very strong feeling he wished I were dead.

I took the second glass slower. Savouring it when I thought Everard wasn't looking.

'. . . about Felicia.'

'Shoot.' I was probably overdoing the false bonhomie, but the whisky was singing inside me.

'Is she? . . . Does she? . . . Is there someone . . .?'

'A boyfriend?'

'Yes.'

'Well, it's a delicate question,' I said, looking at Everard's short, plump frame and plain face and wondering in which parallel universe he thought he had a chance.

'How delicate?' The way he said it, smug like a lizard, you knew he thought he was just the man for delicate love situations. The 007 of the brokenhearted.

I assumed a cryptic look. My mind gleefully shuffling through the lies I could tell – and I'd thought my Friday evening wouldn't be any fun. Everard had leant forward, eagerness shone in his eyes. He thought he was in with a chance. Pity skewered my plans to string him along.

'I think you should ask *her* that.'

'I thought you could tell me first . . . how the land lies,' he said stiffly, realizing he might have just wasted two glasses of his dead father's finest. 'One doesn't want to make an arse of oneself.'

'Indeed one does not,' I said, heartfelt. One jolly old chap to another. How did we British manage to cobble together an empire with such a crippling fear of social discomfort?

I finished off the whisky. It made me happier than sunshine. I put the glass down. Stood up. Patted him on the shoulder.

'Take a chance, Everard. All of life's great achievers do.'

*

At work, Ted Franklin came bustling up to me with a sheath of papers in his hand. 'I'm getting together a petition,' he said. 'About the lighting. She', he stabbed his finger at Andie, deep in conversation with someone, 'won't listen. She doesn't care what this stuff does to your brain.' He waved wildly at the overhead lights. 'I told her we can do without them. It's worked perfectly well in the past. But she', more wild stabbing, 'won't take me seriously. This *is* serious, Sam.' Ted is normally a sensible person. For some reason the subject of fluorescent lighting sends him over the edge.

'You know what these things do. They're the curse of the twentieth century. Did you know what the inventor said about them?'

I did know. Ted had told me this story several times before. Andie gestured at me to get over and start work. I was already late. I edged towards her. Ted followed me.

'. . . never be used in peace time. That's what he said. They were for the war effort. For a national emergency, Sam. We have to do something.'

The night passed slowly. I finished my shift and treated myself to breakfast at the Blue Skies, my favourite hangout.

The Blue Skies is not a fashionable dining establishment. There's no danger of running into supermodels or rock stars within its grimy four walls. In food terms, it's the restaurant equivalent of a pair of velvet flares with a peace sign stuck on the backside. I'm sure the chef reads all the latest edicts about cholesterol and fat and preservatives and the ever lengthening list of things we put in our mouths on a daily basis that can kill us and then he goes straight back to his business of dishing out fried everything with a piece of parsley on the side just for ironic effect. And he does it with pride.

'You haven't been in,' Pat, the waitress, said grumpily as I took my seat. She banged a cup of coffee down.

'I was in Australia.'

Pat sniffed, as though that didn't rate as an excuse in her book and went off to convey my order to the chef.

'I brought photos of Simon,' I said as a peace offering when she returned. I got them out of my pocket and slid them across the table. Pat has met Simon several times but I often think doesn't really believe someone that sweet could be related to me. I'm sure she suspects I hire him for special events to impress my friends.

She wiped her hand on her apron. Reached out for the packet. There were pictures of me and Simon in baggy swim shorts cavorting at various beaches around Sydney.

'He's grown quite a bit,' she said, shaking her head. Looking at me with understanding. 'Such a shame.'

I knew what she meant. 'Yeah. A shame is what it is.'

My pager went off as my meal arrived. It instructed me to call Felicia urgently and left a number that I didn't recognize.

'Sam, thank God.' Felicia sounded overwrought. At first I couldn't tell whether she was laughing or crying.

'What's up?' I said cheerily, before I realized she was gasping as though she was hyperventilating. 'Felicia? What's the matter?'

'Sam . . . I . . .' More heaving breaths.

'Sit down, love. Take your time.'

I waited, hand clenched to the phone, horror scenarios flashing through my mind. Felicia had been at Bruce McCarthy's party. If he'd laid an unauthorized hand on her, I promised myself, I'd make him sorry.

'Sam . . . I'm sorry . . . I can't . . . can you come out here?'

'Where are you?'

'Bruce's place . . . come as quick as you can. Please.' She started crying. Sobbing like a child.

'What's wrong?'

'Something awful.'

Chapter Six

I crouched down beside Bruce. Stepped around the pool of vomit. Felt for the pulse in his neck. The skin was cold. There was no pulse. The smell of faeces, urine and blood was starting to make me feel ill.

I stood up. It occurred to me that I could really have done with a cigarette. Maybe even two. One straight after the other.

Felicia was biting her thumb. 'What do we do? What do we do?' she mumbled over and over.

'How'd he get like this?'

'How should I know?' Felicia snapped, some of her old verve returning. 'Looks like he did it himself.'

She wandered around the room, starting absent-mindedly to clean up the party remains.

'Don't touch anything.'

'Oh, right. Of course.' She brought her hand back as though she'd been stung. 'Of course.'

I decided to check the place over for any other nasty surprises.

I took the stairs, Felicia following reluctantly. There was a small landing with four doors leading off it. The first was Bruce's bedroom. An unmade futon blocked out most of the space. A TV set and a stack of video tapes sat in one corner. There was a full-length mirror leaning against a wall along with a couple of framed art posters. Another wall was taken up with a built-in wardrobe that was partially finished. The shelves were stuffed full of clothes and building equipment. Paint brushes, drop cloths, empty cans. And a half-packed suitcase. I remembered Bruce saying he'd just got back from Los Angeles.

There was a large sash window which looked on to the back garden. The early morning sun seemed indecently bright. I shaded my eyes as I looked out at identical houses on the opposite street. Nobody stirred.

The second room was the office we'd sat in the other night waiting for Bruce's ghost. In proper light I could see Bruce had a shabby oak desk and bookshelves made of bricks and planks of wood. There were magazines, papers and boxes of files jammed haphazardly on to every flat surface. I flicked through it for something to do.

'You told me not to touch anything and you're going through Bruce's papers?' Felicia said, incredulous.

'Just curious.' But I stopped. Felicia was right to be horrified. I had to learn to curb my snooping instincts. And I would. Just as soon as I'd finished looking around.

There was another bedroom, empty except for a couple of ladders and a work bench. Beyond that was a bathroom, newly done out in turquoise patterned tiles. There was nobody in there.

'Let's just leave right now,' Felicia said. 'Nobody will know we were here. C'mon. Let's go.'

I grabbed her, shook her gently.

'I've been in this situation before,' I said. 'Believe me, we have to call the cops,' I said. I guided her downstairs, led her to a crate, sat her on it. 'And when they arrive they're going to want to know what you were doing here. I think we should run over your story so it's straight.'

'Straight?' Felicia snapped. 'Are you implying that I did this?' She looked at Bruce's body, looked away with a shudder.

'No. Just tell me what happened.'

'I came back.'

'Why'd you do that?'

'Just let me tell it, okay?' Felicia shifted her position on the crate. 'I left the party about one-thirty. I went home and slept for a while then the neighbours woke me and I remembered I'd left my scarf behind. My father gave it to me and I'd hate to lose it, so I got dressed and came over to get it. I thought the party would still be going.' She surveyed the room. 'Instead, I found this.'

'How'd you get in?'

'The door was ajar.'

'Find the scarf?'

'On the floor.'

'How did Bruce act at the party?'

'Charming and nice – until his ex-girlfriend turned up. You remember Lindy – she was with Bruce when I met him?'

'The dizzy blonde.'

'Right. She turned up late, a bit pissed, I suspect. She gatecrashed, Bruce told me. They had a row because he was dancing with someone else.'

'Who?'

'Me.'

'What happened?'

'She didn't stay long. She dragged him out in the garden and they had a screaming match. Then she stomped upstairs, got her coat and left, vowing to make him sorry.'

'How did Bruce take it?'

'Sheepishly.' Felicia wound her scarf round her hands. 'I'm in trouble, aren't I?'

'No.' I found the phone.

'Don't bullshit me, Sam. You know how these things go. Am I a suspect?'

'Everything'll be fine,' I said as I dialled the emergency services.

The car swerved into the street the wrong way. The siren seemed indecently loud for a lazy Saturday morning. Two uniformed officers got out, came to the door and introduced themselves. Felicia showed them the body. Soon the plain-clothed team and forensics arrived, elbowed the uniforms out of the way and wrote notes and made sketches in their notebooks. Dusted things and measured.

Another cop arrived. He was the boss, judging by the way everyone deferred to him. He was tall with grey hair and a stomach heading south. There was stubble on his face which either meant he'd been up all night or been yanked from his Saturday lie-in. He introduced himself as Detective Inspector John Jennings and asked us politely if we'd accompany him to Shepherd's Bush police station. Just as politely we said yes.

The uniforms showed us to the car. There were people outside, staring at us. Felicia's composure was steely. She didn't say a word on the journey to the station.

'I've never been in trouble with the cops in my life,' she whispered as we were taken up the front steps of the station. 'I've never ever been inside a police station.'

'You're not in trouble now,' I said. 'They only want to ask you some questions.'

They took us to separate rooms. John Jennings disappeared with Felicia and I was palmed off on to another officer. He took me to a small office and divested me of all the information I had about Bruce McCarthy, which took about five minutes. Then he asked me the same questions all over again. Everything I said was dutifully recorded and noted in the officer's spiral-bound notebook. I fancied a cigarette badly. I asked for one. I got tea instead. It was weak and sugared but I took it. The officer then left me alone and told me to wait for Felicia.

I sipped the tea, in an empty office, watched cops and various other sundry hangers-on go past the half-glassed walls. Thought about cigarettes and wondered if death from lung cancer could possibly be as bad as the pain of giving up.

There was a knock at the door. An attractive

brunette in a black leather jacket, swinging a Nikon camera, stood there.

'The morning press conference is which way?' she asked cheerfully. 'I'm quite lost.' She grinned, showing me teeth that were just as perfect as the rest of her.

'I thought I saw some shabby looking specimens troop that way a few minutes ago.' I pointed down the corridor.

'Thanks.' She waved and was off again. I went to the door to prolong the view of her leaving.

'What are you gawking at, Ridley?'

Felicia had come from the opposite direction. She had a junior cop in her wake.

'Typical. I'm undergoing the worst experience of my entire life and you're lusting after stray females. Sam, you're like an animal, you know that, don't you? Take a look at yourself. You're slobbering.' The jolly good mood didn't quite extend to her eyes. There she still looked shaken and afraid, but she was making an effort, that was something.

We went home. I slept and Felicia rang her mother. I got up at six in the evening, feeling strangely better than I had in days and Felicia suggested we go out for dinner to a new restaurant she'd managed to blag her way into. It seemed a more attractive option than my usual Saturday night modus operandi, where I divided my time between frozen pizza and the least dismal offering on the telly. I went off to find a tie that didn't have a stain.

I felt pleased as we got ready, as though I'd rejoined a club I'd been denied admittance to for a long time. It was Saturday night and I was going to dinner. This was what normal people did. For once I was part of society. I felt warm and fuzzy. I smiled at my reflection and it obligingly smiled back. Maybe things were on the up.

'Cute tie,' Felicia said, sizing me up before we stepped out the front door.

'A present from Simon.' The tie had a cartoon character on it, but I thought I could pull it off in a witty, ironic way. 'Shall we go?' I offered her my arm, mock polite. But the feeling in my gut when she put her hand on my arm surprised me.

We met Everard on the stairs. The frequency of this lately started me wondering whether he'd drilled a hole in his ceiling and was running a spy camera.

'Hellooo.' He wrung his hand, mock surprised.

'Everard, sweetie,' Felicia cooed, her southern, accent firmly in place.

'Would you care to join me for a sherry?' Everard didn't even pretend the invitation included me.

'Honey, we'd love to, but we've got reservations at L'Abattoir.'

Everard looked impressed as he tried to position himself closer to Felicia and wedge me out of the picture.

'My dear,' he said, 'however did you get in there? You must have booked weeks ago. I hear their pig's knuckle is to die for!' He giggled at his bold use of American idiom. 'And the sheep's stomach stuffed with veal tripe and truffles is worth the price of dinner alone.'

I looked uneasily at them both, wondering if I

might not have been better off at home with a soggy pizza.

'Everard, honey, we've got to fly,' Felicia said. 'You know what their seating policy is – in by seven-fifteen and out by eight-thirty.'

'It's so popular, who can blame them?' Everard pressed both hands together in a gesture of supplication.

'Not me.' Felicia smoothly steered us both past him. 'But let's get together real soon. Next week maybe?' That made Everard so happy I thought he'd pass out on the spot.

'Can we skip the Abattoir?' I asked as Everard closed his door behind him. 'I don't like the sound of it.'

Felicia pulled the front door open. Her next words were drowned out in a hail of shouts and a light storm of flash bulbs. I put my hand up to my face, but through the confusion I thought I could hear people shouting my name.

Chapter Seven

'Felicia! Did you sleep with him?'

'How much cocaine did Bruce McCarthy take before he died?'

'How does it feel to find a dead body?'

'What made you go back to the house?'

'What did he look like when you found him?'

'Tell us about the drugs orgy!'

'Felicia, this way!'

They were shouting and jostling and forcing us back against the door. It had closed and trapped us on the stoop. The crowd of photographers surged closer. Someone put a camera close in Felicia's face. I snatched it away.

'Miss Randall has not given you permission to take her photograph,' I said pleasantly, through gritted teeth. He swiped the camera back, looking like he'd like to extend his hand to my face.

I searched my pockets for the keys to get back in the house. The crowd crushed forward, snapping, yelling till they blurred into one amorphous beast. Felicia put her hands up to her face.

The door clicked open behind me. I almost fell

into the foyer, tripping over phone books and sliding on junk mail.

'What on earth.' Everard had pulled himself up to his full height, which while not imposing, had a certain air of authority. I grabbed Felicia in and we used our weight to shut the door behind us. The hacks pounded and yelled.

'Are you all right, my dear?' Everard put his hand out to Felicia, no doubt hoping she'd be feeling faint and would need to be ushered into his flat to lie down and be administered sherry and smelling salts.

'Bastards,' she snarled, pushing her hair out of her eyes. 'How fucking dare they!' She stomped back upstairs.

We waited for the pack to get sick of standing out there, which took some hours. Around midnight the last one left, finally convinced that we weren't going anywhere.

'Thank God that's over,' Felicia said. Then the music started upstairs. Loud with a brisk beat, just the way they liked it.

'That's it,' she said. 'I have had just about enough.' She stomped out. I heard her pounding up the stairs. Banging on the door. I followed because I like a good scrap.

Felicia's knock was not answered immediately. She banged harder. We heard thumping and someone yelled, 'Coming.'

'Hello?' My neighbour wore a sequinned cropped top, combat pants and the dull look of someone who likes stimulants too much. She had to yell to be heard over the music.

'Hi!' Felicia yelled back. 'I live downstairs. Are you going to shut the fuck up?'

'Whaddya mean?' The girl swayed. Put her hand to the door jamb for support.

'Rachel,' a guy yelled from somewhere in the apartment. 'Everything okay?' He shuffled over and stood behind her. He looked vaguely familiar to me but I couldn't place him.

'The music. The music is what I mean. Can you turn it down? For once?'

'It's Saturday night,' the woman said.

'I don't care. I've had a very bad week.' Felicia advanced on her, a mad gleam in her eye. 'Can you understand that? A very bad week.'

The woman looked puzzled.

Felicia sighed. 'Just turn it down, okay?'

We went downstairs. The music stayed loud.

'Ridley. Where's Felicia? There's some fucking frog at her flat. Where's my fucking story?' It was the following morning and the newsroom executive editor John Marlowe was on the phone. Marlowe's a guy who's made bad manners his philosophy of life.

'Good morning, Marlowe. How's Gloucestershire this sunny Sunday?' Marlowe, although a common lad by birth, has married into the set that gets their photos taken wearing sad frocks in *Tatler*. Most weekends he goes to the country to lord it over his estate. During the week he does more or less the same thing at City Radio.

'Where the fuck are you?'

'At home,' I said, thinking that was fairly obvious.

Felicia's pager went off inside her handbag. She pounced on it, plucked it out, still holding the pan she was about to cook eggs in. She frowned at the message, frowned at me. I mouthed, 'Marlowe'. Her frown deepened. Marlowe likes Felicia so much he treats her even more badly than me.

'I mean why aren't you at work. We had to find out on a rival bloody station that two of my staff were at a drugs orgy where some schmuck died.' Marlowe didn't really care about that. Gleaning news from rival stations was pretty much the norm at City. But that didn't mean he should waste a valuable opportunity to rake me over. 'Get the fuck to work. I want you and Felicia all over this story. Find her and get it covered. Understand?' It was probably a good thing that Marlowe didn't know Felicia was staying at my place, then he'd really enjoy hating me. Marlowe had once tried to convince Felicia of his physical charms. Felicia had convinced him, equally firmly, that she wasn't interested. He still bears the psychological scars.

'I'll get right on to it,' I said. 'My Shock Death Horror, by Sam Ridley.'

'Don't piss me off, Ridley. Just do what I fucking pay you for, that's all I ask.'

'Enjoy the shooting,' I said. But he'd hung up.

We ate our eggs driving into the office.

'Ah, the happy couple,' Lyall said as we arrived in the newsroom. 'No doubt you're here about the big story.'

Lyall gave me a look that implied he wanted to know the dirt on Felicia and me as soon as possible. 'Delaney wants to see you. He's got such a grip on this one it's positively frightening.' Lyall pointed to Delaney's office where we could see the man himself waiting. Shuffling through the tabloid papers that no doubt carried a lurid and fantastically false version of Bruce McCarthy's final hours.

Delaney's saving grace as a newsroom manager is that he doesn't do much managing because he's not that interested in anything that won't make him a millionaire by the time he's forty. But he's also astute enough to realize that this attitude is not going to get him far with the suits upstairs, and a full twenty per cent of him would like to have a crack career in a profession that impresses people when he mentions it at dinner parties. So every now and then he selects a story where he can dust off his supply of news clichés and be seen bother his staff by muttering things like 'this one's bigger than Ben-Hur', or 'let's rock and roll'.

If the story happens on the weekend then all to the good: he whips out the pair of jeans that he keeps specially for said occasions, teams them with a natty pink polo shirt and the latest trainers, to show that he's a cool guy and not in the least bit stuffy, and prepares to inflict journalists with his views based on the solid eight months he spent actually working as a reporter.

'Guys, guys,' he said, ushering us in, chuckling. Marlowe had played bad boss so he could lay off with the truncheons. 'We're a little behind the eight ball on this one, but I think we can make up the ground by lunchtime.' He looked eager.

Felicia and I both said nothing, waiting for him to fill the gap. Delaney rode it smoothly. He is a salesman, right down to his monogrammed pink socks.

'There's a time for objectivity and there's a time for subjectivity,' he began ponderously, like he'd run through it for the benefit of his bathroom mirror. 'And I think this story needs the latter. "Me" journalism is what we're talking about here. Make it personal. Make people *feel* what it was like to be there. Make yourself part of the story, Felicia.' He emphasized the last five words with small stabbing movements. 'You too, Sam,' he said, like I was missing out.

Still there was silence.

'Well? What d'ya think?'

'You ever seen a corpse, Alan?' Felicia said.

'Pardon?'

'Dead guy. Stiff. You ever seen one?'

'Felicia, Felicia.' Alan wagged his head from side to side. Condescension so thick you could spread it. I half expected him to ruffle her hair. 'We're not talking about me. This is about *you*. You were there.'

'Bruce McCarthy's last living act was to wet himself,' Felicia said calmly. 'Or maybe it was to shit himself. Because there was both all over his trousers.'

Alan paused. Lips pursed. 'Well . . . of course we don't need too much detail. People will be eating their Sunday lunch.'

'There was blood coming out his eyes. His eyes were bleeding, Alan. You ever seen that? And his ears. Not to mention his arm. Do you have any idea how much blood you can lose from a major artery?'

Delaney clearly didn't.

'He'd been sick too. A great big slippery pool of it beside him.'

Delaney's smile took on a waxy quality. 'I expect your reporting, as always, to remain within the bounds of good taste,' he said frigidly. 'You haven't given any other interviews, have you?'

'To the police,' Felicia said patiently. 'I'm not talking to the press, Alan. Not even City Radio.'

Alan pressed on valiantly. 'What about the party beforehand?' he asked, hope still vibrating in his voice. 'Can you do an in-depth piece about that?'

Felicia appeared to consider it. 'I could talk about the drugs,' she mused. 'That'd be really interesting for our audience. They're concerned about drugs.'

'Yes. Yes exactly. A very important issue.' Alan leant forward eagerly in his chair. At last Felicia and he were on the same page. 'A drugs issue.'

Felicia shook her head in awe. 'You should have seen that place. Coke, dope . . . Ecstasy.'

Alan nodded eagerly. Ecstasy. Ecstasy had a buzzy feel about it. It made headlines, he'd seen them. People had died taking Ecstasy and reporters had seized upon it as a symbol of the Moral Decline of Modern Youth.

'It was a walk down memory lane for me,' Felicia went on. 'Stuff I haven't seen since my folks' parties in the seventies. They were doing all the junk you thought had gone out of fashion once the suburbanites got hold of it. But there it was, all back again. Just like it had never gone away.'

'Drugs. Resurgence. This is good.'

'But of course my memory of last night is fuzzy, I was pretty out of it myself. You know how it is, Alan. You've been around the block a few times.'

He didn't and he hadn't. He looked shocked. Then tried to cover it up. Unsuccessfully.

I concentrated on keeping a straight face but Alan wasn't looking at me. He was staring at Felicia as though she'd just grown an unsightly horn.

'Wonder how that'd go down with the board?' Felicia mused. 'Me being in such a place. They wouldn't care, would they? I mean, you're only my supervisor, not my mother. You can't monitor your staff's activities twenty-four hours a day so I'm sure it wouldn't reflect badly on you.'

Delaney looked as though he'd just sat on something sharp. Our company is so concerned about our private lives that it recently made us sign a document promising not to smoke, drink or take drugs on our own time. I cleverly transformed a snort of laughter into a niggling cough.

Felicia had just presented Delaney with a hydra-headed conundrum and every one of those laughing little faces had the potential to blow up on him. Would it reflect badly on him? Would it? Could it? It danced around him like a demonic Dr Seuss lyric. He'd have to call Marlowe in the shires and ask his opinion. He didn't like the thought of placing the call any more than Marlowe would like receiving it, but he couldn't think of anything to counter Felicia's argument.

'It's a three-par news story, Alan. An accident. A young man who dies taking too many drugs – if that is in fact how he died, and the police haven't said – is of no consequence to anybody except his family and his friends. And I don't think we'll be doing any favours by broadcasting the seedy details, do you?'

She was very, very good. Even after no sleep. Especially after no sleep.

'But drugs is an issue,' Alan spluttered as she walked out. 'We need to talk about the dangers . . . the public . . .'

Felicia cut him dead with her 'oh, please' look. 'They can get their kicks someplace else,' she said, getting up. 'It's not coming from me.'

Felicia dashed out the story while I gave Lyall the details by the coffee machine.

'Fuck the story,' he said. 'I don't care about some party-boy crack head who topped himself. What I want to know is how come Felicia's not staying at her place? And how come she rings you to go out and do the knight in shining armour routine?'

'She's split up with her boyfriend so she's staying at my house.'

Lyall's eyebrows shot up.

'It's temporary,' I said. 'Two weeks, tops.'

Lyall looked at me as though I was mad. 'You're going to kick her out?' he said, aghast. 'You would actually do that?'

'No. She's going to find somewhere. Anyway, I thought you didn't like her.'

'There's like and like.' Lyall's lascivious gaze slunk over to Felicia. 'Besides, now she's snapped out of the

Fifi Whiplash attitude, she's pretty bearable.' His eyes darted back to me. 'You wouldn't have anything to do with that, would you, Ridley? Her rather sudden change of mood?'

I clapped him on the shoulder. 'My oldest friend, I am providing her with a roof over her head. That is where our relationship starts and ends, trust me.'

'I've never trusted you in my life, Ridley,' he said, upset at being cheated out of prurient gossip, 'and I don't intend to start now.'

To make it look as though I was working, I called the cops, who weren't saying much more than the last time I spoke to them. Mostly I browsed the papers, thinking how much easier it would be to work at a place where you could just make things up. The tabloids made Bruce McCarthy's party sound like Satan had been running a pharmacy out of the kitchen.

When I got home I rang Charlie Hobbs, my dear friend on the Metropolitan Police.

'Bloody Ridley,' he said. 'I hadn't heard from you in so long, I allowed myself to hope.'

'Let's catch up.'

'I'm bloody busy.'

'I'm busy too. You make time for your mates.'

'I know what you've been up to, I heard about that McCarthy bloke. How the hell did you manage to get mixed up with him?'

'It's a jolly tale. I'll tell you about it when we meet.'

'We're not meeting. I've got to bloody exercise, don't I? Not only do I have to find enough hours in my day to work, keep the wife happy, make sure the kids are not turning into delinquents, now I have to bloody get out and pound the pavement every day. Doctor's orders.'

I tried to conjure up a picture of Charlie, who is vastly overweight, springing through town in Lycra shorts.

'Dreadful,' I said.

'You don't know the hell I've been through.'

'Why don't I keep you company while you take your exercise?'

'Nobody sees me like this.'

'Come on, Charlie. The time'll go faster if you have someone to talk to.'

He liked that idea. We arranged to meet in Hyde Park.

It wasn't the spectacle I'd been hoping for. Charlie wore a tracksuit, robbing me of the opportunity to see the Hobbs legs bared. And his doctor had advised him that strenuous exercise after so many years of inactivity would be foolish. So we set off on a brisk walk.

It was a warm day for March. Cheerful spring flowers bloomed, dog owners frolicked with their pets and the sun came out from time to time. To complete the picture of a promisingly fecund spring, young couples strolled past, arm in arm.

'You got too tanned in Sydney,' Charlie said. 'Tanning's bad for you.'

We walked in silence for a bit.

'I'm giving up smoking,' I said when Charlie stopped to take his pulse.

'Who'd have thought it would come to this,' he sighed.

'At least I think I've given up. I haven't had one this weekend, even after seeing a dead guy. And there's nothing like seeing a corpse to make you feel like you deserve the soothing touch of nicotine.'

'Now you know why I haven't given up,' Charlie growled. 'I told the doctor I'd cut down, that's all. That's all he can expect from me. I'm no bloody saint. And at least I'm not lying to him. Three a day, that's what I'm down to.'

'That's gotta count for something.'

'So tell me about this bloke McCarthy. Some cop said something about ghosts. They were getting a good laugh out of it. What the bloody hell were you doing?'

'New show.' I told him about it.

'*Lively London*.' Charlie snorted. 'Your career doesn't know where to bloody stop, does it?'

'I took it because I needed the sleep.'

'What kind of an excuse is that?'

'A pathetic one.'

Charlie laughed some more. Picked up speed. I thought I detected a spring in his step.

'He was in a mess, Bruce McCarthy. That's what I heard.'

'You heard right,' I said. 'Coroner must have had fun.'

Charlie nodded.

We were moving at a fair clip now. A brisk wind whisked through the park, stirred up dead leaves and brought a smattering of rain. Those who'd thought ahead put up their umbrellas. We just got wet.

'So what's the autopsy going to say?'

'There were no drugs in that syringe.'

'He was trying something bold and new?'

'Bold. Not new. Household bleach.'

I stopped. 'He was injected with bleach?'

Charlie nodded. 'You know what it does to your organs? It's a nasty way to die.'

Chapter Eight

Detective Inspector John Jennings told a news conference the following morning that a murder inquiry had been launched.

'Any chance it was an accident?' one of the hacks yelled from the back.

'We're not treating it as an accident. Or suicide,' Jennings said.

'What about the woman who found him?'

'She's helping us with our inquiries.'

'Is she a suspect?'

'She's helping us with our inquiries.'

'What was she doing in the house at that time of day?'

'Was she his lover?'

'Question time's over,' John Jennings said firmly, getting up.

I tried to slip out before I got into another situation like the one Felicia and I faced on Saturday. I wasn't quick enough.

'Hey, Ridley. What's the story?' They crowded around me like bullies in a playground. 'Got a few words for your peers?'

'You heard the man.' I collected my gear.

They pressed in on me, badgered me with questions, but I knew to say nothing. That way your words can't be taken out of context and twisted to mean something you didn't intend. After a while they gave up and went away. All except one.

'Fancy being spirited away from here?' It was the brunette woman with the camera. Still smiling, still wearing the black leather jacket. With blue jeans this time, and a red jumper. 'I've got a car,' she said.

I told her my name. She told me hers. Kyle Gordon.

She unlocked the car. 'This story won't last long. Soon they'll be off in another direction like yapping dogs.' She pulled out into traffic, she drove well.

'You old cynic.'

'I've spent six years covering places with real problems like Somalia and Rwanda. It's hard to get excited about parish pump stuff after that.'

'Why'd you come back?'

'I've been too long on the road. You get tired. I started to hanker for home, even though when I got here I wondered what the hell I was doing.' She grinned. I liked her profile. The gentle bump in the middle of her nose. The fringe that wouldn't lie flat. Imperfections that only emphasized her beauty.

'What are you doing?'

'Taking a breather. Consulting the entrails of goats to see what the next stage of my life will be.'

'Any clues yet?'

'A few ideas, nothing definite.'

I thought about asking her if she had a boyfriend and dismissed it as too obvious. Instead we batted *bons mots* at each other as she guided the car London-slow through the traffic.

She dropped me outside work. I suggested a drink. She agreed and gave me her card. Smiled again as she said it had been nice to meet me.

I leapt up the steps. Swaggered into work.

City Radio was slightly shocked by the heady feeling that it might for once be at the centre of the story. Delaney and Marlowe wanted a meeting so I grabbed some caffeine and went to join them.

Felicia had not been looking forward to the day ahead. While I'd been out with Charlie on Sunday the cops spoke to her again. She came back from Shepherd's Bush police station quiet. Not like her at all. She was fretting that even though she had no motive and barely knew Bruce, the cops were going to arrest her for his murder.

It turned out her worries were much closer to home.

Alan was sipping from a cup of his miracle product. Marlowe had his hairy fist wrapped around a huge mug of scalding black coffee. He has fresh Arabica beans roasted and delivered weekly. He makes much of his working-class roots but doesn't neglect to avail himself of the little luxuries that marriage to an heiress has introduced him to: the bespoke suits, the Cuban cigars, the Michelin-approved restaurants. The chalk-striped suit he was wearing that morning made him look like a caricature of a Conservative Member of Parliament.

Felicia, Crosbie and Lyall were all there. Faces moulded into varying degrees of impassivity.

'Sorry I'm late, folks.' Rick Brittan oozed in and grabbed the chair I was about to sit on. I stood, leaning against the wall, flirting with the temptation to accidentally spill coffee down the front of his purple button-down shirt. I Resisted. It would have been a waste of bad coffee.

'You know why you're here. I want this story,' Marlowe said, staring hard at Felicia.

I had a bad feeling. Marlowe looked as though he was spoiling for a fight. Felicia was going to be publicly punished for standing up to him. Punished too for rejecting his advances all those months ago.

Felicia looked him straight in the eye. 'I stand by what I said.'

'You got away with it on the weekend, but that's not going to happen again. It's now a murder investigation. I want a feature piece on what happened at the party, your relationship with Bruce McCarthy, however unsavoury or painful it is for you to talk about it, I want it. Exclusive. We're going to trailer it and we're going to make an attempt to get something we haven't had for a while – people actually listening.'

Delaney looked on, rapt. So this was how heavy-hitters got their reputation. He took a nervous sip of his miracle fluid and then cast an envious eye over Marlowe's Guatemalan espresso. Perhaps that was what gave Marlowe his heft.

Marlowe moved till he was directly in front of Felicia, standing over her. She had to crane her neck to keep his eye. But she kept it.

'There could be a problem legally,' Lyall said calmly, inspecting a fingernail. 'If there's a trial.'

Marlowe glared at Lyall. Lyall rarely makes trouble but he draws the line at seeing colleagues savaged in front of an audience.

'You let me worry about that,' Marlowe said, patronizing and sarcastic. 'I take full responsibility. You run with this as far as it can go.'

'If you're fined for contempt it won't be cheap,' I said. 'Courts are snippy about that these days.' I hoped to appeal to his practical side, City Radio is notoriously tight. Our annual newsroom budget all told comes to about the sum that our rivals spend on sugar for their coffee machines.

'I'm going to ignore you, Ridley, unless you have something constructive to add, which I very much doubt. As usual, you've mishandled this story from the very beginning. Now's your chance to make things good. What do you suggest?' Marlowe snarled.

'I think I can help out,' Rick interjected. 'This is too big for one person to cover. Much better if we pool our resources.' He smiled daggers at me.

I smiled back. A newborn gerbil has better news sense than Rick. I gave him the metaphorical rope in the hope he'd fashion it into a nifty little noose that would fit snugly around his neck.

'Well?' Marlowe barked, rounding on Rick. He had no favourites today.

'I think we should follow up the ghost angle.'

'How very tabloid,' Lyall murmured.

'You,' Marlowe stabbed his hairy finger, 'keep out of this. Why?' he said, spinning back to Rick.

'Makes it wacky. Gives it spin.' Rick beamed around the room.

But even Marlowe couldn't swallow that. 'Give Sam back-up,' he snapped. To everybody else: 'Get all over this. I want neighbours, I want mates. I want to know what sort of man he was. And I want it nailed down by lunchtime.'

Chapter Nine

The woman who answered my knock looked harassed. In the background I could hear screeching children and daytime TV.

'Come in,' she said, after I'd explained who I was. 'If you don't mind a mess. I was just about to make tea.'

The house backed on to Bruce's and was similar in layout. This one was family cluttered in contrast to his bachelor minimal. In the living room the furniture was squashy and well used. Primary-coloured toys were sprinkled over the floor at regular, ankle-threatening intervals. Twin girls of about four reigned over it. A young woman I assumed was an au pair tried to get their attention with toys which they snatched and threw at each other.

'Let's leave them to it,' the woman said. 'We'll sit in the kitchen.' I followed her to a long narrow room that overlooked a well-kept but toy-scattered garden.

'Amy French,' the woman said, holding out her hand. 'That's Bruce's place over the fence.'

She was slim with short black hair, and a high voice. She wore faded jeans and a striped fisherman's shirt. She made tea and sorted out biscuits from a packet and we ate them at a large wooden table stained with juice and children's modelling clay.

'You want to know about Bruce, of course. Shocking business. I still can't believe it.'

'What was he like?'

'Cheery. He was always cheery. Mind you, not that we had a whole lot to do with each other. He came round and introduced himself which is very rare in this part of town. My husband was suspicious.' Amy ran her slim hands through her hair, leaving it spiky. 'Said he was touting for business. I didn't think there was anything particularly wrong with that.'

'Did he have many parties?'

'A few. He'd invite us over from time to time, if I saw him over the back fence. We dropped in once or twice. My husband didn't like them, he said they weren't "our crowd" but I didn't mind it at all. It was nice to meet different people. It happens so rarely these days now that I've been blessed with two angels from heaven,' she said wryly. One of the angels burst out crying, came running in holding a finger to be kissed. She soothed the child and sent her on her way.

'What about Friday night. Did you go over?'

'I would have except Dave, my husband, was working late and I didn't have anyone to sit with the kids. It was Brigit's night off. It was probably just as well because Bonnie was sick later on. I was up all night with her.'

She looked around her sunny, untidy kitchen as if appreciating it for the first time. 'And when I heard what happened . . . God, who would want to do something like that? He must have died in terrible agony.'

'The police think he may have been so stoned he didn't notice too much.'

Amy shuddered. 'Well, that's something, at least.' Her eyes went to the cupboard under the sink. 'I always keep my cleaning gear locked. It's my nightmare that the kids'll get in there.'

'Did you see anything when you were up with Bonnie?'

'I didn't see anything. I thought I *heard* something. I thought I heard an argument. I told the police officer when he came . . . but I'm afraid I wasn't much help. Bonnie was crying and she'd been sick so I opened the window to air her room out. Bruce was shouting at someone, I thought. But I couldn't hear another voice so maybe he was just pissed and amusing himself – once after a party he cut down his clothes line because it suddenly offended him.'

'What time was the argument?'

Amy screwed up her eyes, trying to remember.

'About five, I would suppose. I wasn't too clear. I just tumbled out of bed. I was half asleep, I didn't really check the time.'

'Could the other person have been a woman?' I asked, thinking of the argument that Felicia witnessed between Lindy and Bruce. Maybe Lindy had come back to pick another fight.

'Really couldn't say. I couldn't make out words. And I wasn't really listening, either. I was preoccupied. Not much help, am I?'

After Amy had given me another cup of tea I rang

the doorbell of number 268, Bruce's only next-door neighbour by virtue of the fact that his house was on the end of the terrace.

'Yes?' A frail, older woman looked at me fearfully. Her head was wrapped in a scarf.

I introduced myself, gave her the spiel that I gave Amy. She was shutting the door before I finished.

'I'm sorry, I don't think—' Her eyes were watery and her hand shook. 'I'm not well you see, and—'

I apologized for bothering her. Was about to return to my car when a man came up the path. He carried a paper bag with a chemist's insignia on it. He squinted at me. He was lanky with white hair and a clipped moustache.

'Sam Ridley, City Radio,' I said. 'I wondered if I could ask you some questions about Bruce McCarthy.'

The woman still seemed nervous, but her husband put out his hand. 'Paul Fraser. Won't you come in?'

The woman sat in a large Victorian morning chair and looked out over the garden. The sun went behind a cloud and Paul Fraser turned on a lamp.

'Bad business about next door,' he said.

'It's the last thing you expect,' his wife said. 'At our age we're used to people dying . . . but not like that.'

'Did you know Bruce well?'

'No. Well, only to speak to in passing. He hadn't been here for long. The house had stood empty for a good spell before that.'

'It was nice to have someone move in finally,' his wife said. 'We used to worry about squatters.'

'I'm actually trying to find one of Bruce's girlfriends. Lindy is her name. Did you ever meet her? Blonde hair and a shrill voice?'

Both shook their heads. 'Most of his coming and going was at night,' Mrs Fraser said. 'We turn in quite early.'

The tea was good. I'd watched Paul Fraser make it lovingly, warming the teapot, making sure the water didn't over boil. Pouring it into china cups with matching saucers. The sun came out and went away again. Chunky rain clouds loomed.

'Did you go to his party on Friday night?'

'Good heavens no. Hardly our sort of thing.' Paul Fraser sat at the table and gripped his cup with both hands. 'All those rowdy youngsters.'

'He was a lively young man,' Mrs Fraser said. 'Seemed very friendly. Always ready to chat. I gave him advice about his borders. He didn't have the first clue about gardening, but he was very keen on his house. It was the first one he'd owned.'

'One of the other neighbours said she thought she heard an argument early on Friday morning. Did you hear any shouting?'

'I generally sleep quite soundly,' Paul Fraser said. 'I didn't hear anything.'

'He ever mention a ghost to you?'

'Ghost?' Mr Fraser said, puzzled. 'Oh yes, there was some suggestion that old place was haunted. But that was years ago – when Bradley lived there. I thought it was just a rumour.'

'Bruce told you he had ghosts?' Mrs Fraser asked.

'He seemed quite upset by it when I interviewed him last week.'

'Did he? I would have thought it was just the sort of thing a young man would relish.' Mrs Fraser smiled. 'What harm can a ghost do?'

There was silence while we sipped our tea. Mrs Fraser got up and nipped a dead leaf off a pot plant. Both of them seemed expectant.

'It's a pleasure to have you here,' Paul Fraser said. 'We listen to City Radio all the time, especially when we're pottering in the garden.'

I stared at them. Two actual living, breathing listeners. Our audience. I felt like a person who's just chanced upon the Yeti.

'Crosbie Shaw's our favourite,' Mrs Fraser said. 'She's very good, isn't she?'

I don't often hear the words 'Crosbie' and 'good' in the same breath. It took me aback.

'Well, I—'

'Although she doesn't seem herself lately,' Mrs Fraser went on. 'I do worry about her. She seems tired. The old spark isn't there.'

'She's battling very bravely with a personal problem.' I implied by my tone that was all I could reveal.

Mrs Fraser nodded her head sympathetically. 'There's always something, isn't there? No matter who you are. Being rich or famous doesn't make it any easier.'

After I left them I spent a few minutes knocking on doors without success. Bruce's other neighbours were either all out or not answering their bells. The street looked as though it was coming up, judging by the numbers of skips and building projects on the go. I walked back to the car which was parked outside the Frasers'. I held my Marantz tape-recorder carefully. It deserves respect due to its advanced age. A youngish bloke with a fat briefcase and a spreading waistline got out of his car and walked towards me. He had on a well-cut suit and expensive shoes and a belligerent expression.

'You a reporter?'

I said yes.

'Cops know who did it yet?'

'I don't think so.'

'One of his girlfriends, probably. He had it coming, the way he ran around.'

'And you are?'

'David French,' he said. Amy's husband.

'Would you be prepared to be interviewed?'

'I've got work to do,' he said and turned away.

Chapter Ten

The office was free from predators. Marlowe had gone up to his office and the newsroom, which operates like a self-regulating macro-organism, immediately went back to doing things exactly as if he'd never spoken. I wrote and edited my story for the lunchtime bulletins. I did it quickly. I needed to get home and get some sleep so that I could be refreshed before beginning my *Lively London* shift at midnight. I hoped the madness would be over soon. Two jobs is too much, however mindless one of them might be.

'Sam, old mate.' It was Rick. And he was blocking my way to the door.

'Rick.' I could hardly muster up the energy to be snide.

'I called the cops to see if they had anything new on the ghost angle,' he said. 'They said they didn't know anything about a ghost. Have you been holding out on them?' He clapped me on the shoulder.

I wasn't in the mood to deal with him. My body craved nicotine and rest.

'Stay away from the cops,' I said. 'I've got it covered.'

'I don't think you have, Sammy. I don't think you

have.' Rick chuckled. 'Besides, I'm merely offering a fellow professional a helping hand. This is a big story.'

I walked away, he followed me.

'Hey, mate, not all of us can cope all the time. It's okay to admit that.' He lightly stroked my arm, mock concerned. 'So you forgot to tell the cops about the ghost, that's okay. Rick's here to make everything better.'

I stopped. Slapped his hand away. 'You like clothes, don't you, Rick?'

His hand went instinctively to his tie. Smoothed it down and popped it back between his freshly laundered lapels.

'Sure you do. Well, let me tell you that police work is very hard on your wardrobe. Look at me.' I gestured at my worn suit, shiny in all the right parts. 'This used to be a Hugo Boss.'

Rick laughed. I laughed too. And poked my finger in his chest.

'Don't forget, I know where you live.' I picked up his tie and made like I was snipping it with my fingers. He snatched it back.

'That's Italian silk, old trout. Mind the merchandise.'

'Silk. All the more reason not to take risks.'

I went home and tried to sleep but couldn't. So I returned to the office. It was sad, but I did it anyway.

Felicia came over.

'I've been thinking about Bruce's ex-girlfriend, Lindy,' she said. 'Any ideas how we find her?'

'No. You?'

'I think Bruce said she worked in a chemist's shop. Said she had aspirations to become a beauty therapist.'

'Do we really want to call every pharmacy in London? We don't even know her last name.'

'It's Lee,' Felicia said casually.

'How do you know?'

'The cops told me when I went back for my second interview. They asked me if I knew her. Lindy Lee. The name reminds me of a sixties pop singer.'

There was no way to avoid hitting the phone books. Felicia gave me a work experience person, a sullen, shabby young woman called Fern who made it clear that what she was expected to do was fathoms beneath her prodigious ability. City Radio has had many volunteers over the years. They're of mixed ability, but all come armed with the iron-clad belief that they are the saviours of journalism. I ignored Fern's frown and unresponsive body language. I gave her the phone book and told her to start at the beginning.

We were hours on the phones. Many people simply hung up, thinking that someone asking for a Lindy Lee didn't have enough to do with his days.

I found her eventually at the Clarion pharmacy in Kensal Rise. I spoke to one of her colleagues who said she was out but would be back shortly. I decided to speak to her in person. It was nearly knocking off time, maybe I'd get lucky.

*

'Which nicotine gum do you recommend?' I smiled brightly at Lindy, which wasn't difficult. She'd decided her breasts were her best asset and should be shown. Her white coverall didn't do the job it was intended for.

'This is more expensive, but it's worth it,' she said, pointing a long, purple and green fingernail, resplendent with a silver star, at a row of boxes that promised a cigarette-free life.

'I'll take it. What time do you finish?' I asked as I handed over the cash.

'Who's asking?'

'Sam Ridley, City Radio.'

She sized me up. 'Do I know you from somewhere?'

'No, but you could. Fancy a drink?'

'Whaddyou want?'

'An interview.'

'I'm not doing interviews. I'm in mourning.'

'I can tell.' I looked at her breasts.

'Are you offering?'

It took a second to realize she meant money. 'Could be. Depends.'

'My story's exclusive.'

'I don't doubt it.' I smiled at her breasts so they didn't feel they were being left out.

'I can tell you some stuff about Bruce' – Lindy's spurned-woman anger popped up for a moment before she tamped it down, straightened her shoulders and got a grip – 'if the price is right.'

'Let's talk,' I said. Popped a wad of gum in my mouth. Worked it tentatively. It did not have the same tactile pleasure as lighting up a fag. I had a feeling this giving-up business was going to be harder than I thought.

When Lindy finished we walked to the nearest pub. It was an old-fashioned boozer with old-fashioned customers; suspicious types who preferred drink to talk. I ordered Lindy a vodka and tonic and a beer for me. As I carried the glasses back to our table the eyes of the afternoon drinking crowd were upon me. I was the envy of every man in the room.

'So you and Bruce were mates,' I said disingenuously.

'Yeah, mates. That's what we were.' Lindy's purple lipstick left a neat half-moon around the rim of her glass. 'That thing on? Better not be,' she said of my Marantz, which was nestling on the seat beside me.

'It's not on.'

'How much are you offering?' she said briskly.

'What's your story?'

'I know what he was up to. I made it my business to know. That's why he wasn't so keen to ditch me like he did all his other women. I made sure I had insurance.'

'What was he up to?'

'Like I said, it's going to cost.'

'I've got to know whether it's worth my while.'

'Oh, it definitely is.' She left another purple smudge on her glass.

'How do I know that?'

'Don't waste my time,' she said. 'Either make me

an offer or I go.' Her hand strayed towards her bag the way women often do when they're preparing to leave.

'Don't be so hasty.' I smiled in my most heart-warming way. Some women have been known to go for it.

She didn't go for it. 'I know what I'm worth,' she said. 'I've got to get something out of this, at least.'

'Why?'

'I—' She coloured. 'I just do.'

'You only get out what you put in. What'd you put in?'

'I haven't broken any law.'

'You argued with Bruce just before he died.'

'So what?' Lindy stopped her leaving preparations. For a second or two, I had her.

'You crashed the party, argued with him because he was dancing with somebody else. Later he turns up dead. Some people might think that suspicious.' This wasn't the way I intended the interview to go but I had an overwhelming need to wipe the smug smile off her face. I have grown to hate people who think their proximity to tragedy can be turned into cash if one can find a willing and wealthy tabloid paper.

'Who the fuck do you think you are, accusing me? Just fucking leave me alone. I wasn't breaking the law.' For emphasis she dashed the rest of her glass in my face. The good, old-fashioned way. I blinked and gasped in shock. 'You want villains, go and speak to his mate, Curly. Ask them about breaking the law. I'm just an innocent spectator.'

She slowly gathered her things and walked out of the pub.

There was laughter. Most of it directed at me.

Chapter Eleven

'Why'd you have to antagonize her?' Felicia was stirring something in a large pan. It smelt great. I'd downed one whisky and was making significant inroads into the second. It almost made up for not having slept.

I changed the subject. 'How can you work up the energy to cook after such an awful day?'

'It relaxes me,' she said. 'Not everyone lives like a troll.'

'I do not live like a troll,' I said, half-heartedly. 'Besides, I don't think Lindy was up to anything.'

'Sounds like she's pretty astute to me. Maybe she did the money thing as a way of putting you off. I wouldn't want to be bragging about my relationship with Bruce if I'd been seen arguing with him just before he died.'

'Maybe she didn't know she'd been seen.'

'I was there, Ridley. She must have seen me.' Felicia tasted what she was cooking and then threw in some salt.

'I imagine it was just idle threats. She probably planned to creep into his house and sew prawns into his curtains or something.' Felicia ground pepper into the pan. 'By the way, Charlie Hobbs called for you. He's got the scoop on that guy you asked him about – Curly Ryan.' Felicia left the pot and began setting the table. For three.

'Who's coming to dinner?'

'Everard. He's been asking me for lunch almost every day and I haven't been able to make it, so I invited him up here.'

'Well thanks for letting me know.'

'Shut up, Ridley. He's not so bad, just lonely.'

'He's a supercilious pain.' The alcohol had gone straight to my head. It gave me permission to say what I liked.

'I don't mind him.'

'I do.'

'You don't even know him.'

'That's the way I like it.'

Felicia looked up from her table preparations. 'It's one night out of your life. What's the problem?'

'I don't want him in my house.'

'Well, too late. He's coming.'

'Are you looking for another sugar daddy? If so, you should know he's got no money.' As soon as the alcohol-smoothed words were out of my mouth I wished them back. Felicia just stared at me, dishes in hand. I fully expected them to come flying my way. But she set them down on the table with a bang.

'I'm sorry,' I whispered. I was.

'Forget it,' she said, equally hushed.

'I didn't—'

'Apology accepted.' The tears in her eyes told me it wasn't. 'Just shut it, okay?'

I took my glass and the phone into the bedroom and called Charlie Hobbs. Although he wasn't working on Bruce's murder, he usually knows what's going on. Cops, like reporters, love to gossip.

'Curly Ryan,' Charlie said. 'A builder. Known Bruce McCarthy for some time. Volunteered himself for questioning, so I'm told. Didn't tell them much. He went to the party, got pissed, tried to pull birds and failed, threw up and went home. Want to tell me why you're interested?'

'Bruce's ex-girlfriend says he's a villain.'

'So are most London builders.'

'I'm following every angle I can. The boss likes this one, on account of there might be a direct correlation between it and City's listening figures.'

Charlie heaved a deep sigh. 'If you can't trust hacks to be impartial who can you trust?'

'Are the cops interested in Curly?'

'All avenues of inquiry are being pursued,' Charlie said in a mock-plod tone of voice.

'Where can I find him?'

'I've already told you more than you deserve. What do I get out of this?'

'I would find him anyway, you're merely saving me some time.'

Charlie gave me the address and I promised to buy him a Diet Coke.

I decided to go and see Curly Ryan right away. The welcome I would get from him could scarcely be chillier than the one in my own home, so I said and received a cool goodbye. I passed Everard on the stairs, his plump face alight with joy and his hands filled with flowers and wine. He couldn't believe his luck that I wasn't sticking around. I wished him a good evening. Maybe I even meant it.

Curly Ryan's flat was in the less inviting part of West Kensington. High-rise council flats marched in a chevron pattern on one side of the street. Curly's flat was in a single Victorian five-storey house. The house stood out from the ugly, modern buildings around it like a big, white tooth.

I thought about Felicia on the drive over. She hadn't done anything except clean my flat and make nice food and I had snapped at her because I hadn't slept. And the two shots of whisky hadn't helped. I felt bad. I'd apologize properly when I got home, I decided. With flowers. Like Everard.

I grabbed another piece of nicotine chewing gum. I'd nearly gone through the whole packet and it wasn't making my love of the weed go away. Perhaps I should just start smoking again.

Curly's bell was broken so I knocked on the door. The flat was quite dark but a television droned somewhere, canned laughter punched out periodically.

'Yeah?' A guy wrenched the door open. He had a tinfoil rectangle filled with food in one hand and a plastic fork in the other.

'I'm looking for Curly Ryan.'

His mouth was filled with food so his speech was indistinct, but I managed to catch the word 'pub' and follow the hand signals he made indicating right and left. It occurred to me that I didn't know what Curly looked like.

'Tall. Red hair,' mumbled the direction-giver. 'Can't miss him.'

The pub was big, crowded and smoky. As I stepped into the fug I sensed my lack of real nicotine might present a problem. I shouldered through the crush looking for a tall, red-headed man.

There was one standing at the bar, one huge leg slung over a stool, the other planted firmly on the ground. Talking to a bloke about the same height but slimmer. Curly was a chunky fellow whose nose started off in one direction and finished in another. His eyes were deep set, sheltered by a verandah of red eyebrow. He wore a checked shirt with the sleeves rolled up.

I edged up beside him. 'Hi,' I said. 'You must be Curly. Get you guys a drink?'

'Bugger off,' he said. He blew smoke in my face which wasn't as much of an insult as he might have imagined.

'Suit yourself.' I stayed where I was and ordered a beer. 'I wanted a word about Bruce McCarthy.'

'I said "get lost".' Curly leant into my face.

I smiled genially. 'If I recall, what you actually said was "bugger off".'

'You want a smack?'

'No.' I turned to face him. 'I want to talk about Bruce.'

Curly put his beer down. Ran one hand across his eyebrow. The crowd surged and swayed around us as more people pressed towards the bar.

'Why?' he said at length. 'Why do you want to go doing that?'

Because the boss is sitting on my tail, is what I could have said but I didn't want to burden Curly with the politics of my workplace. Instead I smiled. 'It's a murder. People are interested.'

Curly frowned in concentration. The man at his side nudged him with his glass. 'C'mon,' he said, 'let's go somewhere else.'

'Wait,' Curly said.

We took our drinks and squeezed through to the snug, which was quieter. A couple were sitting there but Curly's mate, with a few well-chosen words, persuaded them they'd be much more comfortable elsewhere. I set up the Marantz, angled the machine towards Curly who drew back suddenly.

'Don't answer any questions you don't want to,' his mate said, looking straight at me.

'And you are?' I demanded, bored with his aggression.

'Pete Walker. We're partners. You speak to Curly, you speak to me.'

'Fine.' I kept the microphone in front of Curly. 'If I think of a question, I'll be sure to ask it.'

'Is that thing going?' Curly asked, nervous in the unfamiliar circumstances. I reassured him and we started with general questions to get him warmed up.

'I've known Bruce for years. We met in Spain,' he said. He had a low voice that was barely making the sound needle register. I pushed the microphone closer. 'We went over to work on the Olympics. Bloody good gig – money was good, beer was cheap. Food wasn't so great – foreign muck – but there were plenty of English pubs in Barcelona. After we came back we kept in touch. We thought about setting up in business – but it didn't pan out. We both got interested in other things.' Curly made it sound like a philosophical split on a par with the Social and Liberal Democrats.

'Why didn't it work?'

'He liked the ponies a little too much for me. Every bookie he's ever dealt with is now living in splendour thanks to Bruce's habit. He'd gamble his last penny.'

'Did he have any other bad habits?'

'He was just a normal bloke. He liked a drink, liked a flutter. Liked a joint or two. Liked the ladies. Never had any problems in that department,' Curly said, his voice shaded with envy.

'What about debts? He have any of those?'

'Dunno. Could have. Pretty likely, knowing him.'

'How long did you work together?'

'Few months. Not long.'

'His girlfriend seemed to think he was doing something illegal.'

'Who? Who said that?'

'Lindy Lee.'

Curly sneered. 'She couldn't get what she wanted from him. 'Course she's gonna say that.'

'What did she want?'

'The key to his front door. She was just a quick shag for Bruce.' Curly sounded like a proud father, reciting his son's achievements. 'He didn't have any long-term plans for her and he told her. He was always up front. The women always said they knew the score but when it came down to it, they never did.' Curly downed the rest of his beer. 'You finished with the questions? I got things to do.'

Felicia was in her room when I got back. The door was shut and the light was on. She didn't come out. There was a message for me to call Kyle. I dialled the number.

'Hello?' she sounded sleepy. I had fun imagining her in black silk underwear and stockings, getting ready for bed.

'What you up to?'

'Just got in,' she said. 'I spent the evening staking out a club where a young Earl likes to spend time and money stuffing the family millions up his nose.'

'Too bad.'

'It's too bad the paper I work for considers this news. But I shouldn't grumble. The money's good and I've just bought a flat. Speaking of which, I'm having the inaugural party next Saturday. Can you come?'

'That sounds great. Let me check.' I paused a few seconds to make her think I actually had a social calendar. 'Yep. That seems to be fine.' I took the address. 'Can I bring anything?'

'Come at eight. And just bring yourself.'

She made it sound like an invitation. I hoped it was.

Chapter Twelve

Felicia and I spent the next day tip-toeing around each other. I saw her in the newsroom but we didn't speak. I'd gone straight to the overnight shift on *Lively London*. I was almost senseless from lack of sleep. Too tired even to drag myself home.

Crosbie Shaw was all a-twitter. She'd been campaigning for a show devoted entirely to stalking and Marlowe had said he would think about it.

'Crosbie's got a stack of clippings,' Lyall said as we refuelled at the coffee machine. 'People are writing stories about her now she's become a celebrity victim.' He sighed and stared deeply into his coffee.

'Sam, I want your input on this.' Crosbie beckoned me into her office. The clips about her plight were spread on the desk. I read them.

Celebrity stalking, it appeared, had become the poignant issue of the week. Which meant that one tabloid columnist had fired off his or her half-baked opinion based on something the middle classes were drunkenly lecturing each other about over dinner and three or four of them had followed suit, quoting each other for ease of research. Before you knew it, consensus had it that society was teetering on collapse because of this insidious canker that needed to be rooted out without delay.

'What do you think?' she asked. 'I need your input.'

Crosbie appeared refreshed since the last time we had spoken. She had taken to wearing her normal work clothes and had put on make-up. Her hair was sitting unnaturally high, doing a pretty good imitation of a test-pilot's helmet, but that was her customary style. She was wearing perfume and had painted her nails red.

'We need to bring the issue to light,' she said, when I didn't reply.

'Sounds like it already is to light.'

Crosbie ignored me. 'Too many women suffer in silence. These people, these stalkers are sick, they need to be exposed. There isn't enough protection for victims. Look what happened to Princess Diana.'

'Princess Diana didn't die from being stalked.'

'No, but her final months would have been much happier if they hadn't been hanging around.'

'Don't you mean paparazzi?' I was finding it hard to keep up with Crosbie's line of thought. My mind, still insisting my body needed nicotine, had formed a little picture of me walking along with a crutch made out of cigarettes. I lost track of what Crosbie was saying altogether, lost in imagining the smell of nicotine. Fern bustled in with a file, put it on Crosbie's desk and stooped over the clippings.

'. . . what do you think?'

I squeezed my eyes shut to see if I had subconsciously retained her words. I hadn't.

'Sounds good,' I said at last.

'You haven't been listening, have you? Not that I expect men to be interested in anything a *mere woman* has to say.' The injured suffragette was a new role for Crosbie whose interest in politics usually extended only to lunching important Members of Parliament after they'd been on her show. I squeezed between my eyes, hoping the nascent headache would disappear.

'Call me if you've got specific queries,' I said and walked out.

My phone was ringing.

'You gonna be in tonight?' It was Charlie.

'Where else would I be?'

'Got something interesting you might want to see.'

'What?'

He just laughed. A dirty laugh. 'Your VCR's working, isn't it?'

'Last I checked.'

'Good. See you at nine.'

I was asleep when Charlie arrived with a small plastic box tucked under his arm and a couple of cans of beer. The box contained a video cassette. There was no label.

'What are we watching?' I said as I loaded it into the machine.

Charlie just sniggered. He went to the kitchen and found two glasses to pour the beer into. I looked at the glass he handed me. 'You've been married too long,' I said as I took it.

'Yeah,' he sneered. 'I've lost some of the uncouthness of my youth. Nice flowers.'

Everard must have found another opportunity to give Felicia lilies. They seemed to be propagating of their own accord. There was even a bunch on top of the television.

'The flowers aren't my fault,' I said. 'I've got a flatmate.'

We sat on the sofa. The credits rolled.

Chapter Thirteen

The plot wasn't much of a poser. It was about a young woman called Heidi who liked to make men happy in the most straightforward way. Lots of men. I think there was a kind of European motif because a lot of the men wore masks like you see on the tourist posters for Venice. The highlight of the movie came when they all wore their masks, and little else, to a great masked orgy. It was poetically called *Humping Heidi*.

'What d'ya think?' Charlie said halfway through.

'I liked the dramatic tension in the first act but I think the exposition's a bit clumsy. And some of the characters need work.'

'I don't get the bit about the ball,' he said. 'Wasn't Heidi supposed to live in the mountains with goats?'

'Perhaps they drew the line at bestiality.'

'I just think it should be thematically consistent, that's all. I mean what's the point of calling her Heidi when she's nowhere near the mountains?' Charlie asked as he rewound the tape. We watched a small speaking bit where Heidi welcomes the participants to her ball.

Felicia came home.

'Hi,' she said. Her eye fell on the television and she forgot about being pissed off with me. It was an eye-catching scene. Heidi was holding forth as the other characters decided they didn't feel much like dancing. Charlie couldn't find the 'off' button so it ran for longer than we both felt comfortable with.

To break the ice, I introduced them. Felicia shook hands uncertainly. Charlie didn't know what to say. I'd never seen him in that position before. He was actually staring at his feet. Or he would have been, could he have seen them.

'The video belonged to Bruce McCarthy,' he said at last.

'What are you doing with it?' Felicia asked sweetly.

Charlie ignored that.

'He's a serious collector. He had about twenty of these.'

'Let me see that.' Felicia grabbed the remote control out of Charlie's hand and rewound to the start.

'It's not exactly hardcore,' she said after a few minutes. 'I've seen worse than this on New York cable.'

'Yeah, good clean fun,' I said, feeling happy that she appeared to be in a good mood.

We heard someone calling Felicia's name. She put down the remote control, went to the window and peered out.

'Oh, God,' she said. 'It's Claude.'

And there he was. Standing under a street lamp looking up at our windows. He was holding something in his hands. I couldn't work out what it was until he started playing it – it was like a piano accordion only much smaller and octagonal. I'd only ever seen them before in tourist posters of France.

'Well, what d'ya know,' Charlie said, joining us at the curtains. 'Who is this wally?'

'Someone who can't take a hint.' I poked Felicia gently. 'Cherie, he's playing your song.'

Charlie looked with concern at Felicia, who seemed to have lost the will to stand straight. She groped for the sofa. Sat on it very small.

'I don't believe it,' she said. 'Please come away from the window. Let's pretend we're not here.'

'He probably saw you come in,' I said. 'He's been waiting. He knows you're here.'

Claude began singing. A mournful song. He had a thin voice but somehow it seemed to clear the traffic.

'You want me to get rid of him?' Charlie asked Felicia. She didn't reply so Charlie leant out the window and yelled, 'Hey! Hit the road, Jacques.'

Claude took no notice.

'It's not so bad,' I said. Felicia glared at me. I remembered I had to be extra nice to her.

'I'll go down there and sort him out,' Charlie said, all official.

Felicia put her head in her hands and shook it from side to side.

'I'll go,' I said. 'You stay here and don't worry. Charlie, can you get her something?'

'Fancy a beer?' Charlie asked. 'I've got some left in the can.'

*

CROSSING LIVE

It had started to rain but Claude seemed not to notice.

'She doesn't want to see you, old boy.' I hoped my display of pukka good manners would persuade him to be a gentleman. 'So why don't you go away.'

'How could you know anything about what she wants?' Claude spat, although incongruously he kept playing.

'I'm taking a wild stab.'

'She's in conflict between her bourgeois conditioning and her feelings for me. She needs to release herself from her puritanical morals.'

'I'm sure that line goes down a treat on twenty-year-old philosophy students, Claude, and good on you. Whatever gets them in the sack, I say. But Felicia doesn't buy it any more.'

'How do you know that?'

'Because she sent me down to tell you to go away. It's over. And however much you play her song she's not coming back.'

Claude appeared not to notice the cogency of my argument. 'I would give her everything. She wouldn't have to work. She wouldn't have to struggle.'

'She doesn't want money. She wants to be married and have kids.'

'I would give her kids,' Claude said.

'You just don't get it, do you?'

Claude stopped squeezing the mini accordion. I wondered if he was planning to wrap it round my neck. 'She's loved me since she was nineteen,' he said. 'Does she think she can walk away from that?'

'Do you see her in the love nest any more, Claude? Go and get another chick to take her place.'

113

'She won't stay away. She'll be back.'

For a short guy with a big hooter he had quite touching faith in his physical charms.

'Yeah,' I said. 'Whatever you say.'

By the time I got back upstairs, Felicia was sipping tea. Charlie sat beside her, patting her on the shoulder every now and then.

'Has he gone?' she asked.

I checked the window. 'For now.'

'Thanks for dealing with him.' Felicia sighed. 'He's been calling me at work and generally making my life a misery. I've refused to speak to him. I can't cope with it right now, what with everything else.'

We sat in silence.

'How'd you meet this bloke?' Charlie asked.

'When I was a teenager I ran away from home. I went to Paris. I'd read Sartre and Camus and had a romantic vision of me sitting in sidewalk cafés wearing a beret.' Felicia laughed. 'Instead I ended up working in them. And Claude owned one of the restaurants.'

'You've been seeing him since then?'

'God, no. *Then* I thought he was way too old. I went back to the States. My parents dispatched my brother to come and convince me I should abandon the bohemian life and go to college. The glamour of living in freezing, rat-infested attics had waned by then, so I went. I didn't meet up with Claude again till about three years ago. I'd gone to Paris for the weekend. For a laugh I went back to the old restaurant and there he was.'

I poured myself a whisky, convincing myself it was what I preferred to a cigarette.

'He told me you'd been in love with him since you were nineteen.'

'I allowed him to think it because it seemed cute at the time.'

'How can he afford to give you a flat?'

'You were here. I turned down that offer.'

Charlie had abandoned his usual air of detached cynicism. 'He gave you a flat?'

'No, he didn't,' Felicia said patiently. 'He has family money, I think. And the restaurants. There are three or four of them and they're very highly regarded.'

'He says he wouldn't mind kids,' I said.

Felicia's head jerked up. 'You didn't—?'

'No.'

'Didn't what?' Charlie asked.

'Nothing,' Felicia and I said together.

Silence opened up. Charlie knew there was a story behind the story but he was too polite to ask. 'If you want me to send a uniform around, have a quiet word,' he said, 'as a favour. I can arrange it.'

'It's okay,' Felicia said. 'Thanks all the same. He'll give up when he realizes I'm not going to play ball.'

'Well, you know where to find me,' he said. 'If you change your mind.' He collected the tape and left.

Felicia and I sat. I sipped my drink. For once there was quiet from the rowdy youths upstairs. I gave thanks.

'I didn't mean what I said about the sugar

daddy,' I said. 'It was supposed to be a joke, but it came out wrong. I'm beholden to the god Nicotine.'

Felicia shrugged. 'It was partly true, that's why it hurt.'

'It's not true.'

Felicia smiled. 'It's a bit true. I had grown used to the way Claude pampered my life. I like having all the little things, you know? The clothes, the apartment. I kidded myself I was an independent woman because I was working.'

'You *are* an independent woman.'

'Yeah,' she said ruefully, 'I am now.' She reached for my glass and took a small sip of Black Label. 'I don't come from money, Ridley. I grew up blue collar. I can do without the nice things, I've done it before. It's the security I'll miss. Claude has a charmed life. He never has to worry about money for a minute. If the business goes belly up there are the trust funds. Not just for him and his wife but for each of the kids. Even if Claude ends up begging on the streets he knows his kids will never lack. What'll happen to my kid if something happens to me? There's no back-up, Sam. I'm the last resort.'

'Nothing like that's going to happen,' I said, drawing from my stock of fatuous answers.

'It's a thin line between good health and bad. Between good fortune and bad. I could slip on a crack in the sidewalk tomorrow and put my back out. I could lose my job, anything. Don't you ever think about that when you pass a beggar on the street? "It could be me." If I don't hustle every chance I get, it *will* be me.'

'Sometimes I feel like I'm already there.'

'Well you do have the wardrobe for it.' She grinned. She got up and kissed me on the forehead. 'Goodnight, Sam Ridley. Thanks for the roof over my head. Maybe I'll do the same for you one day.'

Chapter Fourteen

Bruce McCarthy's funeral was held in a village in the Chilterns. Felicia wanted to go, I had a whole day looming ahead of me with not much lined up to fill it, so when she asked me, I agreed to accompany her.

It was a cold day. The clouds pressed low and promised rain. The sort of day that makes you want to emigrate. I thought of Simon basking in sunshine on the other side of the earth. The pain of it still has the power to take me by surprise.

'I think the sky is falling,' Felicia said as she slung her shoulder bag into the back seat of the car. 'We should go and tell the king.' She seemed more cheerful than she'd done in days.

We collected portable coffees and bagels from a shop in Notting Hill Gate and joined the traffic inching west while Felicia lectured me on bagels in particular and English food in general.

The village where Bruce was to be buried was small and stone-clad and was called Lower Wibble, or some other name that sounded like a comedian had made it up to get a cheap laugh. There was a church, a store that doubled as a post office. And a pub. We were too early for the funeral and just in time for opening. I suggested a pint. Felicia wasn't keen.

'I'm not drinking,' she said.

'You can watch me.'

'I don't think this is a very appropriate way to pay our last respects.'

'Judging from the way Bruce McCarthy lived, I'd say it was an excellent way.' I ordered myself a pint and Felicia tea. She took one sip and proclaimed it undrinkable.

'Keep your voice down,' I hissed. 'You'll hurt the landlord's feelings.'

Felicia's lip curled. 'He has no feelings if he thinks this passes for tea.'

It was obvious we weren't going to agree on anything and so by mutual consent we remained silent. There weren't many other people to look at apart from a couple of tweedy types who looked as though they were bracketed to the bar, but apart from them we were the only customers.

'Isn't rural life nice?' I said brightly.

A woman came in wearing a fur coat, black patent stilettos and a chic black hat with a veil. Obviously not a local. She ordered a double gin on the rocks in a low, raspy voice. She sat at the bar while the publican, leering, pressed the glass against the dispenser and tried to make polite conversation. They chatted about the weather and the woman didn't take off her coat, even though it was extremely warm inside. She drained the gin in two gulps and left. The barman stared after her.

We finished our drinks and walked across a small

green to the church. We were one of the first to arrive. The woman we'd seen in the pub sat in the last row on one side, we sat on the other. The church was freezing. A couple of electric heaters were suspended from the rafters but the cold gobbled up any futile offering they made. The service hadn't even started and already I wished I was back in the airless warmth of the pub. I thought about telling Felicia I'd meet her there after the service, but knew that would have been downright injurious to my health.

So I sat and shivered and watched the mourners file in. They were country folk, mostly, judging from their clothes. Bruce McCarthy had left his roots far behind in his search for hedonism in the big city.

I hadn't expected to see Curly and his mate Pete and at first I hardly recognized them in suits. The builders looked as ill at ease. It was hard to imagine church was something they were accustomed to.

A grey-haired couple walked quickly in and sat in the front row. Dressed in black, bowed and leaning on each other.

'Parents,' Felicia whispered. They were handsome, like Bruce. Age had softened the lines but the bones were the same. She wore a red suit and a white rose in her lapel. He wore black.

The service began promptly and the vicar, a tall, thin man with a nasal voice, spoke in glowing terms of Bruce, whom he had known since he was a devout young Christian. I shivered and waited impatiently for it to end. The vicar invited us to sing a hymn and then hear a lesson which he advised us was something from Corinthians and would be read by Bruce's uncle.

But I wasn't listening to it. Curly and Pete, whom I had a good view of, were staring at the woman in the fur coat and whispering. An annoyed person in the pew in front of them told them to shut up. Curly and Peter looked like they wanted to punch the person in the face. After a tense few seconds they settled back in their seats.

The vicar had started talking again. Then the service was over. We followed the coffin outside where it had started to rain. The pall-bearers loaded it into the back of the hearse, the rain beading their shoulders.

The mourners went to their cars. The hearse moved off slowly to the bottom of the lane.

We got in our car and followed.

The graveyard was on a hill about a mile away. The rain got heavier as we arrived at the gates.

Curly and Pete hunched over and trudged through it like men. Someone produced a black golfing umbrella for Bruce McCarthy's parents. Other people had come prepared with raincoats. The rest shrugged resignedly and prepared to get wet.

'Have you got a brolly?' I asked, searching through the rubble on Felicia's back seat.

'Yes. But it's no good.'

'What do you mean it's no good?'

'It's got Mickey Mouse on it.'

'So what?'

'So I am not gatecrashing a funeral with a Mickey Mouse umbrella.'

'No one will care,' I said, still searching. 'Certainly not Bruce. Besides, you can't gatecrash a funeral.'

Felicia was not to be swayed. 'We get wet, okay? It won't kill you.'

We traipsed through the field to the graveside where the coffin was raised over the grave. The crowd had dwindled to about twenty and the formalities were carried out as quickly as was decent. Water seeped up through my left shoe and down the back of my neck. I huddled next to someone with an umbrella so my right side stayed dry.

The vicar said more words. The coffin was lowered into the ground where a large pool of water awaited it. The mourners made for the blessed dryness of their cars.

'I need another drink,' I said as I dripped all over Felicia's black leather interior. For once she didn't argue. We went back to the pub. A few others from the funeral had gathered there. Felicia and I found a booth as close to the fire as we could. Our clothes steamed.

'That woman seem familiar to you? The one in the fur coat?'

'Nope,' I said.

'I've seen her before.' Felicia studied her Diet Coke.

'At the party?'

'Probably. God, I'm so awful with faces. Did you know the brain shrinks during pregnancy?'

'There she is now, why don't you ask her?' The fur-coated woman had walked in and ordered another drink. She surveyed the room, caught sight of Curly and Pete and went to join them. They listened while she told them something. Then the woman left. Curly and Pete stared after her. Their lips in a synchronized curl.

'That was worth it, don't you think? To pay our last respects,' Felicia said when we got clear of the village and back on the motorway heading for London.

'As long as I don't catch pneumonia.' I turned the heater on full.

'Well, I feel better,' Felicia said. 'The cops aren't interested in me any more. Now we've got closure. We can put it behind us.' She flashed me her best smile. 'We can go home and forget all about it.'

She turned on the radio. Because she's a dedicated professional, it was tuned to City. The reception was pretty weak, about the strength you'd get if you put two overweight hamsters on a wheel and plugged them into a generator.

Through the intermittent static we could hear a voice from beyond the grave. Bruce's voice:

'He's in my house. Every night he's in my house. He walks around, moves things. I see him. In the hallway. On the landing. Going through my papers. It's a sign.'

Chapter Fifteen

Felicia's foot lifted off the accelerator pedal. She pulled over on to the hard shoulder. Turned the volume up as far as it would go. More of Bruce's words came out:

'*What goes around comes around. And I can't escape. I know that now. There's no escape.*'

'Where'd they get that from?'

I was saved from replying by Rick Brittan's smooth voice explaining what I already knew. Bruce McCarthy had spoken to City Radio just days before he died. Even though Rick mentioned I'd done the interview, he still managed to make it seem as though the credit was due to him.

'How'd Rick get hold of your interview with Bruce?' Felicia asked.

'He must have taken it from my desk,' I said, suddenly needing a cigarette more than anything. This wasn't just a whim or passing fancy. This was a serious, no-nonsense craving. A cigarette would make me calm. It'd give me the fortitude I'd need to deal with Rick in a civilized manner and not scoop his eyes out with spoons. Felicia started the car, we moved back on to the fast-flowing motorway. I stared at a billboard which showed sexy, healthy young things enjoying a cigarette. I didn't believe the brand's claims about it improving one's love life but at that point I'd have traded a lifetime of bonking for one blissful packet of fags.

'I take it you didn't tell Marlowe you had this interview.'

'No. The only person I mentioned it to was Andie. She must have said something in passing.'

'Bad move not telling Marlowe,' Felicia said. 'Carry on this way you'll be phoning in traffic reports from Croydon.'

The traffic slowed till we were moving at walking pace. Felicia drummed her fingers on the steering wheel.

'Still, at least this way you have your integrity, right?'

'I didn't say that.'

'You thought it.'

'I didn't think,' I said it slowly as a rehearsal for saying it all over again to Marlowe, 'that any good purpose would be served by playing a recording of a man who wasn't in his right state of mind that night. He was overwrought, probably had had too much to drink and wasn't making much sense. I thought I was doing him a favour.'

'You were. You just weren't doing yourself a favour.'

The traffic started moving again and Felicia went smoothly through the gear changes. 'I take it you didn't tell the cops, otherwise they'd have the tape now as opposed to Rick.'

'I didn't tell the cops.' Why hadn't I told the cops? 'Too much on my mind.'

'That'll go down well with the man in blue in the rubber hose room.'

'I'm a patient man, Mr Ridley.' John Jennings had taken a pencil from behind his ear and was playing with it. Balancing it between his two forefingers. I was in his office. He'd heard about the interview and asked to see me. 'But I don't like being jerked around.'

I said nothing, transfixed by the pencil. I'd gone over the reasons why I hadn't given them the tape. Gone over again my impressions of Bruce the night I'd interviewed him. There was nothing new. Nothing I hadn't told him the first time.

'Anything else you can think of?' he said slowly. 'That might have slipped your mind?'

'No.'

'Get out of here,' he said. 'I really don't want to see you any more.'

I left. Then I went to find Rick Brittan. I intended to make him suffer.

He was at the office, fresh from his triumph.

'Sam, old mate. Cops have just been. I gave them the tape. I'd already made a dub.'

I resisted the urge to shove Rick up against a wall and make his dentistry less cosmetic.

'Why didn't you tell me about it, old man? You heard Marlowe. We're supposed to be working on this together. We're supposed to be a team.' He put an arm around my shoulder. 'But all you've done is give me the bum's rush. So I seized the initiative.'

'Rick, buddy.' I patted the seat beside me. Made him sit down. 'Let me try and make this clear. The next time you go into my drawers, or indeed anywhere near anything of mine, I'll hire a nasty man to go to your house, break all your mirrors, wax the floor with your moisturizer and bring it to a dazzling fresh shine with your designer trousers.'

Rick laughed. He thought I was joking. 'I was playing the ball, not the man, old bean. Didn't you hear me say in the staff meeting that we should play the ghost angle. Nobody backed me then. I just wanted to prove that sometimes Rick is right.' He beamed.

'Bad dress sense is contagious, Ricky boy. Do you really want to be hanging around me for too long?'

Rick's expression flipped to mock concern. 'You seem stressed, Sam. Why don't you take a nice long break? Leave the news game to those who've got the energy for it. After all, the only reason I'm on this story is because Marlowe said so. He thinks you need help so here I am. Ready to help you in any way you need it. Don't take it personally. Think of me as your news butler.'

News butler. I couldn't stand it. I got up. Walked outside. Went to the newsagent. Pulled money out of my pocket. Spied a packet of Camels sitting enticingly on the shelf. Imagined smoking every one. Opened my mouth to order them.

'Sam!' It was Ted Franklin. Clasping a packet of sugar-free mints in one hand, a five-pound note in the other.

'Ted,' I said with less enthusiasm, 'what are you doing here?'

'Working overtime. Thought you were giving up smoking. It's terribly bad for you, you know.'

'Fancy that. You'd think they would have told us.' I slipped the fags in my pocket, relishing the smooth planes, the sharp, shiny corners of the packet.

'I wouldn't,' Ted said, following me out of the shop. 'I really wouldn't, Sam. Do you have any idea how many pollutants our bodies are subjected to in the space of a lifetime? Nicotine is just about the worst you can do. You might as well stick a gun to your head.'

'That wouldn't be as much fun.' I inspected the packet again, realized I didn't have any matches. Turned back to the store.

'Don't do this, Sam,' Ted wailed, fists to his forehead, over-dramatizing like the frustrated actor he is.

'I have to.'

'You don't. You really don't. Think of a new life. One without poisons.'

'I have. I don't like the sound of it.'

'You're over the worst, Sam. It gets better. It gets easier, it really does.'

Ted was practically barring me from the shop. His face shining with the zeal of a proselytizer. I stopped. He knew he had me. He held out his hand. I took the packet. Gave it to him slowly. Savouring the last of it while I could.

'You won't regret it,' he said. 'Fancy a mint?'

*

I wanted to get the hot coals treatment from Marlowe out of the way as soon as possible but he wasn't to be seen. So I went to the movies, hoping it'd take my mind off smoking. It didn't. The protagonist, his girlfriend and the English bad guy all smoked like they had days to live. I could barely pick out the details on the set through the blue haze of cigarette smoke. I left after three quarters an hour and made my way home through the soggy crush of evening commuters.

Felicia was going out when I arrived.

'Crosbie's had a letter from her stalker. She wants me to go over.'

'What is it this time?'

'It's serious. He wrapped it round a rock and threw it through her window.'

'Want me to come?'

Felicia didn't need much persuading. Half of the stress of her job is in playing mummy to the spoilt little princess that lurks distressingly close to the surface of Crosbie's psyche.

'I'm so glad you could come.' Crosbie greeted Felicia at the door of her Georgian maisonette in Primrose Hill, a parody of the welcoming hostess. She looked me up and down but said nothing. Ushered us into the living room and pointed at a hole in the window. They were big, flat-fronted windows but divided up into smaller panes. There were slivers of glass on the floor and a rock about the size of my fist.

'What time did this happen?' I asked as Crosbie picked up a crumpled piece of paper.

'Just before I rang you.' Crosbie handed Felicia the paper.

'Don't touch it, old thing,' I said lightly. 'The cops will want to see it like it was.'

Felicia put her hand behind her back. Crosbie glared at me for the implied criticism. 'I hope people will believe me now,' she said. 'I expect to be taken seriously and not treated like some hysterical female.'

'We're taking you seriously or we wouldn't be here,' Felicia said gently.

'It was such a terrible shock. I was sitting here reading, the room was quiet, no music or television. And there was this sound.' She put the paper down on a large wooden coffee table stacked high with interior design magazines. 'The rock came flying in, I nearly died. I didn't know what had happened. It could have hit me.'

The note was handwritten. I straightened it out with a pencil. *My Dear Crosbie*, it read in round, child-like letters, *You are the star of my firmament. You are a goddess in the news pantheon. I worship you from afar. But I want to be close to you.* It was signed, *Your most loving fan*.

'This the first time he's done this?'

Crosbie nodded.

'He's only been following you before, right? There haven't been any other attempts to get in touch?'

'The phone calls.'

'It seems rather dramatic,' Felicia said. 'I mean why bother with the rock? What's the matter with the mail?'

'Perhaps he wanted to save on postage.' I bent over the rock but it didn't make me any the wiser about the motives of the thrower. 'What I want to know is where you find a rock in London. The whole place is paved over.'

'I can't believe I'm hearing this,' Crosbie hissed. 'Some lunatic attacks me and all you can think about is jokes.'

'Where's your phone?'

'Why?'

'I'm calling the cops.'

'No!' It was almost a shout.

'Why not?'

'I can't deal with them just yet.'

'You must deal with them.'

'He's right, Crosbie.' Felicia backed me up.

'Just give me a little time to recover, okay? I'll ring them tomorrow. Please don't put me through this tonight. It's been such a shock.' Crosbie's shoulders shook and she sank into a puffy white sofa. Felicia looked at me and shrugged.

'It's okay,' she said. 'We won't do anything you don't want us to.'

'I feel so alone, in this place.' Crosbie's voice shook. Felicia sat with Crosbie and put her arm around her. Told her she'd organize an emergency glazier to come and repair the window. I looked around uncomfortably. The flat was decorated entirely in white, even the carpets. I picked up the note by the corners when Crosbie wasn't looking and put it in my pocket. I'd pass it on to Charlie.

'I'll check outside,' I said. Felicia gave me a look that suggested I was better off away from there.

Crosbie's flat looked out over the grassy swathe of Primrose Hill and a good part of London. It was a nice view in the early evening with the lights all twinkly and no hint of the smoggy muck that makes it so dispiriting during the day. I took a deep breath and imagined the air felt cleaner up here.

A small iron fence was the only protection from the street. It wouldn't have required much in the way of athletic ability to lob the rock through the window, it was about four feet away.

I looked up and down the street but I was the only one around. On impulse I rang the upstairs neighbour's bell, and explained the situation.

'Hang on a sec,' he said. 'Be right down.'

A large dog came through the door first. A sleek black and brown beast that had 'don't mess with me' tattooed on its teeth.

'Hi,' the neighbour said, yanking on the dog's chain as it attempted to eat me head first. 'Harry Stephens.'

I told him about the window and tried to keep the panic out of my voice.

'God, that's awful,' Harry said, trying to stay upright as the dog hinted, by launching itself repeatedly into the air, that it would be happier across the road in the park. 'Poor Crosbie.'

'Have you seen anyone suspicious about lately?'

'Nope. And I spend half my life out here. Caesar needs several walks a day, don't you, precious?'

Caesar's doggy ears heard that last sentence as 'get that strange guy in front of you' and changed his tack from the park to my throat. I stepped back smartly. I had no desire to drown in dog slobber.

'But then I'm usually rather preoccupied,' Harry

added, quite unnecessarily, as Caesar strained at the lead once more.

'If you think of anything,' I said as Caesar won and Harry lunged off. 'It's City Radio.'

'I know,' he said and disappeared, lurching, out of the footprint of the street lights. 'We all know who Crosbie works for.'

We waited with Crosbie until the glazier arrived and listened to him opine the state of the nation's young and how it wasn't like it used to be in the old days when people could go on holiday and not have to lock their doors and what this country needed was a strong leader like Margaret Thatcher again and less interference from the Jungians. The logic of his argument puzzled me until he'd mentioned the Jungians a few more times, then I realized he meant the unions.

'Why doesn't Crosbie want the cops?' I asked Felicia as we drove home. 'How does she think she's going to get rid of this greaser without them?'

'She's miffed that they didn't take her seriously when she first complained. Also, she told me she once got busted for marijuana in the sixties while she was at a rock concert. The cops treated her very roughly.'

'Marijuana'? 'Rock concert'? It was a struggle putting Crosbie in any context that even approximated the milieu those words conjured up.

'Apparently she was a wild hippie chick before she settled down to become a crusading journalist.'

*

I slept for a good few minutes before going to work at midnight.

'Sam, get over here. Got a call for you and it won't transfer,' Andie yelled. I was happy to comply. She wore a miniskirt with patent-leather boots, a combination that will always improve my general well-being. 'Do pick up your jaw, darling,' she said in her best Sloane voice, 'it's trawling lint on the carpet.' She handed me the phone. 'This guy wants to talk to you. Says his name's Curly Ryan.'

I took the phone, wondering what the red-haired builder wanted from me.

'You didn't tell me you'd spoken to Bruce,' he said accusingly and without preamble.

'Good evening, Curly. I didn't think it was relevant.'

'What would you know about what's relevant?'

'Apparently not very much. What's your point?'

'What did he mean about being punished?'

'I have no idea.'

'He must have told you.'

'He didn't.'

'I need to know.'

'If you heard the interview you know everything I know.'

Curly clearly believed I was holding something from him. 'I can tell you some stuff about Bruce.'

I tried not to act too interested. 'What sort of stuff?'

'You want the real story? Then we should trade.'

Chapter Sixteen

'See, Bruce was a gambler. He liked the ponies, cards, fruit machines, you name it. He couldn't walk past a betting shop. Just had to pop in and put a few quid on something. More than a few quid more often than not.' Curly sighed, his big, fair face creased in puzzlement. 'That's how we met him in Barcelona. In this grotty little bar just off the Ramblas. He was playing poker and losing. Pete and me were drinking. We'd wandered into the place by mistake. He asked us to lend him some money. Stupid things you do when you're half-cut, we gave him fifty quid. 'Course he lost that as well. We thought it was hilarious at the time. You do when you're drunk and we were making a fair bit of dosh in those days. Bruce promised to pay us back. We didn't expect to see it.'

Pete slid another few of beers on to the table. Curly swept the empty cans off into a large open rubbish bin. The odour of half-decaying food gently permeated the flat.

'So we sort of became mates after that. He's a likeable bloke – *was* a likeable bloke. He'd pay us back and then pay day would roll around and he'd be back in that same dingy bar. Losing as if his life depended on it.'

'I still reckon those games were rigged,' Pete said. 'Geezer who ran the place was dead dodgy. He had the worst rug I've ever seen. It was a whole different colour to the rest of his hair and the bloody thing never moved.'

'Very distracting trying to have a conversation with old Dutch,' Curly agreed. 'You couldn't take your eyes off it.'

I looked at my watch. I'd been half an hour and apart from fond reminiscences of their wonderful trip abroad, hadn't learnt much. The smell from the rubbish was starting to make me feel slightly ill.

'Then he moved in with us,' Curly said, as if imparting some news of great import. 'Was that before or after he got married?'

'Before. Definitely before. Remember he said he was going to pay us back and he went away for the weekend. Came back and went straight to the tables. Lost all the money again. Next thing he turns up with this Russian bird. "Guess what, we're getting married," he said.'

'Never did find out where he met her,' Pete mused. 'Marriage made in heaven. How long did it last?'

The front door opened, bringing a welcome blast of cold air. It was the chap I'd spoken to when I'd first called at the flat. He nodded at Curly and Peter. They nodded back.

''Evening,' he said to me. He turned to Curly. 'I'll have that rent next week,' he said. 'Soon as I get paid.'

Curly nodded, barely registering him. He turned

back to me. 'Bruce and the missus are still married. At least they were till death did part them.'

'Know where I can find her?'

'Somewhere out in Acton, that's what he said. She moved out there and set up her own place. Her name's Lana,' Peter said. 'And she's hot.'

At 6 a.m. I called Charlie Hobbs. I knew he'd be up. He's the kind of guy who always is. I figured if Bruce McCarthy really did have a wife the cops would know about it. And if they knew about it and hadn't told the world, there had to be a reason. I picked up a couple of inferior coffees at the only place open at that hour and waited for him at the gate to Hyde Park. The Hobbs exercise session was taking place early that day.

'Bloody hell,' Charlie said. 'You think it's any help for me to be drinking coffee? And I bet that milk's not skim. You're trying to kill me, you bastard.' He bent down to tighten his shoelaces, sneaking a quick, lascivious look at the polystyrene cups I was holding.

'It is. I have only your interests at heart.'

'I suppose just one can't hurt.' Charlie took the cup and swallowed half the contents in one gulp.

'I hear Bruce McCarthy had a wife.' I matched my pace to Charlie's. It was a leisurely pace.

Charlie finished off the coffee. 'And Mary had a little lamb, so what of it?'

'Just wondered. Cops looking for her?'

'Looking.'

'Haven't found her?'

'Couldn't say that.'

'How exactly couldn't you say?'

'What would you do if your spouse was killed? Even if you hated him, you'd go to the cops, right? Especially if you hated him. You'd go in and play the grieving partner and pretend that the deadbeat scum's passing detracted from the sum of human goodness. Just in case they got the mistaken idea that you were in some way responsible.'

'So what did Lana McCarthy do?'

'Davidoff. She kept her maiden name. First thing she does is check out. She left her flat Saturday morning and hasn't been back.'

Chapter Seventeen

After my shift ended I should have gone straight home and slept but I didn't. I was intrigued by the mystery wife, Lana Davidoff. Why were the cops not saying anything about her? Why had Curly Ryan suddenly come over all informative? These were questions I pondered on the way home, and instead of going straight to Ladbroke Grove I made a detour to Kensal to the pharmacy where Lindy Lee worked.

I bought a couple of packets of nicotine gum, and when I enquired of Lindy's whereabouts the girl behind the counter told me she had phoned in sick. I told her a great pack of lies to get Lindy's home address from her. It wasn't too difficult, young women who stand behind chemist-shop counters are often not hired for their brains.

Lindy lived not far from her job in Kensal Rise. Some say the area is coming up, but only the people that have recently bought property there. The ones who haven't just snicker when they hear it described as the new Notting Hill.

'How did you get here?' Lindy said as she opened the door to her flat.

Lindy didn't look very sick. She looked like she

was about to go out, in fact. Make-up, hair, both were in place. She had on a skirt so short it was a belt in all but name, her frosted blonde hair was teased and primped and held in place by large pink clips. Her clingy blue shirt strained at the buttons and was so tight I could see the outline of her lacy uplift bra underneath.

'Hi,' I said, grinning broadly. 'I think we got off on the wrong foot last time. I'd like to make it up to you.'

'In your dreams. I told you, I'm not talking to reporters unless they pay me.'

I sighed. The Duchess of York has a lot to answer for.

'I wondered if you'd heard the news. About Bruce's wife?'

'What news?'

Normally at this point, I'd have whipped out a fag to lull her into a false sense of security. But those days were gone. And I had to stop thinking about them.

'What about the wife?' The door stayed half-open, her eyes half-curious, half-guarded.

'Let's go somewhere, shall we? We can have a valuable exchange of ideas.'

She left the door open while she collected her things. I waited outside, sizing up the villainous characters that shuffled up and down the street. Best to keep on one's guard up in this part of town or you can wake up in a side street with your wallet and kidneys stolen. It's happened to me.

Lindy's coat was a diaphanous number that didn't

cover any more than the other stuff she was wearing. Despite my fatigue, I immediately felt wide awake and quite cheerful.

'Glad to see you're feeling better,' I said as we walked. 'They told me at work that you were sick.'

'Look,' she said, suddenly aggressive. 'I can't go in there every day, okay? I've got plans for my—' She stopped.

'Plans?'

'Yeah, plans. Is there a law against that?'

'What did Bruce promise you?' I was winging it now. So far out I might catch an updraft.

'Nothing.' She said it too quickly.

'Did you know if he was in any kind of trouble?' I quickened my speed to keep up. She walked fast, despite the lethal high heels. 'He was a serious gambler, wasn't he? Did he have debts?'

She turned abruptly. 'Let's go in here. I fancy a cuppa.'

'Here' was a greasy spoon. It was grubby and steamy and smelt of old cooking fat. We sat and ordered tea. Lindy yanked off her coat, grasped for her cigarettes. Offered me one. I almost took it without thinking. I stopped myself.

'I'm giving up,' I said, mostly as an affirmation to myself.

'Why?' Lindy looked genuinely puzzled.

'Doctors tell me it's bad for my health.'

She shrugged. 'You don't want to believe half the things the so-called experts say. What do they know better than anyone else?'

'You're right; I don't want to believe it, but I'm afraid I must.'

Lindy struck a match so sharply that it broke. A guy in a dirty apron banged two chipped mugs of tea on the Formica table-top.

'Everything okay, Lindy?' he said, looking at me while he said it. He was very well muscled from lifting those tea mugs every day. He wore a T-shirt with the sleeves ripped out for the express purpose of showing that he wasn't to be messed with. The message was wasted on me. I wasn't in the mood for messing.

'Everything's fine, Tel. Can I use your phone?' Lindy finally got her cigarette lit. I pretended I wasn't leaning into her smoke.

'Help yourself, love.' Tel wiped a table down. His swipes looked more like punches. Little muscles at the back of his arm winked at me.

Tel continued to glare while Lindy made the call. I couldn't hear what she was saying, but the conversation was brief. I took a gulp of tea. It was hot but tasted the same way the place smelt.

'Everyfink all right?' Tel sensed a disapproving customer.

'Fine.' I forced a smile.

'Sure?'

'Marvellous, thanks.' I swallowed some more swill, to back up my story. Tel shuffled off.

'How's the exclusive tabloid contract coming along?' I asked Lindy when she got off the phone.

'Mind your own business.' Lindy sipped her tea, leaving a big pink splodge on the cup where it came in contact with her lipstick. 'I've got several offers,' she said defensively, as if I didn't believe her. 'It's just a matter of choosing which one.'

'Good for you. So the information about Bruce's wife will come in handy, then. He did tell you he was married, I take it?'

'You think if he wants to screw me, he's going to casually mention that he's got a wife?' Lindy's long nails scrabbled at a sugar sachet. She ripped it in half and plopped the contents into her mug. Chucked the little papers aside. 'You don't get out much, do you?'

'Nobody asks me any more.'

'Well, he didn't. But I found out.'

'I get the very strong feeling that not much escapes you.' I said it flirtatiously, like it was a line to get her into bed.

She laughed lightly, flicked ash. 'You'd be surprised what's up here.' She tapped her hard lacquered head.

I waited. My hand strayed to the mug of tea but the memory of how truly awful a drink it was made me reverse the action.

'The cops think the wife did Bruce in?'

'The fact that she's gone missing is rather suspicious.' I kept my eye on Lindy.

Lindy busied herself with another sugar sachet.

'She's missing?'

'Left her flat around the time he died and hasn't been seen since.'

'Why would she want to kill him?'

'Why indeed? I thought you might know.'

'Nope.' She stared straight at me.

'Did Bruce see much of her when he was alive?'

'I suppose. I don't know. They spoke on the phone. She would often call him on his mobile while we were out.'

'So they were friendly?'

'Bruce was friendly with everybody. He needed to be, he was always borrowing money.'

'From you?'

'I didn't have any to lend him.'

'From his wife?'

'I wouldn't rule it out.'

'What was he up to then?'

I didn't expect her to answer. Maybe the newspaper offer had receded and she didn't have anyone else to talk to. Maybe she was just a natural-born gossip. She stubbed her cigarette out. Looked at me through the curl of smoke.

'More tea, love?' It was Tel with an industrial-sized pot. He didn't wait for her to reply before filling her up.

'Not for me thanks, mate,' I said as the pot hovered in my direction. I cradled my mug, making it look like I wanted to savour every last drop. Lindy leant closer. I got a blast of a hard-edged perfume.

'What would you do if you looked like Bruce?'

I shrugged. 'Good-looking guy – Model? Act?'

Lindy laughed. 'No, not Bruce. He liked something with a little more danger.'

'Robbing banks?'

She laughed out loud. 'He was a porn actor. He screwed women for a living. A nice little sideline that helped keep the debt collectors from his door.'

Chapter Eighteen

I paid for the tea and left. Or at least made a big show of leaving. In fact I walked a few yards to the Harrow Road and hailed a taxi. I sat with the meter running waiting for Lindy to come out of the greasy spoon.

She wasn't long. She bustled along on her killer heels and didn't have any trouble at all snagging a taxi. I thought a fight was going to break out when two, from opposite sides of the busy road, made a play for her custom.

'Where to, guv?' Yes, London cabbies do still say that.

'Wherever he's going.' I pointed at the cab that had just scooped up Lindy.

'I love it when we play this game,' he said, all sarcastic as he flicked the cab around. Turn on a penny does a London cab.

Ladbroke Grove can be a bitch, traffic-wise. This is because the local authority and utility companies politely like to take it in turns to dig up the same stretch of road. It's a jolly game and I'm sure amuses them no end. I bet they've installed a secret camera so they can get special kicks watching the drivers practise their road rage on each other at the roundabout by the supermarket.

However, it was a quiet part of the day and we slipped through no problem whatsoever. Lindy's cab was tooling along, taking it easy. I had no fears about being spotted because the ubiquity of the black cabs means you never notice them. Unless it's pouring rain and you're trying to hail one. Then they never notice you.

We drove past my place and took a left on Lancaster Road. We went up a couple of blocks and stopped a few yards back from where Lindy's cab halted. She paid the driver and went to a red-brick building and knocked on the door. Someone came to the door and let her in.

I paid my driver.

'Call me any time, Mr Templar, sir,' he said chortling at his joke as he blasted off in a cloud of environmentally unfriendly diesel smoke.

I was interested in who Lindy was going to see. I walked up to the door. The shiny brass plaque was inscribed with the words 'West Eleven Telecine'. I had a vague idea what telecine was and the building didn't afford any more clues. There were very few windows and they were covered by blinds. I stepped across the road to get a better view while I pondered what to do next, when the door opened and Lindy came out with a man.

It wasn't hard to figure out who he was. As dark as she was fair, as thin as she was curved. As frumpy as she was flamboyant. But the expressions on their faces were cast from the same mould and they had a similar little cowlick on their foreheads. There was no mistaking them for brother and sister.

She was telling him something. Big gestures as they walked along the narrow cobbled mews. Occasionally she freed a hand to tug at her micro mini which was aiming for its rightful home around her waist. He strolled casually, hands in pockets, shaking his head. Whatever she was saying or asking for, he wasn't going along with it.

They didn't look behind, which was good. There was no shelter on this residential street. No basements to drop into or trees to dodge behind. And I'd have felt pretty silly doing that, anyway, especially in Notting Hill, world capital of hip.

Lindy and her brother went to a Caribbean coffee shop on All Saints Road, sat in the dark corner at the back and talked some more. There was nowhere I could be unobtrusive and observe them and it's dangerous to loiter on All Saints Road these days. The risk doesn't come from the drug dealers any more. They were moved on after a couple of yuppie restaurants opened and the cops decided it was time to do something about the illegal street furniture. If you hang about looking even part-way suspicious, a marked car will pull up and ask you what your business is. A few years ago you could have got yourself stabbed on this street and many people did. Now the biggest danger is being struck by a Piaggio scooter racing its passengers toward their expensive but fêted meals of roast koala rump with chilli and lime salsa.

I'd been planning to go home and nap but my

pager went off. It was Marlowe. 'Need to speak,' read the terse message. 'Get in here.'

'I'm trying to decide whether "ornamental cabbage" deserves a place in my definitive list of oxymorons,' Lyall announced grandly when I got back to the newsroom. 'It's not exhaustive. Not all of them. Not the tired old ones like "military intelligence" and "journalistic integrity", but the fresh, new ones. I think I'm going to put it right here, next to "family holiday".' He indicated the list he'd pinned up on the cork board behind his desk.

Lyall's a clever guy whose job occupies about the same space in his brain as the bit he needs to decide whether he's going to have eggs or cornflakes for breakfast and so he invents little games to keep himself amused throughout the day.

'Marlowe wants to speak to me,' I said. If there were any scuttlebutt to pick up, Lyall would have already done the heavy lifting.

'What about?'

'My lacklustre performance in getting the Bruce McCarthy interview on air.'

'Hmmm.'

'What should I say?'

'Say: "I'll do anything at all but please don't fire me, Mr Marlowe, sir." I'd also compliment him on the size of his penis, if you can slip it into the conversation without seeming obsequious.'

'I can't beg. There's a principle at stake.'

'You and me.' Lyall flipped his chalk in the air.

Caught it neatly. 'You and me, Ridley. We can't afford to have principles. That's the way it is, modern life. No principles.'

'I don't like it.'

'Get used to it. It's only going to get worse.'

I climbed the stairs to Marlowe's office with a heavy heart.

Chapter Nineteen

It's not a cosy relationship, Marlowe's and mine. We don't rub along together. If you asked us to agree on whether the sun came up in the morning and locked us in a small room till we got a result, only one would come out alive. Some days I speculate that it's jealousy on his part: he may be cosseted upstairs with a pert personal assistant and an expense account, but in his heart of hearts he wishes he were still getting his hands dirty on Fleet Street. He has many stories of his exploits in the old days before the newspapers up and buggered off to some dismal place further down the Thames, when he was a street-fighting lad.

Other days I think the way he treats me is just the sheer bloodymindedness of a poor kid brought up rough who can't get used to the notion that he doesn't have to punch his way through life. But I only think that when I'm feeling expansive: it's hard to maintain much in the way of sympathy for someone who's so consistently in touch with his inner arsehole.

I put up with Marlowe because I need the job. Despite the fact that media outlets in London over the last few years have sprung up like mushrooms on steroids, there're fewer and fewer owners and that actually means less work. Add to that the battalions of bright young things being extruded from journalism schools who're prepared to muck in and give employers the benefit of their inexperience and the picture is downright off-putting. I've been around the block a few times but no one would call me a legend in my own news hour. Even if they did, I've seen hacks more garlanded than me given the bum's rush when the suits upstairs decide they want someone with less lip and a lower daily rate. I've weighed all these factors up in the long, whisky-fuelled nights since my family disappeared to the other side of the world and decided that my priorities are my son and my modestly bad habits. I do what I must to maintain them. Mostly, I do what I'm told.

'What's up, mate?' I sat in a chair in Marlowe's office, looked studiously casual. Marlowe would be looking forward to tearing a strip off me because I didn't hand over the Bruce McCarthy interview. No matter that Rick took the tape from my drawer and used it without permission in ethically dodgy circumstances. Marlowe likes to back Rick because it's the side I'm not on. I waited for the impact.

'Looking pretty smug, these days, Ridley.' Marlowe was armoured behind his giant desk. The hard flat light of winter streamed in the panes behind him. All I could see of him was a blurred outline.

'Things have seldom been better,' I drawled. It was going to be a sideways attack, not the usual head-on.

'You're providing help for the homeless, I hear.'

'That's the kind of guy I am.' I wondered where this was heading. Marlowe fancied Felicia so the fact that she was living under my roof would be a big smudgy mark against my name. Marlowe, who judges everybody by his own slimy standards, would assume the worst. He looked like he wanted to say something about Felicia. He drew a breath, but decided against it. Wise, I thought. Leave well alone.

'Crosbie's told me about her little problem. With the stalker.' He shifted his bulk. Picked up a paper off his desk. 'To be perfectly accurate, she didn't tell me. I had to read about it in the goddamn paper.' Marlowe held up one of the sillier tabloids. *Hack's Stalker Hell*, shouted the headline. 'When I asked her about it, she told me you and Felicia went over to see her the other night.' Marlowe got out of his chair and leant against the window sill. The sun snuck behind a cloud. I could see him again. His expression was hard. 'She's pretty cut up about it.'

'Not enough to go to the cops.'

'She tells me the cops can't help her.'

'I'm sure they'd disagree,' I said, wondering when the conversation was going to get around to my appalling lapse of tabloid journalism standards.

'She wants to do a show on stalking.' Marlowe inspected his nails. It was a strangely effete gesture coming from such a big bloke. 'I think it's a good idea.' He shoved his hands in his pockets as if ashamed of them.

I didn't, so I said nothing.

'But before I agree it, I want you to help me.'

I sat up, shocked. This was virgin territory. Marlowe asking me for help.

'Forget it. I'm not working on *Female A.M.* ever again. The last time was a disaster.'

'I don't want you on the show. I want you to find out who's following her.'

I digested that, it took some time. Then I clamped my teeth together to stop from shouting out 'No!' at levels that would bring the security guards running.

Marlowe could sense my opposition.

'Look,' he said, buddy-like. 'You know the stats as well as I do. Most stalkers know their victims. I just don't want this to blow up in our faces. She's got so much bloody coverage as it is.' He swatted the paper like it was an annoying insect.

I got interested. 'Someone she knows. What are you suggesting?'

'I'm not suggesting anything.'

'What then? You want me to catch this guy? Perform a citizen's arrest?'

'I just want you to check it out. So we know what we're dealing with. Maybe you'll get some solid evidence and we can go to the cops.'

I remembered the note I'd taken from Crosbie's. I had to pass it on to Charlie.

'Will you help me?'

'No.'

Marlowe gaped. It was so long since he'd heard that word he probably had to take a minute to figure out what it meant.

'What?'

'No.' I abandoned my slouch and sat up in the chair. We had to get our eyeline equal if we were to have any meaningful disagreement.

Marlowe came around the front of his desk and hovered over me. 'We're not having a debate here. I tell you to do something, you fucking do it.'

'City Radio pays me to be a reporter, I report. I'm not on your private staff.'

'Look,' he said, shaking a finger.

'No. You look.' I stood up, suddenly angrier than I've been in a long time. 'I work for the same company as you, Mr Fucking Big Shot. I am not at your beck and call. I don't do vigilante work and I do not spy on my colleagues. You get that? So take your finger out of my way before I fucking snap it off.'

Marlowe stepped back, his face a treat. So much for doing as I was told. Must try harder in that department when I got to my new job. If I got a new job. In the past Marlowe had threatened to put the word around after he sacked me. He promised I'd be pretty well unemployable in London and would have to move somewhere exciting like Weston-super-Mare to put whisky on my table. I had no reason to doubt him.

I straightened my jacket. Got ready to walk out of City Radio for ever. I reached the door when something stopped me in my tracks. A sound stranger than anything I had heard.

The sound of Marlowe laughing.

It was as if a horse had asthma. A snuffling, exploding sound that erupted from his nostrils in staccato bursts that made you glad you weren't standing too close. I turned and gaped.

'Come back. Sit down,' he said, waving me back to the chair, wiping away a little tear from his eye. I sat, suspicious. A merry Marlowe; it was too much to take in. It crossed my mind that dear old Tel had put something in that vile caff tea and I was now fiendishly hallucinating.

'Let's start again, shall we?' Marlowe sat too, behind his cherry-wood desk, so vast it could have launched a jump jet. No other City Radio executives had a desk like that, it'd been an anniversary present from his wife. They'd needed a crane to ease it in from an outside window. Marlowe had considered the trouble and expense to be commensurate with his opinion of himself.

'Look,' he said, 'you know Crosbie. She's not too tightly wrapped at the best of times. This thing could tip her over the edge. She refuses to get help from the cops so we have no choice.'

'*We* have no choice? I have a choice and I say "no".'

'This isn't coming from me, Ridley. This is higher up. You know how they love her.'

That was certainly true. Crosbie could do no wrong in the rheumy eyes of the senior management.

'I'm getting pressure,' Marlowe said. 'Crosbie's not happy, then they're not happy. And we need to do this thing discreetly.'

'So instead of one creep hanging around the place she gets two, how nice for her.'

'I'll sort it out with her.'

I said nothing. My expression said plenty.

'Ridley, you'll be doing the company a favour. And I think you owe us that.' The implication was clear. I looked unconvinced.

'We'll pay you extra.'

I was thinking of my credit-card bills from Australia. A couple of nights lurking like a pervert in Primrose Hill and I could wipe them out.

It's true. I can be bought.

'A week's pay,' I said firmly.

'For a few hours' work?'

'That's my price. And I'm off overnights.'

Marlowe sighed. 'Okay.'

For once I had him where I wanted him. All I needed to do now was find out why he'd let me get him there.

Chapter Twenty

There was a rumour going round that Jason Nutter had a proper office somewhere but he did most of his work out of an illegal club in Greek Street. It was downstairs from a newsagent and if you knew the right knock you could get a drink there any hour of the day or night. As long as the owner didn't forget to pay the cops, the place didn't shut and Jason liked it that way. He was of the old school, a gentleman's club was his refuge against the uncertainties of the modern world. Never mind the fact that the place was dark, dirty and charged a fortune for the smallest snort of alcohol, Jason knew he could rely on it.

There was a booth at the back where he sat with his mobile phone to one ear and the transistor radio tuned to whatever race meeting happened to be on that day. Jason's bets invariably lost and he would then drink heavily to assuage his disappointment. The pattern had been set many years ago and he saw no reason to change it. Oddly, he seemed to thrive on what would have been a self-destructive spiral for any other person. His habits didn't affect his business, which operated as smoothly as a shark in a metropolitan swimming pool.

Jason didn't actually make pornographic movies. There were no meetings with directors and scriptwriters nor casting sessions featuring big-breasted girls called Muffy and Bimbi. No cheap filming sessions at hastily converted 'studios' in darkest Essex. Jason did money. He spent all day on the phone talking figures to people who wanted to invest. Talking more figures to people who wanted to make the film. Putting them together like a traditional matchmaker. He didn't even see the films that resulted from his deals. On the rare occasions when he could be bothered to leave the club, apart from Cheltenham and Ascot, where he would turn up looking pretty presentable in a morning suit, he would go to London Zoo. He was especially fond of hippopotami, he once told me when I asked him why there were so many pictures of them pinned to the wall behind his booth. The manner in which he delivered this information did not encourage me to enquire further, so I never found out exactly why this was the case.

'Whisky?' he barked at me as I squeezed into the booth. Jason drank ten-year-old single malt like it was lemonade. The word was he was extremely wealthy but he didn't have any legitimate hobbies to waste his money on. He may have had a flat somewhere but he never seemed to spend any time there. He lurched between the club and the betting shop, which was in a little back street a couple of blocks away. He thrived on the toing and froing of old Soho types. The fact that there were fewer and fewer of them these days was a source of great sadness.

He didn't wait for my reply. There were two glasses on the table and he picked one up. Squinted into it to make sure he hadn't left some in there, then wiped his finger around the inside to be doubly certain. He slopped some precious malt in. I took it and drank. Figured the alcohol would kill off the germs that lived on Jason's hands and make me forget that what I really needed was sleep.

'Sam Ridley. You don't come down so often. Whassamadder? I developed an antisocial disease nobody told me about? No.' He held up his hand. 'Lemme guess. You been busy. Am I right?' He was a thin man who wore his hair slicked back in a fifties-style quiff. His skin, not knowing how to respond to the twin effects of booze and lack of sunlight, was grey and pitted and because Jason didn't eat much it was flaccid, like it had lost interest in sticking to his bones.

'You develop a goddamn social life or something? You going out to dinner parties and the theatre and forgetting your old mates?'

'Never. I've been in Australia.'

'Australia,' he wheezed. 'Australia. Where is Australia, anyway? That outside the M25?'

'Unless they moved it.'

'You look different,' he said, suspicious. 'Healthy or something.' Jason would not have appreciated me mentioning I'd given up smoking. He despised any concessions to longevity and would have held me down and forced a full-strength packet of Camels into my mouth, making me smoke them all while he watched.

'Sun,' I said. 'Just laying down some skin cancer for later life.'

Jason looked relieved. 'That's all right then. I thought for a minute . . . don't be going soft on me, Ridley.' He sunk his whisky in one go. 'So what can I do for you, apart from educate your illiterate taste buds?'

'I need some information about a guy called Bruce McCarthy. He's in the business. Talent.'

'Never heard of him. What's he doing? Who's he working with?'

'Not sure.' Then I thought of the movie Charlie Hobbs had brought over to my flat. '*Humping Heidi*. That ring any bells?'

'Years old,' Jason said. 'A classic. Wasn't involved with it myself.'

'He may have been in that.'

'I'll ask around for you. Why the interest?'

'He had his veins pumped full of bleach.'

Jason wrinkled his nose. 'What is the world coming to?' he said as he poured another glass and waved the bottle over mine. 'Drink up, Sam. Don't lag, you know I hate dawdlers.'

I drank up. Jason refreshed our glasses.

'How come he's in the biz, I never heard of him?'

I sipped from my glass, Jason glared at me and pointed at the bottle. 'It doesn't surprise me. The woman who told me might have been spinning me a line.'

'Women.' Jason sighed heavily. 'You gotta learn not to trust 'em. They either want your money or they want to rip out your heart with their vampire nails and stomp all over it in their high-heeled, patent-leather booties. Trust me, Sam. I know what I'm talking about.' He looked as if he did. I'd never actually seen Jason with a woman, but it wouldn't have surprised me to hear he had one or even two stashed somewhere.

'Always say no, Sam. A woman comes to us for help in our line of work, it's trouble. Always. No shagging exceptions.' It seemed impolite to point out we were in different lines of work, so I didn't.

'They want something from you. That's all.' Jason warmed to his theme, 'And it's gonna hurt you to give it, Sam.'

The whisky relaxed me nicely so after I left Jason Nutter, I went home and slept. When I got up I looked in the phone book and found Lana Davidoff's number. The address was in Acton. I knew she probably wouldn't be there but I set off anyway.

I collected my trusty Renault from outside my flat and was on the road to Acton in no time. The traffic was jammed with commuters and progress was slow. It gave me time to think. Despite all my nosing I didn't have any clearer picture of who Bruce McCarthy was. The people around him gave such disparate views that it was hard to get a composite which made any sense.

The L. Davidoff I hoped was Lana was listed as living at Oak Avenue. It sounded suitably arboreal but, in my experience, the grottier the neighbourhood, the more rustic the street name.

Oak Avenue sported a few listless trees, none of them oaks. They were scrubby things that had seen better days, their health and outlook on life no doubt blighted by the fencing around them that had been filled up with empty cans.

The doorbell on the flat was no more revealing about the person who lived there. The bell simply said 'Davidoff'. I rang it but got no reply. I rang again, just in case. The houses were late Victorian detached. But not very detached. There was only about ten feet between them and the fences were low. As I waited I noticed the net curtains at the next-door house twitch. A sight that gladdens a journalist's heart because as surely as God made little deadlines, it meant a Nosy Neighbour.

Chapter Twenty-One

'Lana? I haven't seen her since Sunday morning,' the neighbour said. She wasn't hard to get talking. She'd met me at the door, demanded to share what she knew of the comings and goings of the neighbourhood. 'She doesn't usually do that. Very reliable girl, normally, very regular. Not like that one who lives at number 23. Does she ever like the men, the parties? I tell you. Not that I'm one to pry, mind. It's just, you can't help it when it's on your doorstep like that, now can you? Goodness me, even if I wanted to block out the comings and goings I wouldn't be able to. Rowdy? That girl makes more noise than a platoon of soldiers. Why, my husband, Jake—'

'Lana,' I said forcefully, to try and get the conversation back on track. 'You said you saw her Sunday? What was she doing?'

'Got up very early, she did. Seven o'clock she was out of here. I noticed her because I was standing at the kitchen sink waiting for the kettle to boil. Jake likes his morning cuppa in bed, he does. I always bring it in for him. Forty years married, I never missed a morning. Jake's proud of me. He always tells his mates, I never missed a morning.' She was elderly, an impression enhanced by the calliper on her left leg. She wore a floral wrap that covered her dress. Her hair was crimped in artificial waves and rinsed candyfloss pink.

'Did you speak to her?'

'Who?'

'Lana. Your neighbour.'

'Oh no, dear. I waved through the window, you know. She waved back. Normally she stops to say hello but she seemed a little distracted. That was the last time I saw her. She hasn't been back, least not that I've seen. And I don't go out much, dear. Not with my leg.'

'Did she have a suitcase? Perhaps she went on holiday.'

'No. She carried her little handbag, like always. A black patent-leather bag. Such a nice girl. Always beautifully groomed. Her hair, her nails, always polished. And good to me. Always got the time of day for an old woman.' She put her hand to her hair coquettishly and for a second I had an echo of the past: a fleeting impression of a glamorous young girl. 'It was odd, I must say. Normally if she went away she'd tell me, you know, so I wouldn't worry. I do worry for the young ones. Things aren't what they used to be. Not like in my day. You don't know who you can trust.'

'Did Lana go away much?'

'No, she was a hard-working girl. She took her job seriously, she did. No gallivanting about like number 23.'

'What was her job?'

'She worked over in Ealing at a beauty salon. Always offering me to come and get my nails done. I've never got around to it. So difficult for me to get out—' She trailed off.

'Do you know which beauty salon?'

'I have the number here somewhere,' she said. 'Lana gave me her card. I remember it said beauty consultant on it. Sounded ever so posh. I must go over there and treat myself. Jake's always saying I should treat myself.'

I waited on the step while she searched in the house. 'Here it is, dear,' she said, emerging a few minutes later.

The card had Lana Davidoff printed on it and a telephone number and the words 'Beauty Consultant'. But it was the sort of card you can get printed out at the train station. All you need is a few quid and correct spelling and you can describe yourself as a circus midget and no one would be any the wiser.

'Has anyone come to the flat since Lana left?'

'Oh, that would have been Annie. She was from Lana's work. She popped by to see where she was.'

'How did she get into the flat?'

'She has a key. At least she must have, because she went straight in.'

'Did you recognize her?'

'No dear. I'd never seen her before in my life. I asked her who she was and that's what she told me.'

'What did she look like?'

'She had dark hair, like Lana. And she wore this beautiful fur coat. Must have cost a fortune.'

I didn't know too many beauty therapists who'd

be able to afford or even want to buy a fur coat. Even with my limited grasp of fashion mores, I knew that fur was about as attractive to most British women as head lice. But I'd seen a fur coat on the woman at Bruce's funeral. What on earth was she doing poking around Lana's place?

Primrose Hill belied my theory about place names. It sounded pretty and it was. A little too pretty for someone like me who only feels comfortable with lumpy asphalt beneath his feet. But for those Londoners who for some reason prefer to kid themselves they're living in a rustic village rather than a mighty metropolis, Primrose Hill delivers the goods. There are the basic amenities: the speciality cheese shops, the dainty French restaurants, the upmarket fashion boutiques and the village green, which in this case looks out on the rest of the city.

I parked the Renault a few yards from Crosbie's place and got out feeling uncomfortable. I wondered if I should knock on her door and announce myself. But Marlowe said he'd cleared it for me. Crosbie knew what I was doing and was okay with it. So I figured it'd be better for both of us if we pretended I wasn't there. Crosbie and I are not soulmates; I don't have much time for malingerers who draw huge salaries and she views me the way a rich woman would look at the guy who comes to unblock the drains.

There wasn't much happening in Primrose Hill. I sat in the car till I got comprehensively bored then I walked around a bit to stretch my legs. I'd forgotten about food, and my stomach started to remind me. I walked up to the shops to see if there was a kebab or hamburger place but there wasn't. No big surprises there. I could have sat down at a tiny table and ordered *coq au vin*, or whatever seventies retro dish is big with the fashionable eaters these days, but there was nothing to cater for more simple tastes.

I walked back to the car. The lights were on in Crosbie's flat but the curtains were drawn. I got back in the car. Calculated how much money I was making from this sordid endeavour and how long I should stay to justify it. Four hours seemed like a fair shake. I checked my watch: twenty-five minutes had elapsed. I made a note to come more prepared in future with things to pass the time.

There was nobody even remotely suspicious around. I was wasting my time. The good burghers of Primrose Hill were either inside, in the bosom of their families, or out at the latest chi-chi dining emporium or alternative theatre experience. Every now and then a late commuter would straggle home, clutching a briefcase and a gym bag, but that was the sum of street life. The upstairs neighbour with the impossibly large dog set off for a late-night walk in the park. He didn't see me slumped in my car and I didn't feel like going hand to paw with Caesar, the mutt with a superiority complex.

I decided to pass the time cleaning up the inside of the car. Mostly this involved arranging the old newspapers into neat piles and clearing out the food wrappers that had slid under the seats. I collected an armful of rubbish and took it to the nearest bin. On the way back I spotted somebody standing outside Crosbie's place with a hand on the gate, staring, like I had been a few minutes before. From where I was, I couldn't tell if it was a man or a woman. The clothing gave no clues, they were trussed up against the London weather in black trousers, a leather coat and a hat. I was convinced it was the stalker. I walked quietly towards Crosbie's place. Still the stalker did nothing. I jingled my keys like I was trying to remember where I'd parked my car. The stalker shot a quick glance. The hat was pulled down, I didn't see the face but the shoulders jerked in surprise. He took off.

'Hey!' I shouted. 'Hey! I want a word.'

Chapter Twenty-Two

The chase was short and I lost. The stalker already had a good hundred-yard lead and moved much quicker. I should be fit, but then I should be a lot of things. Once the adrenaline had worn off I ran out of power. I chased down the side of the park. He made for the open grass, running like a hare to the peak of Primrose Hill. It's a short and steep hill and I was not equipped to take it. My shoes slid in the winter mud. I fell once. Picked myself up. Saw the black coat disappearing over the brow of the hill.

Gasping, I struggled to the top but he had gone.

I slid back down the hill, wet, muddy and pissed off. I thought about going in to see Crosbie but decided my mud-caked legs would not accessorize with her all-white interiors.

It seemed unlikely that I'd scare the guy off for good. Whackos usually deserve their reputations for single-minded obsession and an unfit and not particularly imposing journalist was not going to put the fear of God into him. Nothing short of a court order would keep the guy away, and even that was unlikely. If I got really lucky I could find out his identity and hand him over to the cops. If that indeed was what Marlowe had in mind, and I still wasn't sure I'd had the gospel truth from my boss.

Felicia wasn't in when I got back to the flat, and judging from the fact that my ceiling wasn't shaking, neither were the upstairs neighbours. I poured myself a whisky and sat in the half-dark, thinking about Bruce's runaway wife. I studied the card that Lana had given Mrs Richards. Perhaps she'd simply decided to take a holiday somewhere warm and had forgotten to tell her neighbour. There were a million reasons why she would go somewhere. Illness in the family, an impromptu trip. I inspected each of these prospects in turn and decided the suspicious one was the most likely. Marriage may well be a special institution ordained by God but that doesn't stop hundreds of people bashing, stabbing, drowning or otherwise permanently disposing of their spouses every year.

It's enough to put you off romance.

I sipped more whisky. It didn't have the resonance of the stuff I'd drunk that morning with Jason Nutter, but it was plenty soothing. Black Label's been a good friend to me down the years but nevertheless I found myself wondering when Felicia would be home so we could have a real chat. Bruce McCarthy as a porno star, the missing wife, Sam Ridley as City Radio's paid vigilante, Felicia would shake it all down and sort it out in alphabetical order. After the initial shock of her moving in had worn off, I'd grown quite used to having another body around the place. My thoughts moved to advertising for a flatmate when she moved out. Then I considered the realities of the whole dismal process: the sad ad in the *Evening*

Standard, the interviews and the unfortunate permutations that would undoubtedly arise, and decided maybe not. Life's a disaster lottery as it is; no sense in poking a sharp stick in the side of the Fates.

Early the next morning I dialled the number on Lana's card. It was a message service. I left my name and number and a message about Bruce McCarthy.

Because I didn't imagine in my wildest fantasies that Lana would be tripping over herself to call me back, I listed all the beauty salons in the Yellow Pages. I ignored the murderous looks from Fern, who had not recently picked up any pointers about how to behave civilly and asked her to help me ring the numbers.

'Nice jacket,' I said as an ice-breaker. Fern's dress sense had altered in the last week or so. She'd gone from student scruffy to the French existentialist look – a cool black leather jacket, black top and black trousers.

'Agnès b,' she sniffed.

I had no idea what she was talking about. I handed her the list and told her to get on with it. She sighed heavily and clumped away in her new suede boots.

I spent a good thirty minutes on the phone not finding Lana.

I looked across the newsroom. Rick had arrived. He was leaning over Fern's shoulder, almost touching her but not quite. They were so close that she must have had the full steamroller effect of his aftershave. Rick never stinted on the signals he sent out to the world in general and the opposite sex in particular. He loved to hit on the young women and was often successful because they hadn't learnt to recognize lowlife when it nattily disguised itself in expensive clothes. I watched with interest; they exchanged a few words and Fern laughed, embarrassed, judging by the flush that sprang to her cheeks. Rick patted her on the shoulder and walked away, straightening his lapels. I saw that Lyall had noticed what Rick was up to. The message light on my computer blinked. *There's one born every news hour*, Lyall had typed. There are two levels of communication in the newsroom. The audible one people can see and hear and the electronic subtext that comments on what's really going on. I was trying to think of a witty reply when Fern marched over.

'I found your woman,' she said. Her surly mask was back in place as she threw a scrap of paper on my desk. 'It's not a beauty salon, it's a nail bar.'

'What's the difference?'

She just shrugged and walked off, as though I was beneath contempt.

Felicia was deep in planning for her show and not really in the mood to indulge me. I waited around till she got the impression that I wasn't going away.

'What is it?' she hissed.

'Can you call this number and make an appointment?'

Felicia raised one eyebrow. 'Make your own appointments. You're a big boy now.'

'Around ten will suit me fine.'

'Ridley, I'm too busy. Can't it wait?'

'I might be getting a lead on Bruce McCarthy. Ask for Lana.'

Felicia took the number and dialled it with her free hand, subconsciously inspecting her nails while she did so.

'Hello? I'd like to make an appointment with Lana.' Felicia's mid-Atlantic accent had metamorphosed into harsh South London. Flat vowels and clipped consonants streamed out of her mouth as though she'd learnt them in her mother's womb.

'When will she be back?'

There were series of nods and 'okays' while the person on the other end explained the situation.

'I really wanted to see Lana,' Felicia said. More nods, more uh-huhs. 'And this Dixie woman is good? Because I like to have stencils. And dual colours. You know, blue one side, red the other, that sort of thing. Uh-huh, uh-huh. Okay, well, I'll have a think about it and call you back.'

Felicia replaced the handset. 'Lana's away. They don't know when she'll be back. But should you want a set of false nails with silver stars stencilled on them, Dixie can do it for you. She owns the place and she trained Lana, so she knows everything there is to know about acrylic.'

'Great, I've been trying to decide what my new look should be.'

I took the tube out to Ealing.

The demand for false nails was low that day. The nail bar, a narrow, mirrored room with seats along both sides, was empty. I walked in and startled the dark-haired woman in the pink overall who was tidying bottles of varnish. I told her who I was and who I was looking for, which didn't put her any more at ease.

'Lana's not here,' she said, turning away from me.

'Do you know where she is?'

'On holiday. No law against it.'

'I didn't say there was. Where is she on holiday?' I moved so that she had to face me.

'That's not your business.'

'I'm a reporter, working on a story about her husband. You know he died?'

'Yes.'

'When was the last time you saw her?'

'I don't have to answer your questions. Please leave.' She folded her arms for emphasis. I didn't press her.

'Okay.' I held my hands up. 'I'm going.'

She'd hit the phone almost as soon as I was out the door.

There was a burger place across the street. I hadn't eaten breakfast, so I ordered the works: a burger, fries, a little patty thing that advertised itself as a fruit pie, and two cups of plastic coffee. I picked up a paper, browsed through the morning headlines.

I could see the entrance to 'Dixies Place', as the front sign proclaimed. No customers arrived but another young woman turned up for work. When she arrived Dixie went out on the street and looked up and down. She caught sight of me, watching her through the window of the burger bar. I'd read the comics and was tossing up whether to do the anagram or the easy crossword. I waved. She crossed the busy street.

'Hi,' she said. 'It's Sam Ridley, right?'

I chewed the last of the pie. Held out my hand. Smiled my winning smile.

Dixie didn't smile back. 'Lana wants to speak to you.'

Chapter Twenty-Three

'I thought she was on holiday.'

'She got back.' Dixie didn't let her high heels stop her walking at a clip. It was a dismal day, low, grey skies and spots of rain. Dixie got out a tiny, telescopic umbrella. I shouldered on, getting wet. We walked for maybe half a mile to a street lined with once grand houses that were now shabby hotels.

'It's the Blue Hyacinth,' Dixie said, pointing down the street. 'Room 10.'

She left.

I covered the last fifty yards to the hotel sharpish. There wasn't much shelter and the rain had started to come down steadily. A guy who was parked in a white car on the other side of the road reading a file and eating something that looked like a sandwich glanced at me as if to ascertain the degree of my insanity then resumed chewing. I hated him for being warm and dry while I was cold and wet.

I shook some of the rain off me as I walked up the front steps, straightened my tie. The hotel didn't look like a classy establishment, but receptionists can get funny ideas.

This one could not have cared less. She was

young, loudly dressed and I presumed couldn't hear what I was saying because of the stereo headphones locked on her ears. She didn't bother to take them off to hear me better, or even hear me at all. She waved me in as she popped another stick of gum.

The hotel was badly lit and smelt of institutional food. The carpet was threadbare and the walls covered with a maroon flock wallpaper. The look was completed with the obligatory set of hunting prints: a fanciful vision of jolly old rural England that seems to strike a chord in the hearts of landlords everywhere.

I knocked briskly on the door. It opened right away. A slender blonde woman, dressed all in black, stood on the other side.

Lana Davidoff.

She looked me up and down and I did the same to her. Curly had been right. She had the figure and face of a model. The sort that appears in James Bond movies and knows how to field strip a kalashnikov and crush a bloke between her sweetly moulded thighs.

'Not much of a holiday.' I held out my hand. 'Sam Ridley. Glad you got my message.'

'Come in.'

The room was poky and dark. Brown wallpaper, brown carpet. A single bed and a table made from plastic pretending it was wood. The sole window, which looked out on to the street, was covered by a flimsy curtain.

'Coffee? It's quite good.'

Lana picked up a Thermos, her frivolously

painted purple and green nails providing a wacky contrast to the slim silver flask. I sat in a sagging green chair with wooden handles and watched her pour the contents into two chipped mugs.

I sipped. She was right, it was good. I thought about starting a conversation but decided not to. I wanted to see what she had to say first.

Lana crossed to the window and peaked through the curtains then turned to face me.

'What do you want, Mr Ridley?' She smiled and opposite me on the bed crossed her legs slowly and smoothed the cover down as if suggesting I should join her there.

'I want to talk about Bruce.'

'We have not seen each other for a long time.'

'Weren't you concerned when you found out he was murdered?'

Lana shrugged philosophically. 'Nothing I could do to bring him back.'

'The cops want to speak to you.'

Again the shrug.

Some silence passed. I admired her legs. Her ankles, which were peeping out the bottom of flared trousers were particularly well turned. Her delicate feet were encased in high black shoes. She had wide-spaced grey eyes, shoulder-length blonde hair and lips that movie stars sometimes pay plastic surgeons to construct.

She was looking me up and down too. The view wasn't so good from her side, but if she was disappointed, it didn't show. I finished my coffee. Lana checked the window again. Pulled back the curtains.

'Let's go for a drive,' she said. 'And I tell you some things.'

The rain stopped and the sun punched through the clouds. A shaft of light darted in, pointing up the flaws in the room's interior design scheme. Lana didn't have much luggage, a black patent-leather handbag was the only personal effect in the room, aside from the flask and a packet of cigarettes. She picked both up and put them in the bag.

By the time we got outside the sun had gone away and the rain had started again. A typical March day in London, where we rotate the seasons at a brisk pace.

When we reached the bottom of the hotel steps, Lana tucked her arm into mine. I caught a whiff of floral perfume. We had no umbrella, but Lana didn't hurry. We strolled like a courting couple. I forgot about the rain. I felt the warmth of her and thought some inappropriate thoughts.

'Where are we going?' I asked as Lana unlocked her car. It was a small Ford, a recent model, parked around the corner from where she was staying.

'Nowhere special,' she said and slid into the driver's seat. She turned the key in the ignition. It started smoothly.

'Put on the seat belt,' she said. 'We don't want accidents.'

The car stereo blasted into life with the engine. Drum and bass music filled the tiny space. Lana flicked it off.

'First I drive, then we talk.' She had a sing-song Slavic accent that made her sound like Ivana Trump. Under other circumstances, I could really go for an accent like that.

There wasn't much traffic in the suburban streets of West London. We drove slowly. Lana didn't seem to have a route in mind. I sat and waited for her to get to the point. She wanted me for something, for sure. Maybe she'd heard about her husband's death and panicked and was scared to go to the cops, being a foreigner and coming from a place that doesn't have a shining record of human rights.

'I didn't see you at the funeral,' I said after we'd driven north for a bit.

'I was not there.'

'Too upset, I suppose.'

'No. Bruce meant nothing to me, alive or dead.'

I tried to imagine saying that about my ex-wife, Mary. We'd loved each other and hated each other but indifference was not on our emotional menu.

'You are shocked.' Lana shot a sideways glance at me. We were stopped at traffic lights. Lana indicated a left-hand turn.

'He was your husband.'

'It's the way I feel.'

After we turned, I registered the white car that had been parked outside the hotel was following us. A cop, I was sure. I should have realized it before.

I saw Lana glance in her rear-vision mirror, her face expressionless.

'They tell me Bruce was a porn actor,' I pressed on. 'That how you guys met?'

'We met in Spain,' she said. She made another turn, more sudden. The white car stayed a sedate distance behind us.

'What were you doing in Spain?'

'Looking for a husband.' She smiled her seductive, front-page smile. The search probably hadn't taken much time.

We trundled through an industrial estate. From the signposts, I could tell we were somewhere near Park Royal. Featureless prefabricated buildings passed us. The white car remained steady behind. I was starting to get an unpleasant feeling in my stomach. I started to think about the other possible reason why Lana hadn't gone to the cops, the one where she'd killed Bruce and was now looking for a sucker to help her out of trouble. I began to toss around unfeasible plans to get out of a moving vehicle.

'Know that guy?' I asked Lana when she checked her mirror again.

'What guy?' she said innocently.

'The guy who's been following us since we left the hotel. He was waiting outside.'

'There is nobody following us.'

'This nobody's driving a white sedan.'

Lana shrugged. A habit that, for me, could quickly become annoying.

'I feel used,' I said. 'But I'm beginning to suspect a lot of men who come in contact with you feel like that.'

Lana ignored me. She kept her eyes on the road, driving steadily. Her hands, with their strangely lacquered nails, held the wheel loosely. Her thighs moved up and down as she changed gears. The car picked up speed. We were darting around the back roads, but signs were showing that the North Circular was approaching. Like most big roads in the city, it's usually cramped with traffic.

That day it was moving quite briskly. The white car followed us close into the feeder lane but with a smaller car and some cheeky driving, Lana was able to edge over into the fast lane and get further ahead.

I eased back in my seat, gripping the hand rests. Lana leant heavy on the accelerator.

'What's your plan?' I asked.

'You like asking questions.'

'It's an occupational hazard.'

'Ah yes, the so-called journalist.'

'Not so-called. Actual. I'd show you my press card but I honestly think you need both eyes for the road.'

'Anybody can fake press card.'

'Not me. I worked hard for mine. Foolishly, some might say. It hasn't got me anywhere.'

She wove in and out of the slower-moving traffic, which was every other vehicle on the road. Other cars honked their rage. I sighed. Wondered if it wasn't too late to convert to a soothing religion.

'I mean, people talk about journalism being glamorous. All these youngsters pour out of universities and colleges having seen *All the President's Men* thinking they can change the world, but it's not like that. You end up spending all your life in boring press conferences and even more boring council meetings being fed bullshit by some petty elected official who's misread his mandate from the people and thinks it's the tablets of stone. After a few years of this you lose heart, you start casting around for something else to put the spring back into your step and it's only then that you realize you're qualified for exactly nothing. The world has no use for you. Not a one.'

'Except crime,' Lana said.

'It's never appealed.'

'I don't believe you.' Lana flashed me a smile. She was enjoying this. 'You're involved in this, I think.'

'Involved in what? Bruce's murder?'

She shook her head. 'I rang my neighbour. She said you come right after Chloe had been in my flat.'

'Who's Chloe?'

'You know as well as me.'

'I don't. It must be a coincidence.'

'In my position I can't afford to trust coincidence,' she said, braking just enough to avoid running into the back of a truck. 'If you want to do your own deal, tell them I'm not interested.'

'What deal?'

'I pick you up to tell you this. I am not dealing. I am on my own now. Pass that on.'

'Pass it on to who?' I remembered the fur-coated woman who'd been at Lana's flat and at the funeral. Was that who Lana was talking about? 'Who's Chloe?'

Lana had begun edging back towards an off-ramp. The white car tried to follow but was stuck between two vans. Lana turned off the North Circular, barging another red light. The white car was still stuck. We were away free. Lana laughed out loud.

We turned down some more side streets. We were

somewhere in Neasden or Harlesden. This time Lana seemed to know exactly where she was going.

I checked the side rear-view mirror for a sign of the white car, but there was none. I strained my ears for the blessed sound of sirens but all I could hear was my heart beating.

'What happens now?'

Lana slowed the car further, we were near a large park. We drove in the main gates. There weren't many people around. A few joggers. I thought I saw a cop car drive past, but it took no notice of us.

The car park was practically empty. Lana drew up smartly and turned off the ignition.

'London's parks,' she said. 'I will miss them.'

'Taking a trip?'

She put her arm around my neck, pulling me towards her and kissed me hard, forcing her tongue down my throat. I was expecting a lot of things, but not that. I gasped. Tasted cigarettes and lipstick and her. Reached out for something to get a grip with. Before I'd had a chance to get comfortable, she'd drawn back. I heard a click and felt something cold and hard around my wrist. I looked down. Handcuffs.

'What the hell?'

Lana's pale hand stroked the inside of my wrist as she slipped the other cuff on the steering wheel and clicked it shut.

'Goodbye, Sam Ridley,' she said softly. 'Another time maybe.'

'You can't do this.'

'This will help you relax.' She threw down a packet of French cigarettes and a lighter. Then she slipped out of her seat, shut the door and sprinted lithely away, her bag swinging behind her. Rain spotted the car windshield. I soon lost track of her.

I stared at the cigarettes for a long ten seconds. Then I reached out with my free hand a shook one out, lit it and breathed deep, deep, deep. I leant on the horn as I waited for someone to come and get me, experiencing the sickly feeling I've come to associate with first-rate cock-ups.

Chapter Twenty-Four

'Perhaps I'm not getting the full picture here,' John Jennings said. 'We thought you were merely stupid. Now we find you're actually involved with this woman.'

This was about the third go-around on my version of what had happened. I didn't seem to be making any impact with my story of kidnap and forced flight.

'Any chance of a cup of tea?' I was parched. The heating was on blast furnace setting and the room seemed too small for Jennings, me and Rob Black, the officer who didn't do much except stare like he was imagining me in a cell and him armed with something that hurt but didn't leave marks.

'I could have you arrested. I will arrest you. With great pleasure if you don't tell me the truth. Do you know what that means?'

'Sure. My career soars and I get to appear on lots of chat shows.'

'You screwed up a major police surveillance operation.'

I didn't think one bloke with a sandwich amounted to anything approaching major. Perhaps Jennings was mad because he hadn't thought that a woman would pose much of a problem and then she'd gone and embarrassed him.

'She knew you were watching her,' I said. 'You'd have lost her sooner or later. I was the hapless bugger who happened along. She used us both,' I sighed, thinking of cigarettes, of warm baths, of hot pizzas. 'She's not stupid. Not by a long stretch.'

'Where is she?' John Jennings looked like he had a temper.

'She wouldn't tell me anything, believe me, I tried.'

'Where is she?' He was almost shouting now. I put both hands over my face, pressed the place on the edge of my nose where the headaches always start.

'I don't know.' I said the words so they sounded like 'back off, mate'.

'Right,' Jennings said. He slumped back against the wall, fists clenching and unclenching. No doubt wishing my thorax was between them. He pushed himself off the wall and came back at me.

'I'll put this as clearly as I can. I catch you anywhere near my patch and you'll be nicked so fast you'll have scorch marks. Got that?'

I got it. I had no intention of straying anywhere near his patch again. All it had brought me was humiliation. I'd had enough of this story. I was going right off it, in fact. For the first time in a while, I thought of the photographer called Kyle. She hadn't seemed to find me too repellent. Maybe she'd be up for a night out on the tiles, that date we'd talked about. It'd been a while since I'd been on a date, but that didn't mean I couldn't remember how it was done. The thought of it made me feel good. I smiled.

'Delaney's not happy,' Lyall said when I got back to the office around mid-afternoon. Fern sat by his side. I hoped she was taking the opportunity to learn something. There isn't much about the English language that Lyall doesn't know; he's one of these old-fashioned people who loves grammar and knows how it works. Fern had her usual sneer fixed to her face and was shooting her cuffs in a barely concealed sign of her boredom.

'Where've you been?' Lyall enquired mildly.

'I was kidnapped by a handcuff-wielding Russian sex kitten,' I said.

Lyall didn't take his eyes from his screen. 'I don't think that one's going to work again. It barely passed muster last week.'

'It's true.'

Lyall smiled in a sphinx-like way. 'I'd go straight on in, if I were you. That pond slime he drinks can only keep him calm for so long.'

My session with Delaney was short. The guy doesn't have any authority in my eyes and he knows it, so mostly our disciplinary sessions run along the lines of 'wait till your father gets home', the father in this case being Marlowe. But Marlowe needed me too at this moment, so the fact that Delaney was admonishing me for not filling my daily quota of grist for the news mill was not going to make me sit up and take notice.

To ease things, I made a vague promise to try some of Delaney's swamp slime when the next full moon coincided with the transit of Venus, and that mollified him.

I called Kyle while the good feeling lingered. Her voice sounded warm and pleased to hear mine. In the background I could hear busy newsroom sounds. We arranged to meet and see a movie that very night. I had imagined she'd want to see some Estonian auteur's work of urban confusion and poor family relations, but it turned out she was a sci-fi freak and one of the big screens in Leicester Square was showing something she liked the sound of.

'It's sort of a cross between *Aliens* and *Pulp Fiction*,' she said.

'Excellent,' I said, more in prospect of spending the evening with her than anything the big screen could deliver.

I thrashed out a couple of stories I'd been sitting on for a day or so as a filip to those who said I didn't spend enough time in the office, and then I left.

'You look smug,' Felicia said when she came in. I was lying on the sofa, a mug of coffee balanced on my chest.

'I have a date.'

She looked at me sharply. Put down her briefcase.

'A date, date?'

I smiled.

'Who with?'

'An attractive and interesting woman.'

Stunned silence from Felicia.

'It's not beyond the bounds of possibility,' I said.

'I guess not.' She went to the kitchen and grabbed some coffee for herself.

'What are you planning?'

'We're going to the movies.'

'That's safe. A good choice for a first date.'

'I'm so glad you approve.' I took a contented sip from my mug.

'And then what?'

'I don't know. Dinner I suppose.'

'Chinatown,' Felicia said. 'Let me give you the name of a good place.'

'I'll be okay.'

'You won't, Ridley.' A thought dawned. 'Is this the woman from the police station?'

'Yep.'

'Huh,' she said, slumped down in her seat. 'She's cute.'

'Yep.' I smiled more. Expected her to say something like 'what's she doing with a half-wit like you?' but she didn't. I couldn't fathom the look on her face.

'How come she hasn't been snapped up?'

'She's been out of the country. Covering the world with her telephoto lens.'

'I'll get the name of that place.' She rummaged around in her handbag.

'It's okay,' I said. 'We'll find somewhere.'

'No you won't, you'll end up in some dive with so much MSG you'll be bouncing off the walls for a week. You want it to be right, Ridley,' she said. 'First dates are too easy to screw up . . . God, where did I put my diary, I know it's here somewhere . . .'

At seven-thirty I set off. Excited as a schoolboy,

spiffed and spruced. I even wore a properly ironed shirt. Felicia had stood over me for every step of the preparation, which included pointing out the deficiencies in my ironing technique, making sure my socks matched, that sort of thing. She was rigorous. I kept telling her not to fuss and she kept telling me not to take anything for granted.

'American's are world champion daters,' she said, giving me the final once over before pushing me out the door. 'Trust me, I know what I'm doing.' So I felt confident of my physical appearance, at least. It was as good enough start as I was likely to get.

'Oh, Sam?' I was halfway down the stairs when Felicia came after me.

'I remembered the woman from the funeral. In the fur coat. I remembered where I recognized her from. She was in that porno video that Charlie brought over.'

'They were wearing masks.'

'The voice,' Felicia said impatiently. 'I'm good at picking voices. She was Heidi. I'm sure of it.'

Leicester Square was as crowded and as fetid as it always is. I pushed through the tourists wishing, not for the first time, that every single one of them would find some other place to visit. I think London is the greatest city in the world, but why millions of people make the effort to come every year only to make the well-trodden rounds of the most depressing and over-crowded attractions like Leicester Square and Piccadilly Circus is anathema to me.

Kyle stood near the statue of Charlie Chaplin, wearing the same leather jacket I'd seen her in previously, clutching her forearms and watching a juggler throw sticks into the air. She seemed a long way away. When she saw me she approached with a warm smile and gave me a social kiss on the cheek.

'Got the tickets,' she said.

The movie was a witty, postmodern, post-ironic take on a good, old-fashioned horror flick with intergalactic, amorphous slime standing in for the bad guys. It was funny and we laughed and enjoyed it while we were there but forgot it immediately we left the cinema.

'Where shall we eat?' Kyle asked, grabbing her coat around her. She'd only reluctantly parted with it inside and seemed perpetually cold. 'I don't know anywhere any more.'

'I know this little Chinese place,' I said.

We went there and were plonked at a corner table by an efficiently brusque waitress who threw the menu at me and shouted something that I couldn't understand.

'I'll have a beer,' I said, which was the best guess I could make about what she was getting at.

'Make that two,' Kyle said. She cast a practised eye over the menu. 'Szechuan. Don't get much of that in London. Is it good?'

'It should be. My flatmate recommended it.'

'That's the one I saw at the police station?'

'That's her.'

'So she knew that guy who got killed?'

'Sort of.' I explained how I'd met Bruce and how Felicia and I had run into him.

'Bad luck,' Kyle said sympathetically. 'How's she taking it?'

'She's resilient.'

We ordered hot and sour soup and Kyle chatted with the waiter about the specials. She ordered plate after plate of steaming, sizzling dishes.

We tucked in with gusto, talking, drinking, eating. Grinning at each other like happy kids. She told me how she'd spent the past five years, which was in the 'suitcase as apartment' mode. Roaming the world, first as a freelancer and then in the employ of a photo agency. Her stories were funny, self-deprecating, well told. She was as easy to listen to as she was to look at.

'And now you're back,' I said, finding it hard to believe she was in the same restaurant as me, let alone the same table.

'Now I'm back,' she said softly. 'I'm always cold and in culture shock but I'm here. But I'm burbling,' she said suddenly. 'You're going to go home thinking, what a garrulous bore. Tell me about City Radio. Is it an okay place to work?' With her chopsticks she expertly scraped the plate with the vegetables in garlic sauce clean.

'Okay about covers it,' I said. The waiter came by and asked us if we wanted more beer. We both said yes.

'I'll fight you for the chicken and black bean,' Kyle said.

'It's yours. I couldn't eat another thing.'

'I might as well then, I'm a growing girl.' She shovelled chicken on to her plate. 'So. What's okay about it?'

'The startling insights it gives me into the futility of the human condition.'

'You mean the people you meet?'

'I mean the people I work with.'

The waiter dropped the fresh beers on to the table. I reached for mine and was about to take a swig. Then I remembered: the people I work with.

I was supposed to be at Crosbie's.

It was all too perfect, there had to be a catch: That's what I'd been thinking to myself all evening and I was right. I wasn't supposed to be having Szechuan food with a beautiful and interesting young woman who didn't find me completely repulsive. I was supposed to be lurking around the property of a colleague who thought my close relations had only recently emerged from the swamp.

'What's the matter?' Kyle asked. 'You look awful.'

I put the beer down. 'I have to go,' I said. 'I've just remembered something I have to do.'

'What?' Kyle looked concerned.

I couldn't tell her. It was all too sordid. She wouldn't understand, she'd think I was completely whacko. She'd be right.

'I'm terribly sorry,' I said. That lame English phrase felt stale on my tongue.

'Let me come with you. I've got the car, I'll drive you.'

'It's fine, thanks.' I teased some banknotes out of

my wallet. Put them on the table. 'Please don't worry on my account.'

'Sam . . .' Kyle looked upset, confused.

'I'm sorry,' I said.

'Tell me what's up. Maybe I can help.'

I wanted to kiss her. Instead I put a hand on her shoulder.

'Thanks. I had a great time.'

'Oh God,' she said. 'You're not married are you?'

'Not recently,' I said.

'What is it, then? What's the matter?'

'It's work. I promised my boss I'd do a job and then promptly forgot about it. You took my mind off it.' I smiled ruefully.

She half stood, her scarf in danger of sinking into the dirty plates. 'At least call me when you get home. So I know you're okay.'

'Okay,' I said. 'It'll be late.'

'I'll be awake.'

'Thanks for dinner. I had a good time.'

She smiled uncertainly.

I paid for the meal then dashed up to Tottenham Court Road where I'd parked the car and drove to Primrose Hill.

The park was still and silent, as were the streets. The lights were on in Crosbie's flat. It was just after ten. I'd screwed up. I'd screwed up with Kyle and I'd screwed up with Crosbie. Not that I seriously thought I could do anything hanging around her flat, but at least I could have told Marlowe I'd done it, and collected the extra cash with a free conscience.

I thought about Kyle as I sat in the car, gradually

getting colder. She was a prize. Too big a prize to be interested in someone like me. But she seemed to be, at least until my insulting behaviour tonight. What sort of planet must I be on, thinking it was cool to leave someone in the middle of dinner? I should have just lied to Marlowe, I decided as I turned the car engine on to get the heater up to speed. He wouldn't have known any different. I didn't owe him anything. I should have chosen Kyle over freezing my arse off. It seemed so clear now – what had I been thinking?

I sighed, turned the car engine off. I'd have felt cold no matter what the temperature.

An hour passed and nobody came or went. I decided to take a brisk walk to get the circulation in my feet moving again. This time I wouldn't make the same mistake as last time. I kept Crosbie's place firmly in view as I walked up and down the pavement, swinging my arms, stamping my feet.

A woman came out of Crosbie's place as I was doing a couple of half-hearted star jumps. She looked at me curiously. Walked over, stared at me quite rudely, I thought.

'I thought it was you,' she said. 'Stacy Taylor. We met at City Radio.'

Now that she was closer, I recognized her too. The blockbuster novelist.

'Hi,' I said. Feeling like a chump, trying not to look like it.

'Does it hurt?'

'What?'

'Your unrequited crush on Crosbie.'

I laughed out loud.

'I only ask since it seems rather odd that you're here. At this time of night. In the freezing cold.'

'Think of me as the bodyguard.'

She looked me up and down in a 'yeah, right' kind of way.

'She was quite something, in her day,' Stacy said, leaning against my car. 'I remember thinking I wanted to be just like her. She was bold, she was fired up. She had it then. 'Course that was ten, twelve years ago.'

'What happened?'

Stacy shrugged. 'She started to believe her own publicity. Isn't that the horrible clichéd fate of them all?'

'Not you, I think.'

Stacy smiled warmly. I'd paid her a compliment. 'Want to know something? My publicity is a lie I mostly make up for my own amusement. That way I figure there's no danger of me believing it.'

I looked crestfallen. 'So the story about having sex in the office?'

'Sorry,' she said. 'The devil got into me. Crosbie needed taking down a peg. You won't tell anyone?'

'As long as you keep my lurking a secret.'

'Why are you hanging around? Are you her precious stalker?'

'Crosbie's too upset to work and the boss doesn't like it. He wants me to find out what's going on.'

'Disappointing,' she said, pulling her thick coat around her a bit closer. 'I quite like the thought of you as a stalker.'

'Flattery will get you nowhere. What are you doing here?'

'Crosbie invited me over to share in her problems of stardom. I had a stalker once. Loopy guy who thought he was the reincarnation of Louis the Sun King, he told me in his many letters.'

'What happened?'

'Cops nabbed him. He's in a secure institution, brushing up on his French.' She stuck out her hand. Shook mine firmly. 'Got to get home. Good luck with the sicko.'

'The stalker or Crosbie?'

She just laughed, walked away.

I stayed a couple more hours. Nothing happened. I went home, tired and cold. Forgot that I'd promised to call Kyle.

I would have called her the following morning, but what they wrote about me in the papers took my mind off it.

Chapter Twenty-Five

'You read *The Slur* today?' Lyall woke me from a deep sleep without preamble. 'The Slur' is our name for one of the more inventive tabloids.

'Wha—?' I mumbled.

'*The Slur*,' Lyall said patiently. 'It has a story about you. It's not nice. You should get in here. Wear body armour.'

'Wha—?' I said again. I'm not at my linguistic best before coffee. Lyall had hung up.

I looked at the alarm clock. It was six o'clock. I couldn't take it in. I fell back asleep.

The phone rang again.

'Don't fall back asleep,' Lyall said.

'I'm up. Getting dressed.'

'Sure you are.'

I rolled out of bed, went through the daily ablutions in a blur, wondering what the newspaper had made up about me. It was the same paper that a few months back had tried to persuade its readers that Princess Diana and Dodi Fayed hadn't been killed in a car crash but had been abducted by aliens to spawn a new master race that would eventually come back and rule over us, ditching the dead heads who had the present job. *The Slur*, for some reason, was stridently republican. Buckingham Palace had declined to comment on the startling 'evidence' the paper uncovered, which was a mystery witness who'd seen the white Fiat supposed to have crashed with the Princess's Mercedes being sucked into a large cylindrically shaped spacecraft illegally parked in the Tuileries.

I bought a copy of the paper at the newsagent. I wasn't on the front page, which was something. That honour was reserved for a stripper from Manchester who claimed that Satan had made her pregnant. Satan was described as being magically well endowed and driving a black motorcycle with flames on the tank. No surprises there. I flicked through the pages. There I was, on page five under the heading 'Hack Scuttles Cop Probe'.

An important witness in the police investigation into the murder of Bruce McCarthy <u>escaped</u> yesterday because of the unauthorized <u>interference</u> of City Radio reporter, Sam Ridley. The Slur likes to underline words in case its subliterate readers miss the point.

The police are considering whether to <u>charge</u> Ridley with <u>obstruction</u> after he helped the beautiful Russian wife of Bruce McCarthy to flee the country.

'He wrecked our extensive surveillance operation in a couple of hours,' a police source said.

Sam Ridley <u>barged in</u> on the gorgeous Mrs McCarthy as she was making her plan to escape. He persuaded her to take him along to help cunningly <u>foil</u> the team of police officers who were watching her every move. He provided a distraction that helped her get away.

The police haven't ruled out the possibility that he did it deliberately. 'He could well be in league with her,' the source said.

Claims by Ridley that he was <u>abducted</u> were described by the police as 'an outrageous attempt to lie his way out of trouble'.

There was much more but I couldn't bear to go on. I folded the paper with a sigh. It was going to be a long day. I bought expensive cappuccinos for Lyall and me to fortify ourselves for the trials ahead.

'You talk to anybody about yesterday?' Lyall asked.

'No.'

'Sure?'

'Sure I'm sure. You think I'm going to start blabbing a story like that around?'

'Hmmm.' Lyall twirled the foam in his cappuccino with a pencil. 'Wonder what Marlowe's going to say?'

'Plenty,' I said heavily. This was a gift for Marlowe.

The phone rang. Lyall picked it up. 'No,' he said firmly. 'He's not commenting.' He put the phone down. 'The other papers are already chasing the story,' he said. 'And not just the tabloids.'

I expected that. The line between tabloid and quality journalism was increasingly blurred these days. Now when the tabloids ran a juicy story the broadsheets routinely followed with a hypocritical piece that gave the goggling middle classes all the prurient details but without the social stigma of having to buy a paper with a big-breasted woman on page three.

I bit into my bacon sandwich. It contained just

the right amount of grease and preservatives which normally would have made me feel much better about myself and the state of the planet. But not today. I pushed the other half over to Lyall.

'Hey, big fellas.' Rick Brittan's booming voice reached us both at the same time. We both cringed. 'How's it hanging?' he said in a fake Californian accent. Another of Rick's seemingly endless list of irritating traits is his unpardonably bad American accent. If the US government heard about it, they'd send a hit man. There are days when I've thought about putting in the call myself.

'Sammy, boy.' He put a hand on my shoulder. 'I read in the papers you've been busy.' Rick's perfect teeth made an early morning showing. His permatan looked a little faded. The wrinkles around his eyes were more pronounced than usual.

'You look tired, Rick. Girls keeping you up?'

Normally Rick would have rolled with a jibe like that. Taken it as a compliment even. But he didn't. He giggled and flushed bright red.

I had a flash of insight.

I was up in a trice, getting a firm grip of his expensive lapels.

'You skunk.' We were nose to nose. He knew I meant business.

'Steady on, old chap,' he said.

I had told someone about what happened with Lana. I told Lyall, and Fern had been sitting next to him. I was willing to bet she'd rushed out and told Rick.

I pulled back, no sense in expending too much energy on Rick. I lowered my voice.

'If you pull a stunt like that ever again I'm going to do my very best to make sure your life is short, unproductive and entirely child-free. Get it?'

I gripped harder.

'Steady on, old boy.'

'You steady on.' I shook him. Forced him to step back till he was lodged against a desk. 'Am I making myself clear?'

He met my eye finally. Guilty. 'Yes.'

I loosed his lapels, gave him a light shove. 'Good,' I said. 'As long as that's settled.'

Marlowe got in at eight and wanted to see me immediately, but not at his office. We strolled down to Soho and took coffee at Bar Italia on Frith Street.

'What the fuck's going on? We look like fucking idiots.' Marlowe looked pained, which was understandable. Because of our secret deal about Crosbie he had to back me. Or at least give me a good impression of backing. 'Jesus, I really could do without this at the moment. You know how many unwelcome column inches my staff have generated in the past few days – what with you and Felicia and fucking Crosbie. The bigger picture that's starting to emerge from this is that City Radio is staffed by dupes, victims and IT girls. Anybody would think we were running a PR company. If I wanted to be Max Clifford I'd have done it a long time ago.'

I sipped my coffee. Watched the football game on

the big TV screen at the back of the bar. I don't follow sports, so the teams were not familiar to me, but it helps me to have something to think about during Marlowe's rants, which usually turn out to be offensive. So I stared at the men running around after the little ball and the crowd which every now and then would get to its feet, looking as if it had had a religious experience. Maybe there was something to it then: if you could get that excited for an hour or two every week. Forget about one's troubles and the slog of keeping it together in ordinary life.

'. . . Ridley. Are you listening?'

I snapped back, 'Of course.'

'What the hell am I going to say to the board? Just my fucking luck there's a bloody meeting today.'

'Today?'

'Yes, today, Ridley. Think I would have said today if I'd meant some other time?'

This changed things considerably. Marlowe might not back me if he thought it more expedient that I get served up, sacrificial-lamb style. Besides, even though I'd done him a favour by checking out Crosbie, only he and I knew about that. And he'd probably forgotten about it anyway, in the light of the greater scandal of my own misfortune. I stopped thinking about football, started thinking about some fancy footwork of my own.

'They're going to want to know how this happened.' Marlowe slurped his coffee and wiped the froth from his face with the back of his hand. Despite his words, I had the feeling he was actually enjoying the drama. I suppose being in middle management doesn't provide much in the way of visceral thrills on the average day. 'You're going to have to talk to them.'

There was no point in saying 'no'.

'Rick is the source of this morning's story.'

'Rick Brittan? Jesus. You sure?'

'He more or less admitted it to me this morning.'

'You don't have any proof, though.'

'Not directly, no. But it's got his manicured paws all over it, Marlowe.'

Marlowe slumped. 'Civil war in the newsroom? There's no nice way I can tell the board this.'

I stayed silent. I was busy conjuring up pictures of Rick on the cross, Rick roasting over an open flame, Rick stretched out nicely over the rack. It brought a smile to my lips.

'Get him to explain it,' I said carelessly, as though it didn't matter to me whether he did or not. It'd be interesting, Rick tap-dancing for his career. It'd bring out the showman in him. 'Maybe you could sell tickets. I'm sure the rest of the newsroom would like to hear how it happened.'

'*I'd* like to hear how it happened,' Marlowe growled.

'I told Lyall and Fern overheard. She and Rick have got a hot thing going, or at least she thinks they have, so she told him. He saw a chance to stuff me, naturally he seized it.'

'This is conjecture.'

'I'm right, I know it.'

'What the fuck were you doing with that woman

anyway, Ridley?' Marlowe's look was sly, almost respectful.

'It's a long story,' I said. 'And she had handcuffs.'

'Are you going to be charged?'

'The cops are threatening it.'

'How likely is it?'

'Depends what else they can find to distract themselves.'

'Why are they interested in this bint, anyway? Did she kill him?'

'I don't know. I don't know. She didn't seem the type.'

'What type is that, exactly?' Marlowe said coldly.

'The type to inject someone with bleach. I could see her shooting or stabbing. But bleach – that seems a little too . . . dramatic.'

'You're basing this on one car ride?'

'You can learn a lot about someone in conditions of stress.'

Marlowe looked impressed before he remembered he despised me. 'So what do I tell the board?'

'Give them Rick.'

Marlowe winced. That would be a change of allegiance.

'Free your mind,' I said, getting up. 'The rest will follow.'

'You be there too, Ridley,' he shouted after me. The patrons in the coffee bar turned to stare. 'Three-thirty. In the boardroom. Bring your arse humbled and be ready to grovel.'

*

There was no point in going back to the office. I knew there'd be a stack of messages there from people whom I didn't want to speak to, possibly even people waiting outside with microphones and cameras.

I was in the neighbourhood, so I decided to visit Jason Nutter again and see if he'd come up with anything interesting from his contacts in the pornography business. I cut through to Greek Street and found the grimy door of his basement-level club. Jason was, as usual, ensconced behind a banquette, phone to ear, bottle of whisky to hand.

He waggled his eyebrows at me, pushed the bottle in my direction. But I hadn't built up my coffee reservoir for the day. I ordered some from the surly staff member. It came bitter, weak and cooling. I loaded some sugar in and drank it anyway. Jason spoke on the phone and I looked around the club, squinting through the gloom at the photos on the wall of past and present members of the club in various stages of inebriation.

'Sammy.' Jason put the phone down and greeted me warmly. I noticed the copy of *The Slur* sitting at his elbow. He saw me looking at it. 'Bad business, Sammy. In our line of work one should try and stay out of print.' He looked at me shrewdly. 'Guy you were asking me about? His wife lead you on this merry dance?'

'I'm not sure who's doing the leading.'

'Time you found out, old son,' Jason said. 'I'm gonna help you. I don't like seeing my friends made fools of. It grieves me.' He put his hand to his heart. 'It grieves me in here.'

'I'm not too thrilled about it either.'

'Sure you won't have some whisky? It strengthens the blood.'

'I need my faculties today. Got some important tasks ahead.' That wasn't strictly true; I didn't have any tasks in mind, but an idea was nudging out of the primeval slime that was my cognitive process. 'You ever hear of a guy called Dutch? Ran a bar in Barcelona. Had a rather bad wig.'

'Don't ring any bells. I don't know anybody in bleeding Spain. Or at least not that I admit to.' Jason winked. 'All crooks down there, Sammy. Suntanned bloody crooks. What good's their ill-gotten gains when they're gonna die of skin cancer? One day, out by the pool they'll just cark it. It'll be all over. And what good will their money be to them then?' I watched with longing as he took a drag on a cigarette that had been burning merrily away in an ashtray. 'But I know somebody who maybe can help you. He's got more foreign contacts. I prefer to work within the borders of this fair city, but he spreads his net further afield.' He picked up an ancient Mont Blanc fountain pen, ripped off a square of *The Slur* and wrote a number on it. He pushed it across the table to me.

'Ratty Barker,' he said. 'Theatrical agent to the stars. If he can't help you, nobody can.'

Chapter Twenty-Six

It wasn't too hard to see how Ratty Barker had got his name. The rodent-like cast of his features was evident even to the untrained observer. His black hair was slicked back, nose and chin were pointed. Little dark eyes blinked rapidly. The fact that he was wearing an expensive dark suit, crisp white shirt and smooth silk tie only seemed to enhance the feral impression.

His poky office was over a clothing warehouse in Whitechapel. There was barely enough room for a desk and a filing cabinet and the fold-up chair that I sat in. The walls were decorated with mug shots of his clients. They were the usual head-and-shoulders portraits you'd find in the actors directory. There was nothing in the office that gave any clue as to the specifics of the service that Ratty Barker provided.

I squeezed myself into the chair that was designed for a much shorter person and started with a little light flattery to get the show on the road. 'Jason says you know everyone.'

Ratty Barker smiled. Pressed his hands together like he was praying. He had small, economical movements. The sort of person you'd look at and think 'accountant' rather than, say, 'pornography agent'.

'I been in the business thirty years,' he said with a proud smile. 'It's my job to keep on top of things, know what I mean?'

I told him about Bruce McCarthy and Chloe and *Humping Heidi*.

'I remember it well,' he said. 'Chloe Ward was a luminous Heidi.'

'What's she doing now?'

'Nothing, mate. She retired years ago.'

'Any idea where she went?'

'Found true love, me old soldier, that's what I heard.' Ratty eased his thin body back in his leather chair. 'The new man didn't approve of what she did. So she packed it in. Went off to live in Spain and attend to his own private fantasies. Now there's a story to warm your heart, eh?'

'Indeed. Who'd she marry?'

'Some guy who had a nice little earner going in a bar in Barcelona.'

'Was his name Dutch?'

'Something like that. He must've been rich, is all I can say,' Ratty went on. 'A girl like that, she had a big future in front of her, and I don't just mean that in the obvious sense.' He held his hands up in front of him to demonstrate generous breasts.

'And she hasn't done anything since?'

'Not a dicky bird. What's your interest?' Ratty's curiosity gave his face an even more sinister cast.

'She was at Bruce McCarthy's funeral.'

'She'd have known him through *Heidi*,' Ratty said. 'He worked on that. Did just the one. We didn't hear any more from him after that.'

CROSSING LIVE

'Are you sure?'

'Sure I'm sure.'

'I was under the impression it was a regular gig.'

'Not as far as I know.'

I stood up, loosened one of my cards from my wallet. Wrote my beeper number and home number on the back, because I didn't intend to spend much time in the office in the near future.

'Thanks for your help,' I said. 'By the way, you don't know a woman called Lana Davidoff? She was married to Bruce McCarthy.'

Ratty shook his head. 'Never heard of her till I opened the paper this morning.'

I went to a greasy spoon just around the corner from Ratty's office. I had a cup of tea and a serious think about the state of my predicament. The cops wanted my scalp, my employers wanted my scalp. I was a tabloid star in the worst sense: held up to ridicule by my peers. I had no real story to fight back with. I ordered another cup of tea. Prayed for the gods to give me a sign. They didn't. The only sound I could hear was the low roar of impending doom.

Felicia beeped me. I called her from the phone in the café.

'Thank God,' she said. 'You'd better get over here, there's this really scary guy looking for you.'

'I've already spoken to Marlowe this morning.'

'Don't joke. He's called work three times.'

'How do you know he's scary?'

'Call it a little woman's intuition,' she snapped.

'Who is he? What does he want?'

'He never leaves his name, he just growls down

the phone. And he's got an accent. I could barely understand him.'

'Probably some weirdo who saw the article and has incorporated me into his own little world, rich with invention.'

'You wish,' Felicia said. 'Are you nuts, attacking Rick? Never underestimate that sleaze bag. He'll make you pay.'

'I've got Marlowe on my side for once.'

'Yeah, and I've got the Loch Ness monster in for the eleven-thirty slot. Marlowe won't back you when the chips are down. And if you're not careful, Rick will twist you up in little knots and leave you writhing on the sidewalk.'

'Don't worry, everything's under control for once.'

'Well, what are you going to do?' There was real concern in Felicia's voice.

'I'll be okay.'

'At least tell me what's going on.'

It was tempting. Felicia was a good, steady ally, she'd proved that in the past.

'I'll catch up with you later,' I said. 'I've got some calls to make first.'

I meant to go home to use the phone. It would be quiet there. I should have realized there'd be reporters camped outside my house. I turned into my street and stopped. Not a big crowd, I wasn't headline news. But a couple of hacks with notebooks and a couple of photographers. Covering their bases, probably. Just in case the story turned out to be much bigger; you never could tell these days. With all the conspiracy theories the gullible public were so willing to pounce on, one thing invariably led to another. Before I knew it I could be implicated in the fall of the Shah and the disappearance of Lord Lucan.

I turned smartly. Walked in the opposite direction. I nearly stumbled over a silver Mercedes which was badly parked. An ever-present hazard now the neighbourhood has made good.

'Sam Ridley?' The voice came from behind me.

'Yes?' I turned. A guy dressed in black and wearing reflector shades stood in front of me. I could tell he was bad news, just from the glasses. I meant to run, but there was a large hand resting firmly under my elbow. The pain that accompanied it, due to the pressure on the nerve, was so intense I could barely speak.

'Come with me,' he said.

'Okay,' I said meekly.

We went together to the Mercedes. The windows were tinted. The guy opened the back door solicitously, like we were on our first date. Then he gave me a not-so-gentle shove. I stumbled in, barking my shin.

'Hey,' I said. 'This is just like it happens in the movies.'

I wasn't alone in the back. There was another man, also dressed by Central Casting. This one had on a black suit and black shirt and tie. He also wore Ray-Bans. The very expensive kind.

'Hi,' I said, rubbing my shin. The limo was a

stretch job. I groped my way to the seat facing him.

'So glad you could make it,' the Russian said in heavily accented but precise English. 'I have been trying to reach you all morning.' He tapped on the glass. The car moved off. 'There are many things we need to discuss.'

Chapter Twenty-Seven

A copy of *The Slur* rested on the seat beside him with a photo of me. It was one I'd had taken for the station's publicity, another clue that pointed to Rick as the source of the story.

The man opposite me sat very still. I suppose his eyes were checking me out behind the glasses but if they were they were the only part of his body that moved. His large hands rested on his knees. He said nothing. I couldn't think of any small talk, so I said nothing either.

The big car crept patiently through the traffic. We were heading east, on the Euston Road. Then we turned left and went north, around the back streets of King's Cross.

'I suppose this means lunch at The Ivy is off the agenda?' I murmured.

'What?' he demanded. It sounded more like 'vat'. 'What did you say?'

'Where are we going?'

'Somewhere private, so we can talk,' he said.

'We can talk here. Ask away. You have my undivided.'

He looked at me and then looked out the window, the first body movement I'd seen in fifteen minutes.

The patch of land we arrived at was scrub. An old brick warehouse stood at the back. All around were more anonymous buildings.

'Out please,' my host said as the car stopped. I got out. It had started to rain. I hoped this wasn't going to take long, I had appointments to keep.

He eased himself out with the help of the driver. He walked stiffly, as if in pain. I noticed a walking stick. I eyed the driver. He seemed larger than I'd first thought. And he kept looking at me. Couldn't keep his eyes away, in fact. I had a bad feeling about those looks.

The warehouse was colder than outside but at least it was dry. It had a bare concrete floor and some of the windows were broken.

'Nice place,' I said. 'Real potential.'

'Sit down, please.' The man in black's voice echoed in the empty space.

There were a couple of packing crates in the middle of the room. Me and the boss sat down. The driver stood to one side.

'Who are you?'

'Let's dispense with the preliminaries, Mr Ridley. The only thing you need to know is that my driver is a very strong man. If I tell him to kill you, he'll do it.'

I snuck a look at the driver. He smiled modestly, flattered.

'Bearing that in mind, Mr Ridley, I want you to tell me where Lana is.'

'Lana? I have no idea.'

CROSSING LIVE

The driver grabbed my ear and twisted it till I thought my face would come off. I gasped in pain and sank to my knees. Just as suddenly, he stopped. I stayed on my knees, my body struggling to comprehend what had just happened to it. The side of my head was a flaming ball of fire where my ear should have been. I wanted to rub it to ease the agony, but I was afraid of what I might find. My old shoulder injury started throbbing in fear and dreadful anticipation.

'Where is she?' the boss repeated calmly.

'I don't know.'

The driver grabbed my arm, yanked it out and up behind me until I thought my sinews would pop. The old pain came rushing back. Fresh as the day it happened. I cried out, 'Please!'

This seemed to only inflame the driver. He pulled and twisted harder, if that was possible. The pain was sharp, then hot, then dull. I wanted him to stop.

'Where is she?' the boss said calmly.

I took a deep breath. Talking was almost more effort than I could manage. 'She left me when she ditched the police. I was a decoy, that's all. I don't know her. I don't know what she's up to.'

'You don't understand.' The boss tapped his cane lightly. 'I asked you a question. I want an answer.'

'I don't know.'

The driver kept me pinned while he whipped out a knife. He held it close to my right eye. So close the blade was a shiny blur.

The boss nodded.

The blade hovered closer till I could feel its

coldness against my bottom lid. I blinked involuntarily. Tears flowed. Something else. Blood.

'It's very difficult to judge perspective with just one eye,' the Russian said calmly.

The blade dug into my too-soft flesh.

'I'm telling the truth. I don't know where she is, I wish I did. She made a fool of me.'

The Russian turned away. Panic made me go weak, I slumped. The driver kept his grip with one arm. Kept the knife firmly in place.

'Okay.' The Russian turned back to face me. 'Okay.'

The pressure on my eye didn't recede until the boss lifted his index finger. The hand that held the blade lowered, reluctantly. I breathed again.

The boss made another slight signal to the driver who pushed me forward. I staggered to my knees. I ran a mental checklist of all the parts that hurt. Wiped the blood away from under my eye. Thanked the gods for going in to bat for me.

'Lana has something that's mine,' the Russian said. 'I paid her, she double-crossed me, and took my money.'

'How much money?'

'More than you earn in a year.'

'Not that much then.' He didn't get the joke. I couldn't think what possessed me to make it.

'Look, Igor.' I wiped more blood. Searched my pocket for a handkerchief, couldn't find one so I staunched the blood with my shirtsleeve. 'I never met Lana until about forty minutes before she left me handcuffed to a police car. She used me like she used you. I can tell you the name of the hotel she stayed at when she left her flat, but I'm sure she's long gone from there.' I was nervous, wishing I had something to tell him, anything, to make him go away.

'She thinks she can beat me at my own game. She can't. When I find her I'll kill her for thinking she could try.'

'I'll tell her if I see her.'

If there was any reaction behind the glasses, I couldn't detect it. 'When I find her I'll kill her.' He threw a white card down on the floor. 'And if I don't find her, I'll kill you.'

Chapter Twenty-Eight

'What the hell happened?' Felicia had a chair and some coffee ready. We'd arranged to meet in town, away from everybody who wanted to find me. The coffee shop was in West Soho. Felicia had ordered me a sandwich and I suddenly realized I was starving.

'I was abducted by illegal aliens.'

'Rick's gunning for you,' Felicia said while I chewed. 'He's definitely up to something, the slimy little creep.'

'Nice sandwich,' I said.

'What's the matter with your eye?'

'The guy at the tattoo parlour was having an artistic crisis.'

'Sam, this is your career I'm talking about.'

I'd have liked to tell Felicia I had more important things to worry about, but something stopped me. The Russians were serious. I had seen the stories on the news showing the ways they disposed of the people who crossed them. I was lucky to still be alive. I didn't wish to think about the reasons why they'd let me live. I looked around the café. There was no one there who bore any resemblance to the men in dark suits.

'I'll be at the board meeting,' I said, to mollify Felicia.

'Make sure of it. You know what Rick's like. Look how he managed to wangle his job back. Everybody knew what a useless plonker he was and he still did it.'

'Possibly his finest hour.'

'By the way, a woman called for you. Kyle. To remind us about her party Saturday night.'

'Us?'

'I answered the phone and we got chatting. She seemed like a very nice person.' Felicia did her Mona Lisa smile. 'It's a "flat-warming". We're to bring a bottle of wine but no gifts.'

'Lovely. I'll look forward to it.' If I was still above ground by Saturday.

Felicia looked like she wanted to ask me more about Kyle but she restrained herself. Instead she sat quietly, folding her napkin into ever smaller squares. I finished off the sandwich, swallowed the last of the coffee.

'I'd hate it if . . .' Felicia began. Stopped.

'What?' I realized she was more upset than I'd thought. 'Don't worry about me. I've survived worse than this. I'm the Gloria Gaynor of journalism.' I patted her hand. It was ice cold. I took her hands to warm them.

'I'm sorry,' she said. 'It's pregnancy, I'm awash with hormones. They throw me from one extreme to another; it's like being permanently drunk.'

'I know.'

'Funny, I can't imagine you pregnant.'

'My wife made sure I went through it by proxy.'

We were silent for a minute. Me thinking of my past, her probably thinking about her future.

'Everything okay with the little one?'

'Fine. Everything's fine, according to the doctor. I went yesterday. I'm as healthy as a horse. Nothing to worry about except this vast, uncertain future.'

'It's not uncertain. You can stay with me as long as you like.'

'I can?'

'Sure. What are friends for?' I wasn't sure I was being wise, it had been such an over-stimulated day, I was a little light-headed.

'Right,' she said. 'Friends.'

I left Felicia and went to see John Jennings at Shepherd's Bush. The Russians made me want to have the good old British cops on my side.

'You wanted to know all I know,' I said sitting in a chair without being asked. 'I'll tell you what happened to me this morning if you set the story straight about what happened with Lana.'

'If anybody asks,' he said, impatiently. 'The story is not ball-breaking. The world will have forgotten about it tomorrow.'

'I won't forget it. I've been slandered. Held up to ridicule by my peers.'

'Your peers are no better than you.'

'That's not my problem. I look like a criminal. I'm a lot of things, but not that.'

'What have you got to tell me?'

'Will you refute the story?'

'They won't print it, Ridley. The papers aren't interested in putting the record straight. All they want is sensation and scandal. They don't give a frog's fuck about people's reputations. Why don't you sue?'

'That's a luxury only the rich can afford.'

Jennings looked up from his doodle. 'All right, if anybody asks, I'll tell them the story is an exaggeration,' he said. 'Now what have you got to tell me?'

Jennings took the news that a member of what seemed a lot like the Russian Mafia wanted to kill me with equanimity.

'Did I not warn you not to get involved?' he said wearily.

I ignored his lack of concern for my well-being. 'Who are these people? What the hell was Bruce up to?'

Jennings gave me a look that said even if he did know he wasn't telling me. I didn't have time to stay and try and prise it out of him. I had to be back in the office in twenty-five minutes.

I made it on time. The train came, I caught it. It went smoothly through the tunnel, not stopping for suicide victims or the multitude of mechanical problems that dog the outdated and underfunded London Underground service. With three minutes to go I arrived at the front doors of City Radio and took the lift to the boardroom. I felt in control. Optimistic, even. I'd tell the board that Jennings was going to set things right with the media. It'd be enough for them. They'd love me. I smiled as I stepped into the sixth-floor reception area at one minute to. Sweet timing. It was a good omen.

Marlowe's secretary, Jane Miller, was waiting outside. The doors to the boardroom were closed. She smiled, laid a hand on my elbow.

'They've asked me to tell you to wait outside for a moment,' she said in her soft Edinburgh accent. She handed me a cup of strong coffee as a peace offering.

'Okay.' I took the coffee. 'Why?'

'Rick's been asked in first,' she said, opening the door and letting herself in. 'I'll let you know when it's your turn, okay?'

'Okay.' I sat, sipped more coffee. Wished I could have a cigarette. Thought fondly about the two I had when on the run with Lana. The good old days. But I was able to handle it by thinking of the roasting Rick was certainly getting by the board for his unethical behaviour. For once Marlowe was on my side and he'd deliver Rick on a plate with a side order of fries. The feeling that gave me was almost better than cigarettes.

'Your turn.' Jane Miller popped her head around the door.

I straightened my slouch and my tie. Smiled at my reflection in the glossy wood of the door. Not bad. It would have to do.

The board chairman is a crusty old geezer called Anthony Tobias. He got the top job by dint of his family connections. City Radio is one of the last few remaining independent stations in London. It's been owned by the same people since the sixties when the present chairman's father had a brain spasm and decided there was more to life than baby food factories. The City licence had been up for grabs and

Tobias, pushing middle age and still without much interest in anything that didn't wear a short skirt, had been put in charge by Anthony Tobias senior, in the hope that it'd curb his lubricious ways.

It didn't, of course. It delivered the younger Tobias, a handsome blade if you discounted the weak chin, another chat-up line to add to his less than sparkling collection and subsequently launched the short-lived broadcasting careers of more than a few of his well-endowed girlfriends. Some of them even made it on air, which is a period of the station's history nobody prefers to dwell on.

Tobias was getting on now, but he hadn't lost his lust for anything in skirts. His wife died a couple of years back and it was the signal he'd been waiting for. Although he'd never felt particularly constrained by his marriage vows, he was now conducting his private life with all the restraint of a Renaissance pope. The social climbers on the B-list trod a path to the nightclubs where he held court and guzzled an endless supply of Bollinger. More discreet consumption of expensive white chemicals took place elsewhere. Tobias was nothing if not a generous host.

Rick stood at the end of the table. He smiled, pally-like, one hand stuck in his lapel.

'I've finished,' he said and sat down, a look in his eye like a cat that had been set in charge of an aviary. I glanced at Marlowe. His eyes were lowered and he wouldn't look up. His secretary poured me another coffee and patted me on the shoulder. I've always suspected, despite her icy exterior, Marlowe's secretary had a soft spot for me. I wondered what that pat was supposed to convey. Pity?

I had the beginnings of a very bad feeling.

'You can go now.' Tobias's voice crackled like electricity. It was still powerful, despite his advancing years.

I looked up. I'd just got here. But he was talking to Rick. 'I want to hear what Ridley has to say without you here.'

Rick was taken aback. He opened his mouth to say something and thought the better of it as Tobias waved him away. 'Go now,' he said, impatiently.

All the board members watched Rick leave. Except Tobias. He leant back in his great big status-conferring chair, one arm draped over the back, the other tapping a pencil on his blotter.

I've never particularly liked or respected Tobias. I have the very strong feeling if it hadn't been for his family having bucket-loads of dosh, he would not have found it necessary to stick to the straight and narrow. Tobias has the same sense of the world owing him a living as a lot of lowlifers I encounter. I took a large swallow of coffee and scalded my mouth. It was just what I needed to jolt me into thinking clearly.

The door closed behind Rick. Tobias waved a veined hand at me, his old eyes alight. It was the sort of look I imagine elderly Roman senators would have worn as they gazed into the gladiatorial arena.

'I'm interested to hear your explanation,' he said. 'Do go ahead. Take all the time you need.'

I looked at Marlowe for a clue. But like most

bullies, Marlowe had folded in the presence of a bigger bruiser. He looked studiously at his hands. The other members of the board stared down the table with varying degrees of prurience. Board meetings hadn't been this lively since the previous company accountant had been forced to reveal she had embezzled the entire newsroom budget to buy tutus for her transvestite boyfriend's ballet company.

'I..!' I cleared my throat. Where to start... Should I get right in there and trash Rick straight away, destroy his credibility as surely as he had tried to destroy mine? It was tough to know where to start, there was so much about Rick that was reprehensible. It was tough, too, to get focused. Rick's behaviour didn't seem to be the most pressing of my problems at that moment.

I took a deep breath, plunged in.

'There's a lot of stories flying around. No doubt you'd like to hear the truth,' I said, wishing I knew what Rick had said about me.

'That we would.' Tobias was practically rubbing his hands with glee. 'We'd love to hear that.'

'Well, I'm sure I don't need to tell you not to believe everything you read in the newspapers. And this morning was an excellent example of the misplaced trust the public has in the press to—'

Tobias held up his hand. 'Not that,' he said. 'That's a minor issue, we'll deal with that later.'

Minor issue? I looked at Marlowe. He was deeply involved in doodling a rather large 'M' on his legal pad.

'Minor?' I said. 'I don't...'

'Come, come, Ridley. No dissembling,' Tobias snapped. 'Tell the board why you're stalking another member of my staff.'

Chapter Twenty-Nine

'I... pardon...?'

'Tell the board why you've taken to hanging around outside Crosbie Shaw's house.' Tobias's eyes gleamed. This was the most fun he'd had since he dated triplets who claimed they were cousins of the Krays.

'Stalking?'

'Don't bother to deny it. We've heard the witnesses.' I looked at Marlowe. He looked away. I was screwed. He'd set me up and dumped me in it. And now it would be his word against mine. In other words, no contest at all. I was a dupe, I'd believed him. I took another gulp of coffee. I deserved whatever ludicrous fate was about to be served up to me; it would be a valuable lesson in never trusting the vipers and scorpions who call themselves my colleagues.

'You've been seen, Mr Ridley. Your dirty little secret is out.' Tobias practically purred over those lines. I couldn't be sure I hadn't gone up in his estimation.

'Not all of it,' I said, shooting a glance at Marlowe. He looked distinctly uncomfortable. The picture stopped rolling and I could see it in Technicolor. This was Marlowe's revenge. He fancied Felicia and she'd rejected him and now he was getting me back for having her under my roof. He thought we were sleeping together and he'd set the whole thing up to discredit me. I felt weary. Life was becoming way too complicated.

'I'm sorry to disappoint you. I'm not Crosbie's stalker.'

Tobias didn't look surprised. He expected me to deny it.

'I was trying to find out who was following her. I wanted to help her. She hadn't had any luck with the police. Someone had to do something.'

'You came up with this quixotic impulse all on your own?' Tobias's sarcasm was barely concealed. He was having the time of his life. It did seem pretty feeble, subjected to closer scrutiny. What had I been thinking?

'Me and some other members of staff' – I looked pointedly at Marlowe who'd decided the pattern on his coffee cup merited much closer attention – 'decided it might be best to keep an eye on her.'

Tobias tried to look stern but he was practically salivating over the details. 'After Crosbie gets a rock thrown through her window, you're the first one there.'

'She asked me to come over.'

'She called Felicia,' Tobias said. His information was good, he must have spoken to Crosbie. Crosbie didn't have any love for me. Why should she? 'And she told me you took the note that was wrapped around the rock.'

'I was going to take it to the cops.' I remembered the note. I'd taken it from my pocket and put it in my drawer. There hadn't been time. Too much else going on.

'And did you?'

'This is preposterous. Why would I stalk Crosbie? I don't even like her.'

The board members seemed a little shocked to hear that.

'Did you take it to the cops?'

'No. Not yet.'

'I suppose you destroyed it.'

'No. Look, this is—'

'Who were the other members of staff?' Tobias said. 'Name some other of your concerned colleagues.'

I looked at Marlowe again. He stayed resolutely silent. I didn't want to drag him into this. If he denied it, it'd be his word against mine. No use looking like a worse fool than I already did.

'Admit that this sordid charade is something your perverse little mind cooked up.' The words were of moral outrage, but still I couldn't shake the feeling that Tobias was amused, not to mention titillated.

'Felicia Randall will back me up.'

Tobias's grin broadened into a leer. 'I'm sure she'd say anything you asked her to.' I wondered how on earth he knew that Felicia had moved in with me. But I suppose I shouldn't have been surprised. Gossip often broke land-speed records at City Radio. There were people whose only reason for working there was to spread stories.

'And then there's the entirely separate matter of you tramping all over a police investigation. How do you get time to fit it all in?'

'I rise early. Like Margaret Thatcher.' Nobody around the table looked particularly willing to leap on to my side so I plunged on. 'The story was a fabrication. Made up by Rick Brittan.'

'Do you have evidence?'

'I know it.'

'Why would he do that to his own colleague?'

'It's personal.' I was aware as I spun this out how absurd it must seem. It didn't escape Tobias either.

'Pity you don't put a little more effort into your work,' he said. 'And less into making your employers a laughing stock.'

I looked up and down the table. Blank faces stared back.

'I think we've heard all we need. You may leave now,' Tobias said.

I considered if there was anything I could say to influence them. There wasn't.

It was absurd. I had much more important things to worry about and I intended to devote all of my worrying facilities to that end. This could be sorted out later, somehow.

Marlowe's secretary grimaced ruefully. I shot one last glance at her boss. He didn't look up as I walked to the door. Dignified, that's what I told myself my exit was; sometimes I can convince myself of anything.

Felicia and Lyall were waiting when I got to the newsroom. I flopped into my chair. Lyall prised open my fist, eased a cup of coffee into it. Stood back, arms folded. Regarded me as if he were a doctor and it was his job to tell me I had some virulent tropical disease.

'Stitched up,' I said after I'd filled them in on what had happened. 'Tinsel-wrapped and tied in a pretty bow. It's the look for spring.' I searched around for Rick but he wasn't there. A good thing – I might have been tempted to do something that would pass into newsroom lore.

Lyall continued to look grave, which was worrying. Usually, there's no situation that Lyall can't bring down to size with a tasteless joke. But even he was silent.

'Why the hell did you do a deal with Marlowe?' Felicia asked. 'You know he's as trustworthy as a weasel. He is a weasel, in fact. I should know.'

'How should you know?' Lyall perked up. He hadn't heard the story about the time Marlowe had given Felicia the old 'my-wife-doesn't-understand-me' routine.

Felicia ignored him. 'I can't believe you'd be so stupid as to believe anything Marlowe said. And what the hell induced you to hang around Crosbie's place? Are you out of your mind?' She seemed impatient for an answer, or impatient with me, I couldn't tell.

'How was I to know he was setting me up? He said he was concerned about Crosbie.'

'Lord give me patience,' Felicia sighed. 'All right, here's the story, for future reference. Never trust Marlowe. Ever. On anything. If he tells you he likes milk in his coffee don't believe him. If Jesus Christ descends from heaven and tells you Marlowe's a stand-up guy, don't believe him. Got that?'

'I sense that a certain farmyard building door is open and the four-legged beast is long gone,' Lyall said, ultra-casual, the way he is when he thinks there's dirt to be uncovered. 'So, do tell me what has led to you having such a low opinion of our managing editor.'

'Lyall' – Felicia turned to him, hands on hips – 'right now we have to concentrate on Sam. We have to think of some way to get him out of this mess. We can gossip later, okay?'

Lyall looked suitably chastised. 'Not even the edited highlights?'

'I'm going to go right up there and tell them this is all bullshit.' Felicia turned back to me.

'Don't,' I said. 'It won't do any good.'

'Why not?'

'Your testimony is contaminated.'

'How can it be?'

'They think we're sleeping together, because you're staying at my flat.'

Felicia, to Lyall's and my surprise, flushed bright red. Put a hand to her forehead to brush a lock of hair away from her eyes.

'I . . .'

'How awkward,' Lyall said smoothly. I glared at him.

'Well, I'll just go up there and tell them they're way off base. Can't two people share a flat without people thinking they're up to something?' Felicia seemed to be getting more flustered.

'I think Marlowe did the groundwork on that.'

'You see? What did I tell you? He's a jerk. Oh, this is all my fault,' Felicia wailed. 'What can I do?'

'Tell Uncle Lyall everything. Right from the start,' Lyall said. Felicia wasn't listening.

'I know, I know.' She snapped her fingers. 'We could blackmail Marlowe. You know, with what happened to me? We can go to him and say that unless he plays ball, I'll lodge a formal complaint.'

'That was months ago,' I said gently. 'They'll want to know why you haven't come forward before now. It'll get very messy.'

'I don't care. I . . . I know. Even better. I'll go to his wife . . . no . . . I'll threaten to go to his wife. He'll have to back you then.'

'I think we should all sit down very calmly and think this through. For a start there's no reason to fuss yet. Who knows what Tobias will decide? The old pervert's so twisted he could just as easily give me a promotion.'

'This is no time for jokes.'

'Who's joking? This is the guy who's at Stringfellow's every night of the week with four blondes whose combined ages don't equal his. What does he know about morality?'

'You should know those types are the first to cast stones,' Felicia said, resigned.

'Let's just wait,' I said. 'It can't get any worse. The two people who hate me most have already testified.'

'I disagree.' Lyall held up his hand. 'Time for action.'

'What action?'

'We have to break up that meeting. Give people a chance to cool down, to reflect. I'm going to phone in a bomb scare.'

'What?' Felicia and I both took the bait at the same time.

'Just kidding,' Lyall said, straightening his tie. 'I'm going up there to appeal to them as human beings.'

'Let us know if you find one.' Felicia turned and went back to her desk.

'There's no need, Lyall.' I was on my feet. 'Don't get involved. It's only going to end in tears.'

'There are times in a man's life...' Lyall said sententiously.

'You're a good mate,' I said, touched.

'There is one thing you can do for me, though.'

'Name it.'

'I want the low-down on Felicia and Marlowe.'

'Anything but that.'

'Why not?'

'She made me promise not to say.'

He shrugged. 'Ah well. It was worth a shot.'

He pulled his shoulders back and walked slowly to the lift. A tall, thin man without much hair and a face that looks as if it has to bear the troubles of the world alone. All that's just a cover – the guy's a saint.

'What's he up to?' Felicia said.

'He's promised to save my job in exchange for a juicy titbit.'

Felicia's face darkened. 'You didn't tell him . . .?'

'No. In the end he agreed to do it without the titbit.'

'Oh. So what's he gonna do?'

'No idea. But he's good at thinking on his feet.'

I slid into Lyall's desk and did a little light subbing while he was gone. It was relaxing to look at words. You knew where you were with words. They didn't cheat and lie and double-cross. They didn't take you to deserted spots and rough you up. You could make them do what you wanted. With words, you're the boss.

It wasn't long before Lyall was back. He stood in front of me, staring.

'Bad news?'

'The worst.'

I stood up, somehow it seemed more fitting.

'You're suspended, Sam. For two weeks. No pay.'

Chapter Thirty

Lyall seemed as distressed as if he'd been responsible. 'They want you back up there. To tell you. I'm not supposed to have broken the news. I just didn't want you to hear it from that shit Tobias.'

'Right.'

'You going up?'

'No.'

'Why not?'

'Got things to do. Tell them I've gone.'

'It'll make it worse.'

'Hard to see how.'

'They could sack you.'

'Don't you think this is just the prelude to that?' I said. 'They'll use the time to consult their lawyers to see if they can ditch me without running into a messy legal skirmish. And when they've done that it's *hasta la vista*, Ridley.'

I didn't want to see Felicia or anybody. I ducked out, grabbing my coat and started walking, not really sure where I was heading. All I knew was that the more distance I put between me and that place, the happier I would be. I got on to Wigmore Street and walked west until I came to Hyde Park. It started to rain. I pulled up my collar and strode on. I didn't have any money, that was the problem: no reserves to tide me over till I got another job, if indeed I could find one. After the story in the paper this morning I was the laughing stock of journalistic London. I couldn't imagine even getting in for an interview, let alone hooking a job. I could see the smirks on the faces of my peers as I walked. Could hear the laughter. I cursed Marlowe and Rick Brittan roundly and richly as I passed Tyburn Hill, the site of the old gallows. Strangely appropriate to be at Tyburn at that time, considering I, too, was a dead man. Even if the Russians decided to spare my life, what kind of existence would it be? The only chance I would have of getting a job would be to leave the city that had been home for half my life and bury myself in some dire provincial town that called itself chic because it had two wine bars and a warehouse conversion.

I shuddered. I hate wine bars.

The rain had pretty well driven the other park users out. There were a few hardy dog owners and joggers and some tourists no doubt delighted thinking they were getting the complete rainy London experience. I walked beside Rotten Row, not caring about the smell of horse manure. Not caring that I was drenched.

I walked till my shoes were tiny reservoirs and water seeped through my clothes and down my back. I was shivering when I got home. Hair plastered to my head. Clothes covered in mud and horse shit from the park. The clutch of newsmongers had gone from my house. Chasing another five-minute news wonder, no doubt.

There were messages on my machine. The first from Marlowe. I fast-forwarded through it, I had no desire to hear anything he had to say. The second was from American Express about my unpaid bills. The third was from another credit-card company. I had no idea how I was going to meet their demands. I drank deeply from the well of self-pity. Discredited and broke. Discredited and in debt – even worse. I stripped off my wet clothes and ran a bath.

I poured a whisky while I waited for the bath to fill.

Upstairs, my neighbours were stomping about, preparing for another evening of meaningless excess. For once, I didn't care about the racket they were making. I put on an old Jimi Hendrix record and turned up the volume. 'Hey Joe' bounced around the walls of the flat. Usually, the song never fails to lift my spirits but tonight it didn't work the old manic-depressive magic.

I got in the bath, it was lukewarm. I'd run out of hot water. I poured some of Felicia's bubble bath in to try and disguise it, but it left me feeling colder than I'd started. There was no temptation to linger.

It was time for the local.

My local, as I have already mentioned, has undergone some changes in the past few months. It's not the honest boozer it once was. I no longer recognize anybody who goes there. For a while after the refit the regulars struggled manfully along, pretending that nothing had really changed. You'd see them at the end of the bar with a pint of Guinness trying to look like they didn't mind techno-thrash. The trust-fund babes loved it – the sign of working folk indicated to their sheltered way of thinking that they were participating in the real Notting Hill. But the regulars almost all gave up after a week or two. It was just too embarrassing to be seen entering the pastel palaces. They'd move on to another pub that hadn't yet been caught in the cross-hairs of a developer. I could see a time in the future when, like endangered wild animals, we would gradually be herded into smaller and smaller areas and then rounded up and taken to an approved sanctuary where tourists would come to gawk.

Today, however, I didn't care about interior decor. I intended to drink, not absorb the ambience. I ordered a whisky and sat in the corner. Although it was not yet five the place was crowded. That's what happens when your clientele don't have jobs to go to.

I had ten quid in my pocket. It wasn't much but enough to make me forget my troubles for a while at least. I started with a double.

The couple next to me, young girls in Lycra flares, platform trainers and hats with ear flaps that did nothing for them, were remarking in excited tones that a supermodel and her boyfriend had just moved into the neighbourhood. I tried to tune their conversation out but, as often happens, the more you try to do that, the more you can't ignore it.

'They're having the most fantastic alterations done,' one girl trilled. 'An indoor swimming pool in the garden and a Buddhist prayer wheel in the conservatory. And they're having the whole interior designed so that it's, like, *feng shui*.'

'Cool,' said her friend.

'I read in *Hello!* that she spends like an hour every day meditating, that's how she stays thin.'

'Does that work?' asked the other, credulous one.

I went back to the bar and resisted the bartender's attempt to sell me a cocktail whose name alluded to a sexual act. I took the drink back to my seat. Perhaps after I'd drunk it I'd have an inkling of what to do. How to find Lana and make her pay for shortening my life expectancy so thoroughly.

'... they've had ten builders.' The woman was continuing her description of the supermodel house makeover. 'There's an army of them. They told me she's going to be moving in less than a month. Not only that, but they've bought that vile old caff round the corner and are going to turn it into a vegan wine bar.'

'Wow,' murmured her friend, her attention caught by a guy in sunglasses with yellow lenses that gave him the look of a randy, bug-eyed insect.

Builders.

The empty-headed girls had done me a favour.

Curly and Pete. They'd been downright obstructive until after Bruce's funeral. Then they'd fallen over themselves to point me in Lana's direction.

They knew what she was up to, I was sure of it.

My knock was answered by the same bloke as last time. He had a large kebab in one hand. I explained that I was looking for Curly and Pete and he explained that they wouldn't be home from work yet. I asked if I could wait. He said 'yes' although I could tell he really wanted to say 'no'.

The interior was dingy and made my place look like something *Architectural Digest* would be pleased to feature. The clutter was truly impressive. And so was the dirt. The flat stank of grease and old curries. The furniture looked like something even Oxfam would reject and there was not a clear surface to be found.

'Sorry for the mess,' my host mumbled. He pointed towards the sofa and then as an afterthought decided it would be best if he cleared a space to sit. He dumped some debris off the furniture and on to the floor and beamed at me.

'Thanks,' I said. I sat gingerly. The springs in the couch seemed about to surrender. I thought it best not to offer them any inducement.

The bloke with the takeaway told me his name was Craig.

'I remimber you,' he said, in a thick Antipodean accent. 'From the ither day.' He finished the kebab by stuffing it in his face and then I noticed he was in the middle of packing, or rather throwing things into a backpack which stood gaping on the floor.

'Leaving tomorrow,' he said. 'Hitch-hiking through Uzbekistan.'

'Why bother?' was the response that sprang to my lips but I didn't say it. I'd been young once. Perhaps I too would have considered it a capital idea back then.

'Yeah,' he said enthusiastically. 'Me and a few ither jokers decided we've hed enough. We'll come back over the summer, earn some more hard currency. But there's no point stucking round here when the wither's so piss poor, and there's not much work.' He sniffed a pair of underpants before chucking them in with the rest of his clothes. 'Yer money goes further in the bloody Third World.'

'How do you know Curly and Pete?'

'Met them at the pub and they offered me the spare room. It was cheap and I needed a crash pad. The last place I stayed got condemned. Then I laboured a few days for thim. My old man's a builder back home so I know enough to lie my way around a site. Money's pretty easy and the work's a doddle. First few days the ither jokers on the job were telling me to slow down, I was working too fast. Bloody Poms. Don't know the meaning of a hard day's graft.' Craig shovelled some more food into his mouth, some of it fell into the pack. He picked it out and ate it. 'I'll tell you,' he said, 'if you want a job done, then get somebody else. These guys couldn't organize a piss up in a brewery.' He made a half-hearted attempt at folding a shirt, gave up and consigned it to a wrinkled voyage.

'Did Craig and Pete talk to you about Bruce McCarthy?'

'That guy who got done in? Yeah, bloody big shock for them. He was their mate – after a fashion.' Craig tamped down the clothing, which was threatening to burst out the top of the pack even though there was a large pile on the floor still waiting to go in. 'Even though Craig and Peter thought Bruce was a crook.'

'What sort of crook?'

'They told me Bruce was one of those jokers who liked to take money from old ladies for work that didn't need doing. He'd pocket their life savings, tell them he was going to build them a brand-new roof and they'd never see hum again.' Craig shoved a sweatshirt with the name of a rugby team into the pack then brought it back out and folded it in half. 'That's what broke up their business partnership, I thunk.'

'Curly and Pete ever speak about a woman called Chloe Ward?'

'They talked about women non-stop. Always trying to pull and never succeeding.'

'This woman was a business contact. Wears a fur coat.'

Craig's face broke into a lascivious smile. 'She came round the ither day looking for thim. They were trying to avoid her.'

'Why?'

'It was nothing unusual, they're always trying to avoid people. Y'know, start work on a job and then take another one, tell a bunch of lies to the first lot and try and keep the two people happy while pleasing nobody.'

'Did Chloe say she was a client?'

'Nope. She just handed me her card and told me to tell them it'd be worth their while to get in touch.'

'Do you have that card by any chance?'

'It's on the board by the fridge.'

Chapter Thirty-One

Chloe Ward's house was in a mews just off Kensington High Street. It was closed and dark. The security system was state of the art. Even my very amateur eye could tell there would be little benefit to crossing the threshold uninvited.

I stood outside in the winter darkness, feeling cold but thinking more clearly than I had in a while. Chloe Ward was the key to this. The more I thought about it, the more sense this made. She'd been at the funeral talking to Curly and Pete, who'd suddenly come over all forthcoming about Lana. She'd been at Lana's flat. She wanted to find Lana as much as I did.

'Mr Ridley.'

She was standing right behind me. A petite woman in a fur coat almost as sleek as it must have looked on its original owner. She carried a Harvey Nichols food bag and glossy leather purse.

'What a coincidence. Cocktail hour. Fancy one?'

I followed her indoors wondering if I was going to run into her heavyweight husband, Dutch, or whether he was running things back in Barcelona.

'Can you make a martini?' Chloe shucked her coat and bag. She wore a plain suit in dark blue.

'Pouring whisky is about the limit to my bartending skills.'

'Never mind. I'll make us both one.'

I sat while she mixed and stirred and poured. She carried two v-shaped glasses – opaque from their time in the freezer, sprayed vermouth in with an atomizer and offered me my choice of vodka. I chose a Swedish one.

She placed a plump olive in each glass and brought them on a tray to where I was sitting. She sat opposite me, took a small sip from her dainty glass. I did the same. I tried to recall what she'd looked like naked in *Humping Heidi*. Too much had happened since then, the vital parts were a blur.

'What happened to your eye?'

'I fell on a knife.' I swilled the unfamiliar drink. It kicked back.

'What are you doing with Lana? Has she cut you in on the deal?'

'What deal? I don't know anything about a deal.'

'You spoke to Bruce before he died and I hear he was in confessional mode. Probably drunk too, if I know his habits of late. He was inclined to let things slip in that state of mind.'

'He didn't.'

'I could almost believe that,' she said. 'But you keep hanging around, Mr Ridley. First Bruce, then Lana, now me. So tell me what's going on,' Chloe said softly, loosening a button on her rather prim jacket. It seemed suggestive, but I suppose ex-porn stars could make picking their teeth seem suggestive. 'I think you've got an eye for the main chance.'

'I don't know anything.' It was a tired refrain but the only one I knew the words to.

'You're cute when you're playing dumb.' Another button fell. I was catching more than a glimpse of an expensive silk camisole and lightly tanned skin. 'But let's drop that now, shall we? Tell me where the rent-a-wife is.'

'Rent-a-wife?'

'It wasn't a love match. Lana wanted a British passport and Bruce needed the money. They married in Barcelona. She gave him ten grand. It was well over the market price at that time. But Bruce never could turn down a lump sum – his skill for getting rid of money was so well developed.' Chloe arched an eyebrow. 'You shouldn't trust Lana, you know. Don't get seduced by those skinny thighs.'

'You might as well be speaking a foreign language.' I smiled winningly. 'I'm a reporter chasing a story.'

She shrugged as if she would let that ride for the moment. The wind rattled the windows.

'We're in for a rough night,' Chloe said, polishing off her martini. 'Can I get you another?'

I stuck with the one I had. I've never developed a taste for fancy drinks.

Chloe made herself another drink and sank back down into her well-stuffed sofa, twirling the fresh drink between her fingers.

'Like my art?'

The pale room was dominated by a large bronze statue of a man with an erection that would have made a stallion feel insecure.

'What do you think?' she asked. 'Art or pornography?'

'It depends on how much it cost.'

'Alexi found you, didn't he?'

'How do you know?'

'He's got this thing about eyes. He doesn't see very well himself. He likes to spread it around, so to speak. You're lucky. They let you live. Why did they do that?'

'They don't want to close off any potential routes to Lana.'

Chloe slid on to the seat next to me. 'Bruce was bringing a film back from America,' she said abruptly.

'A porno film?'

'It's worth a lot of money. A *lot* of money. He was supposed to deliver it to Alexi.'

I felt my eye. It was puffy. 'But Bruce was murdered and Lana stepped in. Resourceful girl.'

'Not that resourceful. She double-crossed Alexi. She only gave him half the film.'

'Why would she do that?'

'I have no idea what she's up to,' Chloe said, exasperated. 'Maybe she screwed up, maybe she's trying to increase the price. All I know is there are some very angry, very dangerous men who want to find her. If they think you're involved they'll crush you too, without a moment's thought.'

'Your point is?'

'If you know where the other half of that film is, I'll pay you well.'

'How well?'

'Fifty thousand pounds in the offshore bank account of your choice.'

It had a nice ring to it. I made a show of considering.

'What makes you think I know?'

'You know,' she said, but her body language was telling a different story. She was taking a punt. She was desperate, just like me.

'Besides, how could I enjoy my riches, buried in concrete slippers?'

'If you get me the film, I'll get Alexi off your back.'

'What's to stop me dealing with them direct?'

'I wouldn't do that.'

'Why not? They'll be almost certain to offer more money.'

'These guys are like radioactive waste – best handled from a distance,' she said. 'You don't know how to deal with them. I do.'

She was in charge, a woman with a keen mind. Bruce didn't seem like the type who'd have the contacts to set up a big deal with the Russians like this. But Chloe did, or rather Chloe and her entrepreneurial husband.

'And you met in Barcelona?' She didn't say yes or no but it made sense. Bruce racks up some gambling debts in a bar and meets Chloe and Dutch who see his potential and offer him a chance to get clear.

'Why didn't he stick with the pornography?'

She considered whether or not to tell me and decided to.

'He didn't like it. He only did it for the money. He preferred . . . less messy things.'

'But you offered him other jobs after that? 'Cos you got out of the business too. Got married. What other businesses is your husband in?'

She didn't say but she didn't have to. There's lots of industries tied in with pornography. Drugs, pirated films, money laundering, all sort of things. Bruce would have made a good courier, so handsome and innocent looking.

'Think about what I'm offering,' Chloe said to dismiss me.

The rainstorm started just as I reached my car.

There were lights on at my place when I returned. I felt glad. Felicia would be there, she might have even cooked something splendid such as her mother's lasagne, which she sometimes does when her mates need comfort food. It's as good as medicine. The thought of it made me weak with hunger. I hadn't had food in a while.

I parked the car, struggling a bit with the lock. The trusty Renault is very sound mechanically, but bits were starting to fall off the body. The lock had been sticky for some time now, since some local halfwit bandits thought they could open it with a screwdriver and take it for a ride. I happened to catch them in the act and chased them two or three blocks before they got too big a lead on me. They hadn't been back since, and I hadn't done anything about my intention to have it repaired. I turned up my collar against the rain.

Felicia was sitting in the living room, filing her

nails and reading a book. She jumped up when she saw me. Paused. We stood, about two feet apart. Each wondering how the other was going to set the tone.

'You're okay,' she said finally.

'Yep.'

'I was worried. Where'd you go?'

'Walked around a bit. Got wet. Paid a few calls.'

'This is a disaster,' Felicia said. 'A disaster. I'm going to talk to Crosbie, there's no way this can continue.'

'Don't worry about it. It'll sort itself out.' I'd almost forgotten the threat of sacking now that the threat of death had lodged itself firmly in my mind. Why had Lana put one over the Russians?

'A man threatened to kill me today,' I said, forgetting my resolve not to tell Felicia. I got the whisky from the kitchen. Laid down a slab in a glass. A big one. My arm hurt. My eye hurt. The whisky would help.

'Sam, please stop kidding around. This is no time to be flip.'

'It's true. Remember the guy who called up looking for me? Well he found me.'

'Why?'

'They've got it into their heads that I'm working with Lana.'

'I don't get it,' Felicia said. 'This is all to do with Bruce?'

'Bruce was up to something dodgy when he died. From all accounts, building didn't pay enough to maintain his lifestyle.'

'What was he doing?'

I told Felicia what Chloe had told me.

'How would the wife find out?' Felicia said. 'They didn't even live together.'

'God knows,' I said, slugging some whisky. It was something worth pondering. How did she know what was going on?

'Lana somehow found out what Bruce was up to and killed him so she could take over.'

'Wouldn't you?'

'Oh, yeah, Ridley. Sure I would. I see myself an international smuggler and cold-blooded killer,' Felicia said scathingly. 'Look, I think you should let the cops deal with it. Your most important concern should be keeping your job.'

'No point having a job if I'm not alive to enjoy it.' I finished off the whisky. Thought about having a cigarette. I did need one, more than ever. I searched through the kitchen drawers in the vain hope there was a forgotten pack lurking.

'I can't believe you're being so irresponsible.' Felicia swiped her belongings up from the side table. She'd laid out tiny bottles of polish and files and fluffy balls of cotton wool. She gathered them up and put them in a wicker basket.

I shut the drawer. I'd had an idea. I took Felicia's well-manicured hand and looked at it, finger by finger. Then kissed it in a courtly fashion.

'Are you drunk?' she demanded.

'No, just very clever,' I said smugly. 'I know how Lana found out what Bruce was doing.'

'How?'

'Fingernails.'

Chapter Thirty-Two

I thought about Lindy Lee as I drove up to Kensal Rise. I thought about her extravagantly decorated purple and green fingernails with the little silver star in the middle. Lana had had the same design. Maybe it was coincidence. Maybe one of the girlie magazines had announced that purple and green fingernails with stars were the way to get and keep your man while having great orgasms, so every woman under twenty-five had rushed out to get hers fixed.

I was prepared to bet not.

I was prepared to bet Lindy and Lana knew each other and had hatched a plan to get rid of Bruce and hijack the deal that would make them wealthy women.

Only something had gone badly wrong.

Lindy's house was dark. That was good. I wasn't counting on her being home.

I walked up to the front door and knocked, sizing up the place at the same time. It wouldn't be too hard to get in. In fact, I might even enjoy the chance to practise my housebreaking skills.

The street was quiet and dark. A couple of the lamps had expired and shed patches of dark. Two young men bounced by, shouting and gesticulating at each other in a teenage patois that I couldn't make out. I leant against the bonnet of my car, waiting for them to go.

The street got quiet again, I pushed myself off the car and strolled up Lindy's short, shabby front path. Rang the doorbell. Gazed about innocently, for the benefit of anybody who might be looking on.

Nobody was. There were lights glowing at windows but most had curtains firmly drawn. No cars drove by and I was now the only person on the street.

I pushed the door. It was cheap and sat loosely in the jamb. Not much resistance for a resourceful, part-time housebreaker. Standing on the threshold of somebody else's place, going in without permission, always gives me a warm, fuzzy feeling. I pulled on my leather gloves.

It took seconds to get inside. I used a credit card and some old-fashioned brute force.

There were no lights on, the house felt empty. It smelt of brassy perfume and old toast. I walked down the short hallway to the living room. There wasn't much light but my eyes got used to it.

The room had been trashed. The chintz suite had been slashed, stuffing lay strewn on the floor. Chairs and tables were overturned, china ornaments had been smashed. The television and video recorder were intact but Lindy's CD and tape collection was scattered about in pieces. Prints had been ripped off the wall and the backs torn off them. Books and magazines had been ripped up, their pages scattered.

The kitchen was in much the same state. The

contents of the cupboards were over the floor and the work surfaces. Food packets and been opened, crockery broken. The floor was carpeted with pasta shells, soup mix and flour.

Upstairs, Lindy's bedroom presented a similar scene of destruction, her pink little-girl decor an odd contrast to the overall mess. Her bedding and clothes were tossed about. Even the mattress and duvet had been shredded.

I sat on the wrecked bed. Had whoever had been here found what they were looking for? There was no way of knowing. Maybe Alexi the Russian was a step ahead of me. Perhaps he'd already found Lana and forced her to confess what she knew about the movie. She'd given them Lindy's name and they'd come here and taken care of her.

But I couldn't imagine Lindy putting up much resistance. There would have been little need to create all this mess if they knew what they were looking for.

That meant the film was still at large. All I had to do was find out where.

I let myself out. The street was quiet. Nobody about. Nobody taking any interest in me. I allowed myself a moment of optimism. Perhaps the Russians didn't seriously believe I was involved in this. Perhaps they'd just been covering their bases. Maybe I'd misheard him when he said he would track me down and kill me.

It was a moment only.

It ended when I felt the pressure of a big, hard fist in my solar plexus.

Breath rushed from my lungs. I doubled up, felt like I wanted to vomit.

The guy didn't give me time to get upright. He kicked the ripped muscles in my shoulder. He kicked hard. I stumbled backwards and fell amongst the rubbish bins. I hit my head on the stone wall. I was hovering between consciousness and blackout. My assailant lifted his boot, was about to bring it down on my face. I was wedged between the bins. There was no escape. Even if I could get the energy to raise myself.

The boot hovered. It was a big one, I noted irrelevantly. Size ten at least. It would hurt if I was still awake to feel it. I felt as though the universe was about to fold in on me. I would lie back and let it, I decided, closing my eyes.

'Hey,' the guy said. 'I know you.'

The boot lowered. A huge hand reached down and grabbed my shirt. Dragged me up. 'What are you doing here?' he asked roughly. It was Terry, Lindy's friend and the café proprietor who served the worst tea in the world.

'Where's Lindy?'

'What were you doing in there?' he repeated stubbornly.

'Looking for Lindy. Is she about?'

'You broke into her place.' He pushed past me, went in.

'Christ,' he said when he saw the mess. 'You did that? I'm gonna bloody kill you.'

'I found it like this.' I sat on a chair, the feeling-sick part of the evening had not passed.

He didn't believe me. He hovered, fists on hips, wondering what sort of a beating would compensate for the chaos he saw.

'Lindy's in trouble,' I said.

'You seen her?' he asked. The fists bunched, slackened. There was worry on his face as he remembered why he'd come.

I shook my head. 'Not since that day at the caff. When was the last time you saw her?'

'Two days ago. She normally comes in every morning for a cuppa. I checked at work, she hasn't been there either.' He sat gingerly on a ripped chair. 'Usually she lets me know what she's up to.'

I nodded, trying to concentrate on the problem. Trying not to think about how awful I felt.

'What are you doing here?' Terry asked.

'I think Lindy's involved in something much more dangerous than she realizes.'

'You filth?'

I gave him my card, extracting my wallet with difficulty. Everything hurt. He flipped the card over. Slipped it into his top pocket.

'What's she up to then?'

'I think she's involved with someone who's ripped off the Russian mob.'

Terry looked dubious. 'Lindy's a good girl.'

'You ever see her with a woman called Lana? Blonde, Russian accent?'

'Yeah. How'd you know?'

'A rough guess. Where'd you see them?'

'She was in the caff last week. Turned a few heads. First time I seen her.'

'She's Bruce McCarthy's wife.'

'What's she doing wiv his wife? She told me it was all over with Bruce.'

'Romantically it may have been over, but I think Lana and Lindy had business.'

'What are you getting at? Lindy's not involved in anyfink bad. She couldn't be.'

'What were Lindy and Lana talking about?'

'I dunno. I don't listen. I serve tea and sandwiches.'

'See her with a tape?'

'What sort of tape?'

'Like a VHS.'

'No.'

'She mention Bruce McCarthy?'

''Course. She was really cut up about him getting killed. They used to go out. He was a useless swine. Didn't treat her right.' The way he said it made me think he had romantic designs on Lindy. They'd make a contrasting couple – her tarty glamour and his well-muscled roughness. Terry looked like an ex-boxer. He certainly punched like one. I rubbed my stomach. It was on fire. It'd been a hard day for my body which hadn't been in great condition to begin with. 'Did she say anything about the party she gatecrashed at his house the night before he died?'

'Nope.'

'Any ideas where she might be now?'

'This was the only idea I had,' Terry said, looking around him.

'She got any family?'

'None she's on speaking terms with.'

'Friends? The woman she works with?'

'Spoke to her. She knows nuffink.'

We sat in silence.

'She'll show up,' I said eventually.

The look on Terry's face showed he really wanted to believe me.

I met my neighbours on the stairs along with thirteen or so of their closest mates. They were dressed to party which meant I had a few hours of silence lined up, as a special treat. I said hello, they mumbled something unintelligible. They probably needed all the concentration they had to manoeuvre the stairs in their four-inch platform soles and dark glasses.

Felicia was in bed. There was a message from Marlowe on the machine asking me to call him. I ignored it. I'd had enough of Marlowe. I took a couple of painkillers and fell asleep on the sofa.

I woke at 3.30 a.m. when the upstairs party started and listened to the thumping of the music. I had a glass or two of whisky, found some earplugs and crawled into bed.

'Why aren't you at work?' I asked Felicia when she came out at nine the next morning dressed in a sweatsuit and trainers.

'It's Saturday,' she said. 'Try and keep a grip, Sam. And don't forget we have a party.'

I groaned.

'It's just what you need. Meet some new people.'

I groaned again. I thought of the beautiful and

eligible Kyle and wondered whether she could have come along at a worse time.

'What shall I wear?' Felicia mused half to herself as she made coffee. I sat up groggily and rubbed my eyes. 'Nothing fits me any more.' She handed me a cup of coffee and began slicing bagels.

'I've been thinking about it and I'm pretty sure I can persuade Crosbie to put in a good word for you. I'm meeting her for coffee this afternoon. This accusation is so absurd, I'm sure she'll see that. Bagel?'

'Yes, please. It's not absurd when it's made by the managing editor. And what's in it for her if she puts her neck on the line for me?'

'You don't know until you try,' Felicia said, popping the bagels under the grill. 'Who knows, under all that Armani might be the heart of a saint. We know how much Crosbie admired Princess Diana. I'm going to try that tack . . . point out to her that it's her chance to be a friend to the needy and all that. Garlic cream cheese? Or chives?'

After Felicia left for her yoga class, I decided on a whim to revisit Bruce's house. It was the only place I could think of that might give me an idea of what to do next. I'd told Terry I'd give him a call if I came up with anything concrete about Lindy. But I'd sounded more confident than I'd felt. The truth was, I didn't have the first idea what to do.

As I pointed the Renault west, I checked behind me for the Mercedes, but nobody appeared to be following me. I whistled a little song. Perhaps the Russians had already found Lana. Perhaps the other tape had already changed hands and nobody was interested in me any more.

It was a nice fantasy that lasted clear to Shepherd's Bush.

There was one cop car on Bruce's street, parked roughly, front doors open. The front door to Bruce's house was open, the police tape broken. I went in.

The place had been given the same treatment as Lindy's. The cops were upstairs; I stood downstairs. I could hear them talking to each other, trying to figure out why anyone would want to break into the house of a dead guy.

I didn't stay. There'd probably be more cops arriving any moment and I'd answered enough police questions.

The wide street was still quiet. No kids played on the pavement, no men washed the family car. A couple of teenagers went by, both wired up to the same personal stereo, then there was a woman with a shopping trolley and that was the sum of the traffic. The houses were a uniform style. The contents of the front gardens ranged from rejected appliances to shrubs. There was nothing to see. I sighed, turned back to the car. Approaching me were two elderly people. She had her arm resting on his. When they got closer, I recognized Bruce's next-door neighbours, Paul Fraser and his wife.

'Oh, hello,' he said, struggling to remember where he'd seen me before. 'What are the police doing back here?'

'I think the house has been broken into.'

We exchanged a few platitudes about the state of the modern world.

'Have they arrested anybody yet?' Mrs Fraser asked. 'The police aren't giving much away.'

'I don't think so.'

'He had some very strange friends,' Mrs Fraser said. 'It wouldn't surprise me—'

'The police have been here a couple of times,' Mr Fraser cut in. 'They ask lots of questions but they don't tell us much in exchange. They say we don't have anything to worry about, but that's not much comfort, is it?'

'I'm sure they're right.'

'It would be so much easier if we knew,' Paul Fraser said. 'Nothing like this has ever happened before. It's not exactly a grand neighbourhood but even so, there's never been a murder.'

I went back to my car. I'd just opened the door when Amy French pulled up at the pavement, her car loaded with supermarket bags.

'Hiya!' she said cheerily. 'What brings you—?' Then she saw the cop car. 'Oh dear. Not more trouble?' She killed the engine. Got out.

More cops arrived, went in the house. The original two came out. Told us there was nothing to see and got us to move on. I offered to help Amy unload her shopping.

'That'd be great,' she said. 'The other half's taken the twins to see his mother. I'm totally superfluous to that scenario – the old bag can't stand me. Now that I've produced the little darlings, I might as well be dead.' Amy's broad grin indicated she didn't particularly care for her mother-in-law's good opinion. I got in the car and we drove the hundred or so yards to her house where I helped her unload more food than I'd ever seen in my life.

'I must have an incurable case of housewife-itis,' she said after we'd staggered in with the last load. 'I get a couple of hours free and what do I do? Go to an art gallery? Meet a friend for coffee? No. I head straight to the supermarket. Got to keep the pantry stocked, otherwise the world will see me as a failure. Fancy a cuppa?'

'Thanks,' I said, craning my neck to see over the fence into Bruce's garden.

'If you want a better view we can go upstairs,' Amy said. 'I can see clear into his place. And the Frasers'. No secrets on this street.'

'I was just talking to Paul and his wife,' I said.

'Wife?' Amy put a large china pot and some home-made biscuits in front of me. 'Oh, Margaret's not his wife, she's his sister. She moved in with him after some cowboy builders took her for her life's savings.'

Chapter Thirty-Three

I put the cup down carefully.

'What did you say?'

'It was a while ago now,' Amy said. 'But she really did get done. Took the guys to court but they'd done something tricky with their assets so the judgement didn't stick. Or maybe they didn't even have any assets. Anyway, they got off scot-free.'

'Was it Bruce?'

'Bruce? No, I'm sure she would have mentioned if it was Bruce. Besides, I don't think ripping off old women was his style – now young women, that was a different story.'

There was a familiar figure standing waiting outside my place. I wasn't surprised, traffic outside my flat was so heavy these days it was getting to the stage where I'd have been disappointed if there was no one to meet me.

I went straight up to him. Put a firm hand on his shoulder

'Claude, old man,' I said in a jocular English way, 'Felicia's not in. And she's never going to be in for you ever again. Sorry. Life moves on. Get another mistress, I'm sure Paris is bulging with candidates.'

He glared at me. 'Don't think she will stay with you. She is on the rebound,' he said, clutching a bunch of expensive flowers to his chest. 'She will come back when she returns to her senses.'

'Of course she will. All you have to do is go back home and wait like a good chap.' I smiled patronizingly. This guy was seriously starting to bug me. I've never been able to work out why the people least qualified to draw the conclusion that they are the gods' gift to humanity are the ones who unerringly reach it.

'I'm not going anywhere until I talk to Felicia.'

'Enjoy the wait.'

'I can't believe she chose someone like you over me,' he said just as I was about to cross the street. I turned back.

'Pardon?'

'You're not exactly a catch.' Claude looked me up and down scornfully. It was true, the contrast was quite marked, even though the premise it rested upon was false. I didn't have the heart to set him right. In fact, the urge to confirm his misunderstanding became almost irresistible. I stepped back on to the pavement.

'It is amazing, isn't it? Who can ever figure women out?' I smiled down from my superior height. Claude probably cleared five foot five with big heels on. 'She's so irrational – wanting a man all to herself – not wanting to share him with his wife. Felicia is funny like that.'

'My wife has nothing to do with this.'

'Apparently not.'

'Claude?' Felicia had arrived carrying two bags of groceries. 'Sam? What's going on?'

'Felicia, I need to talk to you. Just half an hour, please.' Claude tried to foist the flowers on to her but she didn't have a free hand to take them with. She looked back and forward between us and the flowers, pained.

'Just half an hour,' Claude said again. 'Then I will go. I promise. Felicia, I can't let you make this mistake. I can't let you live in these conditions. You must come back to me.'

'What conditions?' I demanded. 'She's not living in conditions. I have a perfectly nice flat.'

Claude ignored me. Felicia ignored me. She looked like she'd just woken from a very long sleep. I feared she would do something she might regret.

'Felicia, darling,' I said, putting my arm around her. 'Let's go inside.' I took one bag away from her and guided her across the street.

'What? What are you doing?'

'Saving you from yourself. He thinks we're together now,' I said. I whisked her inside before she had a chance to protest.

'And you let him think that? How dare you!'

'I was doing you a favour. I thought you didn't want to see him again.' I shut the front door before Claude could see us arguing. We walked up the stairs in silence.

'You had no right, Ridley.' Felicia dumped her groceries on the floor as soon as we got in. 'You're as bad as Claude. No, you're worse. At least Claude has a life and doesn't pretend he's a superhero, about to save the world. You're sad and useless, Ridley. You play all these stupid boy-reporter games to cover up your own inadequacies. You picture yourself as a hero so you don't have to see yourself as you really are . . . a lonely and pathetic man.'

I blinked, too shocked to say anything. She seemed shocked as well. She gaped like a goldfish and put her hand to her forehead. I checked the window. 'He's still out there. Run on down and take his thirty quid's worth of flowers. I'm sure he has lots of other expensive gifts lined up back at the penthouse.'

'Mind your own bloody business. You don't have the first idea of what it's like for me.'

'I thought you wanted to be rid of him. I thought you wanted a life where you at least had some dignity.'

On the street Claude had dumped the cherry-red roses in the nearest bin. He walked off up the street, eyeing up the young girls who walked past.

'He's going,' I said. 'If you hurry you can catch up.'

'Thanks for your support.' Felicia grabbed her bag. 'Oh, and just for the record? You don't know the first thing about me.' She slammed the door as she stomped out.

I stood there, appalled at what had just happened. Where had that come from? How had we suddenly managed to get so pissed off at each other? I went to the window and watched Felicia catch up with

Claude. They stood in the middle of the footpath while the market crowds surged around them. She was saying something to him and by the smug expression on his face, it was something he liked the sound of. I couldn't watch any more.

I decided it was time for a drink. And a smoke.

Several drinks and a few fags later I was at my new local, an insalubrious den tucked away off Portobello Road under the motorway overpass. The place hadn't seen a lick of paint since 1954, the locals looked as venal and ugly as the mongrels that accompanied them and the alcohol was of the strictly inferior type. But I have a sure-fire method for dealing with all of those things – I drink until it doesn't matter.

At eight-thirty I stumbled out, vaguely aware that I had somewhere to go, but not remembering where it was. I walked south on Portobello, stopping at a fish and chip shop for something to belatedly line my stomach. My throat felt raw from the now unaccustomed cigarette smoke. My stomach was tender from the combination of that and the booze. I felt awful about the things Felicia had said about me. Above all, I was confused at how we'd managed to get so angry with each other.

The tourist crowds were long gone. Instead the bars and restaurants were filling up. People moved about in twos, threes and fours. They took no notice of me, scarfing fish and chips from a paper sack. They had places to go, friends to meet, lives to live. I was alone on a Saturday night.

Sad and pathetic. That's what Felicia thought I

was. I pushed the accusation down but it bobbed up like a plastic bottle in a swimming pool.

Sad and pathetic.

I finished the chips and threw the paper into a bin. I was not sad and pathetic. I had a rich and interesting life. I had friends. And a young son who loved me. Apart from the fact that I had no job and was held up to public ridicule, and could soon be languishing at the bottom of the Thames in unsuitable footwear, I was a lucky guy. And I did have something to do tonight, if only I could remember what it was.

The flat was empty and dark. I stumbled around, found the light switch and took off my jacket. It'd spilt tomato ketchup down the front. And the whole ensemble smelt of tobacco and alcohol. I stepped into the shower, it'd help me think.

I got out, brain still blurred from the whisky and dying for another fag. I told myself no. I had to give up. Today was an unfortunate lapse. I had to start afresh. Think of lung cancer and not contributing to cigarette companies' already bulging coffers. There was a principle at stake. I dried myself and found some sort of clean clothes.

I prodded my gums. I combed my hair. I took a couple of Alka Seltzer. I burped.

Then the music in the flat upstairs started and I remembered.

I had an invite to a party.

The party of a gorgeous and intelligent woman who didn't seem to find me completely repulsive.

'Huh!' I said and pointed my finger at a Felicia who wasn't there. 'I'll show you.'

Felicia had written Kyle's address and number on the calendar hanging in the kitchen. I took a copy of it and set off to find a taxi to take me to Clapham. We stopped on the way at an off licence and I bought a packet of mints and a bottle of Australian sauvignon blanc.

The city looked good that night. The sky was clear and a new moon reflected in the waters of the Thames. The taxi-driver let me off in Kyle's street and I followed the sound of the music.

Kyle opened the door. 'Hey,' she said. 'Glad you could make it.'

She was wearing a red Chinese silk jacket, black trousers and red satin shoes and her long hair was dressed up and fixed in place with chopsticks. She leant towards me and kissed me on the cheek.

'Not half as glad as me,' I said, half-wishing Felicia was here to witness how very wrong she was about me.

We did a tour of the flat, which was large and comfortable. It was painted in bold colours and decorated with African artefacts. There were about twenty people there and from snatches of conversation I heard, most of them were in Kyle's line of work.

We ended up in the kitchen where she poured me a glass of wine. I had intentions of monopolizing the hostess but the doorbell rang, and she left to answer it. I gazed out on to the tiny patio where a Japanese garden was taking shape.

'Fancy a drink?' Kyle was asking the new guest.

'I can't, thanks.' The voice sounded familiar. I

withdrew my attention from the garden. 'No alcohol for me. I'm pregnant.'

It was Felicia. Looking knock-dead gorgeous in a black party dress and high heels.

'Hello, darling,' she said, crossed the room and kissed me hard on the mouth. 'Sorry I'm late.'

Chapter Thirty-Four

I don't know who was more surprised, Kyle or me. Felicia tucked her hand into my arm and nuzzled my cheek. Shock kept me frozen in place. Kyle, who'd been holding a bottle of wine in one hand, put it down slowly. 'Well, I think we have some orange juice here . . .'

'That'll be super. Don't want to interfere with Sammy Junior's brain cells at this early stage,' Felicia said gaily, hugging me closer.

I opened my mouth but for once could think of nothing to say.

'Later, maybe,' Felicia said. 'After all, he will be his father's son. We can't expect him to live an abstemious life. But just for the meantime – you know, give him the best start we can.' She smiled cosily at me.

The doorbell rang. Kyle looked relieved as she darted to answer it.

'What on earth are you doing?' I pulled my arm away from Felicia.

'Getting you back,' she hissed.

'What for?'

'For telling Claude that we were an item.'

'I didn't tell him, he assumed it. And I let him for your sake, to stop him pestering you.'

'And for Everard. He invited me down for drinks and launched himself at me and when I said I wasn't interested he said you'd told him I fancied him!' Felicia's eyes were hard and angry.

'It was a joke,' I said, feebly.

'Well now you know what it feels like,' she said. 'You stay out of my life and I'll stay out of yours.'

I didn't need Nostradamus to predict the rest of the evening would be a disaster. Kyle was puzzled and cool and had too many hostess duties for me to get her in one place to explain. Felicia flirted gaily with all the good-looking men in the room and I sat in a corner and was buttonholed by a bloke who worked in some obscure branch of television who tried to impress me with his importance. It was not a vibrant exchange of views. I allowed him to spout on about telecine and tape-reproduction facilities, he allowed me to drink.

After we'd exhausted all areas of common interest, he left me alone with the bottle of wine. Some kind souls would attempt conversation but they gave up after a few minutes. I noticed a tall fellow in jeans and a checked shirt trying to corner Kyle from time to time, which did nothing but add to my feeling of general misery. At about midnight, I decided that I'd had enough of having a social life. It was time to go home. The party was revving up nicely, someone had put some excellent rhythm and blues on the CD player and people had rolled up the Persian carpet and begun dancing. I wove on out to the kitchen to put my glass away and encountered Kyle and checked shirt in a clinch. He had his hand at the back of her neck. A strand of her hair had come down. She had a hand on his bicep. In my drunken state it seemed an affront to all that was good and decent. I tapped checked shirt on the shoulder and demanded he unhand her.

'What?' he said.

'You heard me,' I slurred. 'Leave that fair damsel alone.'

'Listen, mate.' A finger hove into my view. I tried to focus on it but couldn't. I realized I had passed the stage where I could even vaguely pretend to be sober. I was wild drunk. There seemed no point in further talk so I took a swing at him.

Everything spun.

I was spinning and spinning, the lights too bright, the music too loud. The roar in my head swamped everything. I was out of control. I put a hand out to steady myself and found no support. I stumbled and would have fallen except for a very firm grip on my upper arm.

'Get lost,' checked shirt said and he steered me towards the front door. I turned to get a last glimpse of Kyle. Her face was a mask of pity and horror. Then I was outside on the street. Lying on the street. And the bloody world would not stop spinning. I rolled over. I picked myself up, unsteadily. It was a good night for a walk. I would walk off the drink. I'd feel better when I got home. My head would be clear and I wouldn't have a hangover in the morning.

'Sam! For God's sake, what's the matter with you?'

Felicia.

'I'm tearing drunk,' I said. 'And I don't care.'

'I saw that guy toss you out. What did you do?'

'He was all over her! All over her. I jush thought someone should put a stop to it.'

'What'd you do, Sam?'

'I hit him, I think.'

'You think?'

'It's checked shirt's fault. He had his paws all over the ravishing Kyle. I had to put a stop to it.'

'So you said.'

'So I did. I did and went and sh . . . showed him.

Felicia looked at me for the longest time, staring, hands on hips in her usual stance. Then she turned me back the other way. 'It's been quite a day, let's go home,' she said. Her car was parked nearby. She helped me in and drove us back to Notting Hill. We didn't speak.

The next day I awoke with the horrible feeling that my skull had been trepanned without my permission. A hard, throbbing ache seemed to make my head vibrate of its own accord. I rolled over in my bed, hoping perhaps that it would go away if I lay quietly for a minute or two longer. It didn't. I lay very still, it still didn't go.

The smell of fresh coffee was breezing from the kitchen as I made my slow way from the bedroom to the couch. Every sinew, every corpuscle cautioned me not to be so ambitious in the mobility department so early in the day. But I was determined to be master of my body.

'I went out and bought extra Nurofen,' Felicia said coldly. She had a bag and was on her way out. 'They're on the counter.'

'Okay,' I said. Then I lay on the sofa and wondered if I had died and this was hell.

Sunday passed in a daze. Felicia didn't come back all day. I got up about five and went out for a curry. I fell asleep early and Felicia must have come in late.

Monday crawled around and I still couldn't shake the hangover. But since I didn't have a job to go to there was no special reason why I needed to. I got up after Felicia left for work and pushed a couple of eggs round a pan.

Terry called when I'd almost convinced myself the first batch of morning painkillers were working.

'Lana's here,' he whispered, 'asking about Lindy. Get over here. I'll try and delay her.'

Chapter Thirty-Five

I got to Terry's café fast. The hangover made me blasé about the rules of the road. I felt as though I was suspended in a protective bubble as I screeched up Ladbroke Grove, weaving deftly through the traffic. My responses seemed as sharp as if I'd never touched a drop. The car became a performance engine, responsive to the lightest touch.

The place wasn't busy. There was an elderly woman in a knitted hat and Lana. She had her back to me, staring at a mug of tea which she held in both hands. Staring in horror probably, if her tea was as bad as mine had been.

I nodded at Terry, he nodded back. I slid into the seat opposite Lana. I obviously looked as bad as I felt because Terry took pity on me and plonked a coffee in front of me.

'Hey, Lana,' I said casually. 'Fancy meeting you here.'

She started, looked like she was about to run but held her ground. She was scared stiff, that much was clear. But she was trying not to let it get the upper hand. One cool chick. In other circumstances I might have found her interesting.

'Whose idea was it?' I asked casually. 'Yours or Lindy's? Did you introduce her to your husband, knowing that an opportunity might come up to muscle in on his business? Or did it all happen by chance?'

Lana was grinding her teeth. She kept glancing around to check who else was in the café. When a gust of wind blew the door back, she nearly jumped out of her skin.

'I favour the chance theory myself,' I said. 'Because you weren't in touch with Bruce, were you? It was a marriage of convenience. Until you found out Lindy knew him. And when Lindy started talking about stories of his get-rich-quick schemes and you decided it was time to get reacquainted.'

Terry sat down beside her. Lana was now wedged between us. 'She doesn't know where Lindy is,' he said. 'I told her she was going to show up, that's why she's still here.'

'She tricked me, little bitch,' Lana said. 'And now we will both be killed. She has no idea what she is dealing with.'

'And you do. All those contacts from before the days when you decided to go straight. You know Chloe from Barcelona, don't you? Were you in the same business then?'

Lana ignored me. She turned to Terry. 'I will divide the money with her, I promise. Just tell her to bring me disc. Otherwise we are both dead. Alexi will find her and he will kill her.'

I put my hand to my eye. Terry seemed unmoved by Lana's talk of generosity.

'I will share it with her. I always intended to. I did deal myself because I did not want Lindy in something dangerous,' Lana said defensively.

Terry and I smiled. 'That's so sweet,' I said. 'You're only thinking about her.'

'What sort of money are we talking about?' Terry growled.

'Half. I will give her half, as we agreed. If she brings me the disc I will give her the cash.'

Lana gathered up her handbag. 'She can call me on this number.' She put a white card on the table. I picked it up.

She walked out of the café, looking nervously in both directions before hailing a cab.

'Why was she talking about a disc? I thought movies came on tapes.'

'You're behind the times, mate. Everything's on disc these days,' Terry said. 'Tape's a thing of the past. Digital disc is the future – perfect images.'

An idea was jiggling around loose in my brain. I could pin it down with a cigarette. I'd have just the one. One couldn't hurt. I'd start giving up again tomorrow. I shovelled some change into the cigarette machine on the wall. Terry brought me another coffee and some fried food.

'I feel better,' Terry said as he watched me eat. 'I think she's okay. I'm sure she's okay, isn't she?'

'Sure,' I said. Though I didn't feel sure. What if the Russians had latched on to Lindy somehow? It didn't seem likely, but who knew?

The phone rang just at that moment. We both jumped. Terry leapt across the room with the agility of an old boxer. Grabbed the handset. From the expression on his face I could tell it wasn't Lindy.

'She'll call me soon,' he said. 'I know she will.'

'Ask her where the disc is,' I said. 'She should get rid of it, it's not good for her health.' Or mine, I could have added.

'She's a greedy so-and-so,' Terry said. 'Can't help it. Runs in the genes. They're all crooks, her tribe.'

I put down my fork. Smiled broadly at Terry.

'What?' he said. 'What'd I say?'

'You've given me an idea.' I took a cigarette from its pristine packet in an extravagant manner. I'd jolly well earned it. I lit it, drew deep. Felt calm. I was such a clever, clever chap. Despite everything. I was clever and I was going to live.

'I think I can find Lindy and the disc. Fancy being a hired heavy for the morning?'

'You okay?' Terry asked as we drove back to Notting Hill. 'You look bloody awful.'

'Never felt better,' I said. 'She's got a brother, right?'

'Yeah. Twin brother. But she hasn't spoken to him for years.'

I turned off Ladbroke Grove, tooled over Portobello, quieter on a Monday but still cluttered with people seeking the Holy Grail of hip.

'I think the fact that he works in a tape-reproduction place may have been enough to heal the breach,' I said, recalling the drink-sodden conversation I'd had at Kyle's party. 'Lindy's brother could take that disc and reproduce it many times over.'

Terry whistled. 'And have it on the black market in no time. But that doesn't make sense. If she's only got half a movie, why would she bother? It's no use.'

I pulled up outside West Eleven Telecine. 'Maybe Lana and Lindy didn't know the movie Bruce brought back from LA was on two discs. Maybe they both thought they were getting one across each other. Maybe Lindy doesn't know what the hell to do with it now.'

'I told her she wasn't cut out for scamming,' Terry sighed. 'She never listens. She always thinks she's going to hit the big time. Dunno why she can't play the lottery like everyone else.'

'I'd like to see Mr Lee.' I smiled at the receptionist. 'I want to talk about hiring duplication facilities.' It sounded plausible and the woman behind the stainless-steel desk didn't seem to think there was anything wrong with it. She took us to his office. Left us there. I went in first.

Lindy's brother came towards us, hand outstretched. 'Jeff Lee,' he said.

Terry darted around me, grabbed Jeff Lee's outstretched hand, twisted it up behind his back and pushed him face first on to the coffee table. 'Where is it?'

'What?' Jeff gasped, no doubt a little shocked by the turn events had taken.

'Steady,' I murmured. Terry wasn't listening.

'You put your sister up to this?' he growled. 'Now she's in deep shit, so hand it over.'

'Please,' Jeff said. 'Let me stand up.'

'Go on,' I said.

Terry reluctantly eased up. Jeff stood up straight but Terry's tattooed forearm remained snaked around his neck. Jeff looked thoroughly frightened. I watched where his eyes went. A square rectangular box sat on his desk. I moved over to the desk, sat casually.

'Who are you?' Jeff struggled to regain his composure.

'Friends,' Terry snarled.

'Try not to irritate him,' I said. 'He punches hard. Used to be a professional. Where's Lindy?'

'How should I know? I'm not in contact with her.'

'Now, we know that's not true,' I said. 'Because I saw you together just last week. Where is she?'

Terry's arm tightened. Jeff squealed.

'She said she'd call me. She hasn't. I don't know how to get a hold of her. It's the truth.'

'Where's the disc? She leave it with you?'

'No.'

'It's no use to you so you might as well hand it over. It might save your sister's life. Because if we don't get it back to the people who paid for it, pretty soon they're going to come looking for her.'

'I haven't got it.'

Terry began forcing Jeff's head on to the glass coffee table. 'This isn't going to be pretty,' he said to me. 'You might want to look away.'

'Wait!' Jeff said. 'You're friends of hers, right?'

'The best,' Terry growled.

'Well I'm sure . . . in that case . . . I'm sure she . . .'

Terry loosened his grip. Jeff got shakily upright.

He edged around his desk, pulling a key from his pocket and unlocked a drawer. Slowly, with Terry and me watching for any sudden movement, he pulled out a single CD in a white cardboard sleeve.

'That it?' Terry snatched it.

'Yes,' he said. 'Yes.'

'You sure?'

'Yes.'

'Make any copies?'

'No.'

'Sure?' Terry shook him again.

'No. I mean, yes.'

'You didn't make any copies?'

'No,' he said weakly.

'Let's go,' I said to Terry. He left Jeff reluctantly. 'You'd better have told the truth,' he said. 'Or I'll be back. A lot.'

'Take it,' Jeff said as we left. 'It's no good to you. You'll see.'

The cheery receptionist wished us a nice day as we sauntered out of the building into the cold sunshine.

'I think that went well,' I said, turning the disc over in my hands. Wondering what was on it.

'We still don't know where she is,' Terry said gloomily.

'She's headed for the hills like the smart girl she is.'

'What are you going to do with that?' He pointed at the disc.

'Have a look at it,' I said. 'Then hand it over to the cops probably. Want to come?'

'I really don't care. I got a business to run. Besides, Lindy might call.'

He refused a ride back. I watched him walk away and decided Lindy could do a lot worse.

'Stacy Taylor,' I said to Felicia. She was at work.

'The novelist? What about her?'

'Got her number? I need to speak to her.'

'Why?'

'I'll explain later.'

'We really need to talk, Ridley.'

'Yeah,' I said. 'I'll be home tonight.'

'Good,' she said.

I phoned Stacy and she didn't appear to mind that someone she'd only met twice wanted to invite himself over. The reason I'd called her was because her husband made films. I asked her if she had a machine that played discs and she said she did.

It was that simple.

Home for Stacy was a Victorian artist's house in Brook Green. A tall brick cottage with high windows that let in all the thin winter light there was that day. She greeted me warmly and showed me through to the 'back shed' which was a converted stable with a nest of hi-tech video equipment.

'Not strictly necessary,' Stacy said as she showed me in, 'but the boy does like his toys. What have we got here?'

'A movie. It might be a blue movie, I'm afraid.'

She lifted one eyebrow. 'Good. I can use it for research.'

Stacy put the disc in a machine. A crystal-clear image came up on the wide-screen monitor.

We watched. The pictures playing before me were the last thing I expected.

Stacy turned to me and said, 'Where the hell did you get a hold of *this*?'

Chapter Thirty-Six

I'd expected a seedy porno movie. Instead, on the screen, declaring his love for an androgynous young actress, was Hollywood's hottest new star, a young man whose name I couldn't recall but whose face was more familiar to me than my son's. He was on every billboard in town. I'd seen the trailer for this movie, his latest, in the cinema the night I'd gone with Kyle. It was called *Brutal Impact*.

'Whoa,' Stacy whispered as the hero finished declaring his love and went off to cleanse the world of wickedness. He had an improbably large gun and was stripped down to his undershirt – the Hollywood shorthand for 'I mean business.'

'I'll be really interested to hear how you got this.'

'Somebody I know.'

'Then you're moving with the wrong crowd.' Stacy pointed at the screen where the hero was incinerating a warehouse with a flame thrower and then killing five or six bad guys who were considerate enough to wait in line before attacking him. 'This movie hasn't even been released here yet.' Stacy leant against the bench with her arms folded. She looked at me curiously. 'Do you have any idea what this means? It's stolen, right? Inside job by the looks of things. Studios normally guard against people waltzing off with their multimillion-dollar investments.'

'It's stolen,' I said. 'That's a pretty safe bet. It was on its way to the Russian mob but it got sidetracked.'

'Delightful.' Stacy reached for her diary. 'Don't stop it on its merry way. Hand it back.'

'To the cops?'

'The studio. They'll take it, no questions asked. They might even be grateful.'

'Like a reward?'

'I'll call my husband and see if he knows anybody at the studio.'

I sat in a leather director's chair while Stacy spoke to her husband. She wrote down a name and phone number. And I thought of all the things I could do with a cash reward. It would certainly ease the pain of being sacked from City Radio. I'd take some months off and see my son. I'd rent a cheap flat near him and pick him up from school each day. I'd give him fatherly advice about his rollerblading technique and try not to squabble too much with his mother.

Maybe life wasn't going to be so bad after all.

Stacy put the phone down. 'Henry's going to phone someone he knows and he'll contact you,' she said.

The call came moments later.

'Here,' she said, handing me the phone. A deep-voiced American was on the other end.

'Trip Wainwright,' he said. 'I hear you may have just saved our studio a very great deal of money.'

'Might have done. It's only half a movie. I don't know where the other half is.'

'But it's a loner, right. Are you sure there are no other copies?'

'Pretty sure,' I said.

Trip Wainwright barked with relief. 'Thank God,' he said. 'Thank God.'

'You know about this?'

'A certain gentleman has insisted we pay him several million dollars to stop him flooding the market with pirated tapes before *Brutal Impact* is released here. He can't do it with half a movie. And he hasn't been back to us since the initial demand.'

'Which means he knows there's a problem.'

Trip barked again. I realized it was a laugh. 'Mr Ridley, you are not going to find us ungrateful.'

'Good,' I said. 'This guy says he'll kill me if I don't hand it over to him.'

Silence on the other end while Trip thought busily.

'You've spoken to him?'

'Let's just say I gave him my full attention while he beat the shit out of me.'

'That's just a threat,' he said. 'Once he knows he can't extort any money from us he won't hang around.'

'I'm pleased you feel so confident.'

'We have the disc, there's nothing he can do.'

'Except take his revenge on the person who spoked his wheel.'

Small silence from Trip. 'Don't worry,' he said.

But I did worry. I worried all the way into town

to the studio offices in Soho. I was in an impossible situation. I had no doubt the Russian would kill me. He'd be so angry he probably wouldn't even need to work himself up to it. It'd be one of the those messy routine things, like washing the dishes after a big meal. The other thing was, I could identify him. In the event that the cops ever got a grip on it, I'd be a juicy witness.

I stopped at a phone booth. Called Lyall. Lyall always knew what to do.

His wife, Kate, answered.

'Hey, Sam,' she said in her warm, sexy voice. 'Keeping busy?'

'Whatever your husband's told you, it's not true.'

She laughed. She's a happy woman. Her husband and her kids adore her and they're not the only ones.

'Lyall about?'

'Still at work. Unless he's having an affair with a pert-breasted twenty-year-old.' She laughed again. Lyall would inject strychnine before he'd do anything to hurt her and she knows it. I can never think about their relationship without feeling jealous.

The office isn't too far from Soho. I didn't think it'd matter if I made a slight detour.

Lyall had just left. I logged on to my old computer and checked the wires for tomorrow's temperature in Sydney. Warm and cloudless. It was the middle of the night there. I pictured Simon in his cluttered room, face down, arms spread out at his sides the way he always sleeps and wondered what it would be like to see him every day. I was sure my ex-wife would raise no objections to me picking him up after school – she has a punishing career and works very long hours. Having me around would save on childcare expenses. And with the money I could get for the movie I wouldn't need to work for a while, if I stretched it out. The pound was strong against the Aussie dollar. I'd get a little flat, nothing fancy. An old banger of a car, Simon didn't care about that stuff. He'd just be happy to have me near. I'd be happy to be near. I fell into a familial reverie.

Ted Franklin bustled in. 'It's too bright in here, wouldn't you say? Still fighting to get these fluorescent lights removed. Been doing a few experiments. Unofficially. I'm no scientist but I decided I've got to have evidence.'

'Do what you like with the lights,' I said. 'I'm going home.' But when I said 'home' I didn't think of Ladbroke Grove. I thought of the golden place by the sea where my son lived. Home was Simon. Simple as that. And I'd soon be with him. Nothing else mattered. I'd hand over the disc, receive my fat reward and be on the next plane to Sydney.

'How's that kid?' Ted asked, as if he'd peered into my mind.

'He's fine.'

'Good,' Ted said. 'Australia; healthy place for a kid. Have they checked his school out for asbestos?'

I reassured Ted on this point and he went back to his work. I picked up my jacket. Looked around the newsroom. If I played my cards right I might not ever have to come back here. A whole new life could be waiting. The thought of it pepped me up. I would begin again.

My phone rang.

'Sam?'

It was Felicia.

'Thank God I found you.'

'I'm just on my way out,' I said cheerily. 'Catch up with you when I get home.'

'I'm not at home.'

'Where are you?' I heard the fear and strain in Felicia's voice and an intangible, intuitive sense of dread settled in my stomach.

'I—'

There was a pause. Then another person spoke.

'Mr Ridley.' It was Alexi.

'What have you done to her?' I shouted. Ted looked up from his desk.

'Nothing. She is healthy and well. But I can't guarantee this unless you give me disc. We found Bruce's girlfriend and her brother. Quite easily. The trail leads clearly to you.'

'Let me speak to her again.'

'You can speak to her when we meet.'

'Okay. Where?'

'Bruce McCarthy's house. In one hour.'

I took the disc out of its cardboard sleeve and held it by the edges. Suddenly I didn't want the thing anywhere near me. It was contaminated. If I had fifty of them and they were worth a million each I'd still give every single one up to have Felicia back in one piece.

It was all my fault. She'd met Bruce because of me. Gone to his place. Found his body. Now she'd been kidnapped and was probably being tortured by the former Soviet hulk who no doubt collected body parts as a hobby.

And she was pregnant. I shivered.

I was supposed to hand the disc over to Trip Wainwright. I was already late for the meeting. Perhaps I should call him and explain what had happened. He'd understand, of course he would. He wouldn't mind his million-dollar investment going to the Russian mob so they could extort even more money from the studio.

There was no choice. I put the disc in my pocket.

Ted wandered by. 'Going to try some experiments with the lighting later on,' he said. 'Nothing too fancy, just to satisfy my curiosity. Hard evidence, that's what we need if we're going to win this battle.'

'Whatever,' I said. His batty mania was more irrelevant to me than ever.

'Sam Ridley?'

I turned. Two men I'd never seen before stood there. One held out a badge. It looked official. It was probably what got him past the security guard.

'Tony Price,' he said. 'My colleague, Alastair Waring.'

I said nothing, measuring them. They looked like cops in their grey suits and raincoats. They were both pushing middle age, greying but in good condition. Slim physiques and shiny skin, few wrinkles, no bags under their eyes. Ex-cops maybe. Got into something more lucrative and less stressful, such as private muscle.

'We work for the studio. Helping them recover

stolen property. You're expected. They've rolled out the red carpet and were a little disappointed you didn't show up on schedule.'

I looked at my watch. Not that late. The studio must have been worried that I wouldn't do as I'd said.

They were right to worry.

I couldn't take on two of them. They were in good shape and were probably concealing delicate but deadly weapons somewhere. I couldn't throw myself on their mercy. They might be understanding but they wouldn't be prepared to risk their multimillion-dollar movie. The cops would be called and Felicia would be found days later, trussed in a drain somewhere.

I didn't want that.

'I was on my way,' I said.

'Got the disc?'

'It's right over here,' I said. Walked back to my desk. One foot in front of the other. Trying to think of a plan.

I walked twenty slow steps. Counted every one of them. Thought about making a break for it. How far could I get?

The disc was in my top pocket. But I reached down as though to get it out of the drawer. Perhaps I could overturn my desk, create a diversion and dash.

'There's a lot at stake here,' Tony Price said pleasantly. 'You haven't had a better offer, have you? Because there is no better offer.'

I nodded. I understood the threat. My head

pounded as I eased open the draw. I instinctively drew a deep breath, as though I was going under water for a long time.

And as my hands gripped the rim of the desk, the world went black.

Chapter Thirty-Seven

It was confusing. Dark. I thought I was in pain. There was shouting. Perhaps I'd been shot. But I hadn't heard a bullet. I didn't think I'd felt a bullet. Then I realized. The lights had gone out. Price had lunged for me and I'd fallen against the sharp edge of the desk. Waring was in there too, trying to grab my arms.

'Sam.' It was Ted, shouting across the darkness. 'Hope that didn't inconvenience you. I'm just going to turn the lights back on now, okay?'

'No!' I shouted. I had the disc. There might be a way out of this. Emboldened, I punched Tony Price in the stomach. 'Sorry,' I said. 'I have no choice.' I dodged Waring. Had to move while I had the advantage.

I dropped to the floor and wormed out of there. Fast as I could.

I broke cover and ran for Ted, dragging him to the floor.

'Stay away from that light switch, okay?'

'What—?'

'Who else is in the building?'

'Nobody, just me at the moment. The reporter is

out and the newsreader's having a quick pint before the next bulletin.'

'Keep it dark for a bit, okay?'

'What's all the racket? Who are they?'

'Don't worry,' I said. 'They won't hurt you. It's me they're after.'

I chanced a look over the desk. From the dim light of the computer screens I could see Tony Price and his mate through the desks. Sooner or later they'd get to me, the room wasn't that big.

There are two doors to the newsroom. I figured I could creep around the side of the room, past the offices and out towards the fire escape which was at the back of the building. I had no idea where the fire escape led to, because I'd never had the opportunity to use it. For some reason when we do fire drill the company likes us to use the stairs. I thanked the gods for the clutter of the room.

'Come on, Ridley,' Price said. 'What are you playing at?'

I thought I saw a gun in his hand. Waring wasn't to be seen, which meant he was probably covering the exits.

I didn't reply.

A hand clamped me on the shoulder. Ted's.

'He's got a gun,' he said. 'I'm sticking with you.'

I motioned to Ted to follow me and started crawling towards Crosbie's office. She also had a fire-escape exit.

It was a short distance that stretched to forever.

I reached Crosbie's office. The door was shut. Slowly I put my hand up to pull on the handle. Eased it down gently. It didn't squeak, it was silent and smooth. Just as gently, I pushed.

'He's coming this way,' Ted hissed in my ear.

Ted and I scampered inside like a couple of crippled crabs.

Ted shoved a rubber doorstop under the door.

'Come on,' I said. I lunged for the window and grabbed the lever, yanked it open. Ted picked out one of Crosbie's hard hats – a souvenir from some revolution or other.

'In case he fires that gun,' he said, fastening the strap.

The fire escape was maybe seven feet away. I leapt. Got out of the way to let Ted do the same. He was poised on the ledge. Looking so scared it was almost funny.

'You can do it,' I urged.

Ted flapped his arms at his sides. Looked back over his shoulder as Tony Price started thumping Crosbie's door down.

'On the count of three,' I said, trying to stay calm. Trying not to scream at him. Concentrating on staying where I was instead of fleeing in panic.

'One . . . two . . .'

The door burst open and Ted took flight at the same time. He landed on top of me. We rolled down the first few steps together. Picked ourselves up. Stumbled down the rest, the sound of footsteps behind us. We hit the ground running, across the well formed by four buildings that backed on to each other and out through a lane. Price and Waring were behind us, running.

CROSSING LIVE

We sprinted through the back lanes that cluster at the intersection of Tottenham Court Road and Oxford Street.

'In here,' Ted said. He dragged me into a basement bar that I hadn't even known existed. The place was packed, the noise level deafening.

Ted found the phone. 'I'm calling the cops.'

'Ted,' I said. 'The cops are on their side.'

Ted looked as though I'd just confirmed his every seething suspicion about the corruption endemic in modern life.

'What do we do now?' he whispered. 'What do they want?'

'This.' I held up the disc. 'It's worth a lot of money.'

Ted rubbed his eyes with both hands. 'I don't get it,' he said. 'What's this got to do with the news?'

'It's a complicated story. Why don't you wait here? You'll be safe.'

'Where are you going?'

'I've got an appointment.'

Ted shook his head. 'I'm going back.'

'They might be waiting.'

'Don't be silly,' Ted said. He straightened himself up like a soldier about to go over into no man's land. 'I've got a bulletin to put out. The news must go on.' He marched through to the front door of the pub.

I waited for the coast to clear. If I gave them long enough Price and Waring might think they'd lost me and leave.

They came into the bar.

I saw Tony Price before he saw me. The room was

so full that every time the door opened the crowd ebbed and flowed like a lazy tide.

Tony Price edged patiently through. The room wasn't that big but neither was there any space to manoeuvre. It was slow going. I couldn't tell if he'd seen me. I crouched lower, the barman gave me an odd look.

I checked my watch. I had twenty minutes to get to Bruce's house. Plenty of time under normal circumstances, but these weren't.

Tony Price was maybe ten feet away. Scanning the room. And he'd seen me.

Chapter Thirty-Eight

I bought myself some time by leaping up on the bar, running along it, dodging pints and wineglasses. The patrons protested. I apologized. Tony Price barged through the people that separated me from him.

I jumped off the bar, nearly pushing a couple of people over. Apologized again. Only five feet to go till the door. Forgetting all civility, I shoved.

I burst out of the pub. Waring was waiting. He stood in my way. Desperation made me bolder than I would normally have been. I put my head down and tackled him. It wasn't bad for a standing start. It must have been because it hurt me like hell and had him doubled up on the pavement. I stepped over him. No time for gloating. I ran down Hanway Street and turned on to Tottenham Court Road. Price and his mate were still on my tail but there was nothing much I could do. I'd think of a plan to lose them and save Felicia. Sure I would. Something brilliant would occur to me any moment now.

I dived down the steps of the tube, fishing in my pocket for change. Ran to the ticket machine, banged the money in, waited an eternity till the pink rectangle dropped into my hand. Price and Waring got there as I hit the escalators.

I ran down the moving steps two at a time, took the 'no exit' tunnel to the Central Line.

There was no train on the platform. The signs said one would be along in three minutes but London Underground's minutes don't bear much resemblance to the laws of time that the rest of us live by.

There were maybe ten people on the platform including the guy filling the chocolate dispenser. Price and Waring would have taken a line each, so one was bound to turn up here any minute. There was nowhere to hide.

I retraced my steps and waited in the corridor. Nobody showed up. Maybe they'd both taken the Northern Line. I allowed myself to hope. If I caught the train now I could still make it to Shepherd's Bush on time.

The whoosh of litter and a blast of stale, warm air meant the train was on its way. Still no Waring or Price on the platform. I descended the steps. The nose of the train was in the tunnel. I heard running feet. Could be nothing. A punter trying to make the train. I moved down the platform. Tried to look small besides two Scandinavian tourists with stuffed backpacks.

With a wheeze of brakes the train drew to a standstill and Price and Waring burst on to the platform. The doors didn't open. I pressed the button. They still didn't open.

They spotted me. Sprinted to close the distance. I nipped into the train before the two women with the backpacks. They got on together, blocking the doors. Price and Waring were closing the gap. The women got in, laughing, dumped their packs right in the way. The doors started to close. Price lunged at them. Got an arm through. The doors stuttered, closed again. Price tried to wedge the rest of his body into the too-small gap. I grabbed it, pushed it back out again.

'Safety precaution,' I said. 'Don't want you spaghetti under the train.'

Slowly, the train moved off. Only eight stops to go.

I had no doubt Price and Waring would have backup. A couple of guys, maybe three, waiting at the next stop. Or the one after that. I'd bought myself some time but it wasn't going to do me any good.

In the carriage the usual eclectic collection of Londoners and visitors was displayed. A 'youf' with his personal stereo playing loudly for the benefit of everybody else in the carriage. Two elderly women in floral dresses and grey leather shoes. The backpackers, underdressed and tanned. A worker in a suit, no doubt heading home from a shitty all-hours job, looking gloomily at a magazine.

More people got on at Oxford Circus, none of them seemed to be looking for me. I relaxed a little. It was ten to eleven.

Queensway. Two men were waiting on the platform. Peering into the carriages. The Scandinavians gathered up their things. I stood up with them.

'Hello,' I said to one of the women. 'Would you like a hand with that?' I put on my best voice and gave a slight bow. The quintessential charming Brit.

'Why, thank you,' she said in English less accented than my own, 'that would be delightful.'

'My pleasure,' I said, hoisting the bag on to my back. I nearly buckled. It weighed like a dead horse.

The train stopped. The chap on the platform was two or three carriages along. Walking briskly my way. I was counting on him not looking for a backpacker. I stepped off the train, not looking any direction except forward. Walked deliberately up the steps towards the lift.

From the mirror suspended above the platform I could see him searching the carriages. He nearly got in one, but didn't. He kept coming.

I started the stairs, the pack pressing down on me like a great guilt. The chap on my tail reached the end of the platform, realized I wasn't on the train. He looked up the stairs. He didn't say anything. He just came after me.

'Got to fly,' I said to the woman. I dumped the pack.

'Hey!' she shouted, but I was already halfway up the spiral stairs.

The man behind me increased his pace.

I'm not fit. I'm really not. I'm too busy abusing myself with cigarettes and alcohol and bad food to be bothered with gyms and jogging. But that night my body didn't know it. That night I was Ben Johnson on speed-enhancing drugs. I cleared the steps, not even realizing there was no air in my lungs. I slammed my card in the machine and jumped over the barriers before it had time to open. I dashed out on to Bayswater Road, saw a young bloke about to get in a cab, yanked him aside and said, 'Sorry, mate. Matter of life or death.'

'What'd ya do that for?' the taxi-driver grumbled.

'So you could get fifteen quid for taking me to Shepherd's Bush.'

'Get in,' he said.

I had five minutes.

We did all right till we got to the roundabout. There they were digging up the road. The traffic was clogged on all the approaches.

'Shit,' I said, banging my hand on the window in frustration.

'Look's like you'll miss your appointment,' the cabbie said. 'Not much I can do.'

I looked at the empty stretch of road heading into London. We could do it easily on the wrong side of the road.

'I'll make it a hundred quid.'

The cabbie scratched his chin.

'A woman's life is at stake.'

'I can't afford to get no ticket.'

'Two hundred.'

The cab snaked out of the queue. On the wrong side of the road. At the roundabout, the cabbie turned right instead of left. Also the wrong way. A cacophony of horns advised us we were doing the wrong thing. Traffic steamed past us, horns wailing. The cabbie was enjoying himself. His flagrant traffic violations were punctured by shouts of 'yee-ha,' and 'ride 'em'. He cleared the other side of the roundabout, narrowly missing a truck and a bloke on a scooter. We sped up the wrong side of Shepherd's Bush Green, drivers shaking their fists or a single finger. The cabbie slapped the steering wheel. I thought I heard him humming a few bars of 'Rawhide'.

On Uxbridge Road, the cabbie eased back on to the left-hand side of the road and became a regular driver again. 'What street you want?' he said, lapsing into Cockney sullenness.

He pulled into it. I got out my wallet. Threw all the cash I had and my business card at him. 'Call me for the rest,' I said.

'Hey!' he shouted, but I had to go.

I was already late.

Chapter Thirty-Nine

There were no lights on at Bruce's house. No sign of the Mercedes.

I banged on the door. No reply.

'I'm here,' I yelled, in case they hadn't heard the banging.

Nothing.

I banged and yelled till my fists were sore and my voice was hoarse. There was only silence from inside the house. Maybe I'd got the message wrong. Either way it didn't matter. Felicia was dead because of me. I kneaded my face with my hands, wondered how I would begin to cope with this. Then I pulled myself together. They wouldn't kill her until they had what they wanted.

And I had the disc.

'Mr Ridley?'

It was Paul Fraser, from next door. 'I heard the noise. What's happening?'

'Can I use your phone? It's an emergency.' I needed to call the cops, the movie studio. Anyone.

'Of course. Come in.'

The Fraser house was dimly lit. We padded down the corridor into the kitchen.

'It's right there,' he said. 'Is this about Bruce?' He seemed tense.

'Sort of,' I said.

'Someone went into the house tonight,' Paul Fraser said.

'When?'

'About an hour ago.'

'They come out?'

'Not that I've seen.'

'It's very important that I get in there too. They've got a friend of mine.'

Paul Fraser nodded sadly. 'I'll show you.'

He took me out to the garden, lifted a plank back off the wooden fence and slipped through the gap. We were in Bruce's garden now. In an upstairs window I thought I could see something moving. A black shadow against the darkness.

'You were Bruce's ghost, weren't you?' I asked as he led me round to the kitchen door, took a key from under a pot and unlocked it quietly. 'What were you looking for?'

'When the law isn't fair sometimes it's necessary to break it,' he said.

I went in on my own. Told Paul Fraser to keep clear and not call the cops.

Through the kitchen there was little light. I walked gingerly.

I felt my way to the living room. Then there was light.

I was drenched in it, blinded by it. I put my arm up to protect my eyes.

'Give us the disc.' It was Alexi.

'Where's Felicia?'

'She's safe.'

'I want to see her.'

'She's upstairs.'

'I want to see her.'

'Show him.'

The light slammed off. I closed my eyes tightly, trying to banish the psychedelic colours that danced in front of me.

'Sam?'

'Felicia? Are you okay?' I still couldn't see anything. I tried to trace her position from her voice. She was on the landing, I guessed.

'I'm fine.'

'Hand over the disc and you'll be reunited,' Alexi said.

'Bring her down here.'

'Let's go up together, shall we?'

'I want her down here.'

'You don't have a choice.'

'I'm going to take the disc out of my pocket and put it on this chair,' I said slowly with assurance. I was pretending. 'And Felicia is going to come down those stairs and we're going to walk out of here together. So bring her down.'

'You leave the disc on the table.'

'Felicia, are you okay?'

'She will be,' Alexi said. 'You both will be.'

I had no leverage and he knew it. I took the disc from my pocket. Laid it down on the chair.

'If I find you've hurt her, I'll find you and make you sorry,' I said.

Alexi seized the disc.

I dashed up the stairs, stumbling because I couldn't see.

Felicia was sitting on the bed in Bruce's room. Her back was very straight but her hands and feet were taped together. I snatched at the bindings.

'Did they hurt you?'

'No.'

'Everything's okay,' I said. 'You'll be fine. We're going to go now. I'm taking you home.'

I unwrapped the last of the tape and eased her off the bed. Coaxed her towards the door. Started her down the stairs.

She was looking past me. Downwards, aghast.

The Russian and his sidekick were laying down a liquid carpet. Of petrol.

The Russian walked to the door, bent down with the lighted match.

'Please don't,' Felicia said. 'I'm pregnant.'

The Russian didn't even look up at us as he applied the match to the petrol.

The flames took off with a hollow sucking sound and within seconds the ground floor was covered in fire. There was no safe way to descend the stairs, unless Bruce had an asbestos suit in his wardrobe.

Felicia sank to the floor, moaning. 'I'm terrified of fire,' she gasped. 'I can't deal with this. I can't!'

'Come on.' I grabbed her, pulled her up.

Bruce's bedroom was no good. The windows opened but there was a sheer drop to the street below.

The second bedroom was similarly laid out, with no viable means of escape. I dragged Felicia, crawling and choking now as the flames raced up the stairs into the bathroom. There was a small frosted window that refused to open. I picked up the chrome wastepaper basket and threw it through. Picked away some of the jagged glass as I peered out. About ten feet down was a narrow brick ledge. It was another ten or twelve feet to the ground.

'I'm not going out there,' Felicia said. 'There has to be another way.'

'I'll help you down.'

'No,' she said. 'I'm going back. Someone will have called a fire truck. They'll get me from the window.'

'This is the only way.'

'I can't do it.'

'You can. You have to.'

She backed away, panicked, coughing as the smoke invaded the small room.

'In a few minutes we'll be unconscious from the smoke. Is that how you want to die?'

I could hear sirens. 'See?' Felicia said. 'The trucks are here. They'll have one of those cherry pickers.'

'You can't go back.'

'The upstairs isn't burning yet.' She backed out of the bathroom, pushed the door open, the paint had begun to blister. She blundered on to the landing. The heat was searing. I held my sleeve across my mouth. Grabbed her again, pulled her back as the place where she was standing was engulfed in flame.

We shut ourselves in the bathroom. I ran the taps, drenched the towels and everything I could find.

'We can't wait any more,' I said as gently as I could. 'We stay here and fry or we try and get out. Decide in the next three seconds.'

Felicia sniffed. Straightened up. Crying, she hoisted herself up towards the window. Scrambled for a grip, cut her hands.

'What about the baby?' she said.

'Mother comes first.'

'I can't. There's nothing to hold on to.'

'There's a window ledge about three feet over, try and grab that.'

'It's too far.'

'Try.' I grasped her round her knees. Smoke curled at my feet, weaving its way under the barriers I'd placed at the door. I almost swooned from the heat.

Felicia got her hands on to the sill and for a few awkward moments was suspended horizontally, screwing up her courage. She eased herself out and took hold of the ledge. I held her for as long as my injured shoulder and the shards of glass under my armpits would allow. She inched herself down till she couldn't take her weight any longer. She dropped about three feet, landed on the ledge, teetered for a minute then got her balance.

I breathed relief.

I wrapped towels around my hands to protect them from the jagged edge of the window. Sized up the situation. I was big and the window was small. I eased myself up on the sill.

The bathroom door caught alight and the small room filled with smoke and heat. I wriggled ineffectually, trying to get myself enough height to grab the window that I'd told Felicia to hang on to. My hand gave out and I fell back into the room.

I landed neatly between the bath and the toilet. Blood poured down the front of my jeans where I'd scraped my skin on the broken glass. I'd lost all feeling in my injured hand. It was too hot. Too smoky. My lungs felt tight. I started to choke. I lay as low down as I could. The floor was wet but the water was heating up fast. Flames were devouring the door and making steady inroads into the walls. Tiles cracked under the heat.

I pushed myself up. The heat had become so intense it felt as if my skin was peeling back.

As the flames skimmed towards me, I hauled myself on to the toilet seat. Knocked out the rest of the window glass. Levered my way up till I was sitting on the window ledge. With my useful hand I reached out and grabbed the other window ledge as firmly as I could. One hand and a shaky grip wasn't going to hold me there, but there were no more favourable options. I dragged my legs out with sheer will power, dangled for a minute on the one hand and dropped into space as a burst of purposeful flame and black smoke spurted out of the window.

The ledge broke my fall, which was the best that could be said for it. I landed half standing but couldn't get balanced and toppled still further. Felicia reached out to grab me but I pushed her away.

It seemed to take a long time, the last bit. I felt as though I was falling for ever. The point where my soft body slammed into hard concrete I don't remember at all.

Then I heard voices and sirens. I tried to make sense of it all and couldn't. I passed out.

The first thing I saw when I came around was Tony Price talking to a uniform. I was in an ambulance. It was surrounded by fire trucks and police cars. There were many different types of flashing light to make my head swim.

Tony Price came up. Stood looking stern.

'They had Felicia.'

He shrugged. 'We got them,' he said. 'No thanks to you. A neighbour called the cops.' He held up the disc.

Felicia had been tended by a paramedic. She came over. Tony Price looked her approvingly up and down.

'Maybe I'd have done the same thing.' He strolled off, hands in pockets.

'Everything okay?' I asked.

Felicia looked furious. 'Ridley, how can you ask me that after you've just thrown me out of a burning building? My God, man, I could have been killed. My baby could have been killed. There are days when I do not believe you're for real.'

I grinned. Everything was okay.

The paramedics wanted me to go to the hospital but I said I felt fine. I almost did. A little woozy from the smoke. But not too bad, considering. And I had something else to attend to.

Chapter Forty

I knocked on Paul Fraser's door. He invited me in.

David French was sitting at the kitchen table.

'My lawyer,' Paul said.

I sat down. Paul put a glass of water in front of me. I slurped it greedily.

'I won't tell about you breaking into Bruce's place,' I said. 'I can't cast any stones in that direction. And I can't imagine you killed Bruce if you planned to sue him for stealing your sister's money. What would be the sense in that?'

Paul Fraser cast a look at David French.

'Bruce was going to give Curly and Peter up, wasn't he? That's why they killed him. They were the ones who cheated old ladies, not him. He didn't need to, he had extra money with illegal courier work.'

'He'd agreed to testify,' David French said. 'He had done some work for Curly and Pete and knew a bit about their business. A couple of people, including my client, have had High Court judgements against them in the past but they haven't been able to make them stick because the assets couldn't be found.'

'Bruce knew where they were,' Paul Fraser went on. 'He was helping us build our case.'

'All because of the ghost?'

'I had a look through his papers a couple of times,' Paul said. 'At the beginning, after Margaret recognized Curly Ryan going into Bruce's house. It wasn't right, but it had to be done, we thought they must have been still involved somehow. Bruce caught me once – I thought he'd gone out. I thought the game was up, but he didn't have his glasses on and I realized he couldn't see at all well without them. I simply walked out. Later, he asked us if the house was haunted and we told him it was. He thought he'd seen a real ghost. After that, the idea seemed to seize him. He wanted to believe it. He was anxious to make amends.'

David French chimed in. 'We now know Curly and Pete own the whole building they live in, which is worth several hundred thousand pounds. We'll get the money out of them one way or another.'

The cops offered me a lift. I had them drop me at work. I decided to ignore the fact that I was suspended without pay. The story was mine.

Just before dawn John Jennings rang me. 'You don't deserve this,' he said, 'but I'm going to tell you anyway. We're making an arrest in the Bruce McCarthy case.'

'Curly and Pete?'

'Charles Ryan and Peter Walker to you.'

'What happened?'

'An eyewitness who'd been wrestling with her conscience decided to come forward. Chloe Ward.'

'I'll just bet.'

'The threat of a prosecution for smuggling was enough to make her realize the benefit of a mutually cooperative arrangement.'

'How did she know who killed Bruce?'

'Bruce was working for her. He was supposed to call her immediately he got back from the States with the discs. He didn't because an evil fairy had planted a greedy seed in his heart, and he was thinking of ways he could make the deal more profitable for him. Chloe Ward was suspicious, went over to his place in the middle of the night and saw Peter and Curly leaving.'

'Why didn't she go in?'

'That was her mistake. She wanted to find out what he was up to, she didn't think he had the nous to do anything off his own bat. She decided to wait and see. The irony was, Curly and Pete didn't know anything about the movie. They just wanted to shut Bruce up before he blew the gaff on them. Chloe could have nipped in and taken the discs and continued with the original deal with Alexi and everybody would have been more or less happy.'

'Except Bruce.'

'Instead, Lana and Lindy had planned to swipe the discs from Bruce early the next morning because they knew he'd been sleeping off a serious hangover. Lindy had created a big scene at the party he held the previous night and had found out where the disc was. Lana went over in the morning and picked it up.'

'Too bad for them there were two discs, not one. Why didn't Lindy take it the night before?'

'Bruce didn't know she knew Lana. If Lindy took the disc Bruce might have suspected. If Lana did it, no blame could attach to Lindy. And Lindy knew what Bruce was up to because he'd asked to be introduced to her brother. He was thinking about duplicating the discs and putting them on the market himself. Lindy's brother told him it wasn't practical unless he had all the infrastructure in place. You've got to do something like that damn fast because once a pirated movie gets on the market there are a thousand other crooks who'll do what you did and before you know it, it's on sale at every car-boot sale in the country and your margin is nothing.'

'So Bruce had probably decided the quickest thing was to do what Chloe had paid him for. Lindy and Lana decided it was now or never.'

'Curly and Pete went over to Bruce's the night he died but he had company. So they waited till everyone had left and went back.'

'They argued. That's what the neighbour, Amy French, heard.'

'Probably. We've checked out their van. They had it steam cleaned but there's traces of Bruce's blood type in the floor carpet.'

'And when Chloe finds out Bruce has died, she figures out Lana's stolen the discs. Or guesses. Lana had the contacts and Chloe knew her from when they hung out in Barcelona. Chloe tackles Curly and Pete but they say they didn't take the discs, didn't even know they existed. She forces them to help her find Lana. It is her profit margin, after all.'

'They call me because they figure a journalist on a story is not going to keep quiet when he gets an interview with the wife of a murdered man.'

'It was clumsy, but it worked,' Jennings said. 'Nobody said they were geniuses.'

When I came back from the studio Marlowe was at my desk.

'Not a bad story,' he said.

'It'll come in useful for the job hunting.'

'About what happened at the board meeting. That stalking business got way out of hand.' He had the grace to look ashamed but not the grace to apologize.

'Yeah, well. I learnt important lessons about who can be trusted.'

'It was Rick, you know. He told them.'

'Rick? How did he know?'

'Good question. I didn't tell anyone but you.'

'I really don't care,' I said. I didn't. I started packing up my things. I was leaving.

'Your suspension's been revoked.'

'Gee, thanks.'

'I spoke to Tobias. We've agreed we want to keep you.'

I'd already said thanks, there didn't seem to be anything else to add. I wasn't even sure if I wanted the job back. Too bad there wasn't going to be a reward from the movie studio after all. That cash would have come in handy. I could have afforded to tell Marlowe what I thought of him.

You have a son, I reminded myself.

Lyall brought me coffee after Marlowe left. 'They found that girl, Lindy, in a deserted warehouse in King's Cross,' he said reading from the wires. 'They beat her up, but she's going to live. You know it was a complete coincidence she knew Lana while she was going out with Bruce McCarthy? And look what it got her – makes you wonder if there is a god.'

Poor Lindy. Poor Terry. I made a note to pop over to the caff and drink some toxic tea with him.

'No doubt Alexi and his chum'll be extradited to Russia, convicted in a flashy show trial and before long a generous, well-placed bribe will have them out on the streets of Moscow,' Lyall went on. He dropped the wire copy on my desk.

'Thanks. I feel so much better.'

'This woman called for you.' It was Fern, who'd crept up as usual. She smirked as she handed over the piece of paper that had Kyle's number on it. I looked at the number Fern had written down and the message, written in her round hand. It gave me a thought. I opened my drawer, looking for another piece of paper.

'You hear about the young boy who cried wolf?'

I sat down in Crosbie's office uninvited. Crosbie looked up from behind her bifocal spectacles. She was browsing the latest *Vogue*.

'What are you talking about?' Her hand strayed unconsciously to a file at her side. I opened it. It was full of newspaper clippings. I leafed through them.

'The whole thing was a wheeze, wasn't it? To get attention. To get people talking about you, writing stories about you in the tabloids. A little bit of media coverage. Boost your profile. Is your contract up for renewal?'

Crosbie's face fashioned into an expression of shock and outrage. But her eyes were wary.

'You were jealous of Stacy Taylor and her success so you hired Fern to make a few phone calls and write a note. Loiter a bit outside your place in case anybody bothered checking. Fern was a mistake, by the way. She's screwing Rick and will do anything for him. I know because that's how he was able to tell the board that I was your stalker. Nobody else knew except Marlowe. You paid Fern, I take it. She certainly seems to have a nice new wardrobe of clothes. Was it worth it for the press coverage?'

Crosbie snatched the file back, snapping it shut. She smiled condescendingly. 'Don't be silly, Sam. You've been under a great strain. Try and take a few days to rest.'

I took out the note the stalker had written. The one I'd meant to give to the cops and hadn't got around to. I sighed. Two can be patronizing.

'I saw her at your house.'

Crosbie made a valiant effort keeping the smile in place. 'So she came to visit me? So what? I don't think anybody's going to believe these preposterous allegations.'

'Why'd she run off, then?'

Crosbie shook her head like I was suffering a massive delusion.

'Marlowe wanted to find out what was going on so he asked me to check it out. He was suspicious about you wanting to have a show about stalking and he didn't want City Radio looking any more silly than it already does.'

'I don't have to listen to this,' Crosbie said gruffly. 'Get out of my office.'

'Want my advice?' I stood. 'This would ruin you if it got out. You'd better be very, very nice to Fern. Do whatever you have to do to make sure she keeps her sullen mouth shut.'

I laid the note Fern had just handed to me alongside the stalker's. The handwriting matched.

'This, too, is pretty sloppy,' I said.

I went home. Felicia was already there. Putting things in boxes. Most of her stuff was gone. My flat seemed light and airy.

'Hi,' she said, awkward.

'Hi.'

'How are you?'

'Fine. Where're you going?'

'I've found a place. In Bloomsbury. Nothing fancy but it'll do.'

'Oh. I didn't know.'

'We haven't had much time to chat.'

'No.'

'I didn't thank you. Y'know. For coming to my rescue.'

I shrugged. 'Thanks aren't needed.'

'Yes they are.' Felicia stacked some boxes. 'That woman, Kyle, called. I straightened everything out. She was very understanding. She's a nice person.'

'Yes, she is.'

'You gonna call her?'

'Yes. I owe her an apology.'

'You gonna go out with her?'

'No.'

'Why not?'

Because she's not you, I wanted to say. 'Because she's firmly fixed in my mind with the most humiliating evening of my life' was what I did say.

Felicia grinned. 'You *were* disgraceful,' and she started laughing.

I hadn't put enough distance between me and that night to find it that amusing but after a bit her pearly giggle became infectious. We laughed so much we grasped each other for support. Then we realized what we were doing and sobered up instantly.

I wanted to kiss her. I didn't. I stood there, so close I could breathe her perfume and built pictures in my mind of what we could do together. They were silly ideas. I put them aside just as quickly as I thought of them. Me and Felicia? It was absurd. She wasn't interested in men like me. She liked rich men. Well-educated and successful men. Men with status. Even by a rough count I wasn't in the ballpark. She knew it too. She stepped back, began stuffing more things in a box.

Above our heads we heard the stomping that meant the neighbours were home and were about to crank their stereo up so the whole street could enjoy it. But they didn't. They walked around a bit then there was silence.

'They haven't played it loud for three days now,' Felicia said, looking smug.

'I'm assuming you had something to do with that.'

'Maybe.'

'Did you call the cops?'

'Cops have better things to do. No, I sat them down and had a quiet chat. Made them see reason.'

'Just how was that, exactly?'

'It was easy after I recognized him.' Felicia squeezed the box shut. 'The guy's the leader of a band called The Funky Dildos. There've been a few tangles with the law because he has a drug habit that would floor an elephant and now he's on probation. It's a wanky celebrity probation, but it is probation none the less.'

'But there's no law against having parties while on probation.'

'No. But I told him if the noise didn't quiet down I'd tell the cops I saw him selling heroin to children.' Felicia banged the top of the box with a flourish. 'Not a squeak ever since.'

I helped her take her stuff down to the car. Fussed around getting them in the right way, trying to sort out the thoughts that were swamping around my brain.

'Okay, then,' she said when we'd got the car packed. 'See you at work.'

'I . . . yeah. Suppose we will.'

'Thanks again.' She leant forward to social kiss. I caught her face in my hands. Meant to kiss her on the mouth but diverted to the weasel option of the forehead. She seemed confused and stepped away. Stood as if waiting for me to speak. I wanted to say something but there was nothing that wouldn't sound banal or ridiculous.

'It's been—' I started, but we both started together. Halted.

'—interesting,' she finished.

'Yeah,' I said. 'Interesting.'

'I haven't lived with anyone for a while,' she said. 'Claude didn't really count.'

'No.'

'You're not bad,' she said.

'Not bad? This is the thanks I get for rescuing you from a burning building?'

'Fancy dinner in Chinatown? My treat,' Felicia said hesitantly. 'You know, as a proper thank-you.'

'Okay. I know this great place.'

'You do not.'

'I do.'

'Only because *I* told you. You don't know the first thing about food, Ridley. I'd rather accept restaurant advice from a golden retriever than from you.'

'That's not fair. I'm a connoisseur of pizza.'

'The ones that come in frozen cardboard boxes.'

'Don't they all come like that?'

Felicia smiled as she slid behind the wheel. Her fabulous, thousand-watt smile. 'I'll call you later.'

'Okay,' I said, letting a sliver of hope through.

I waved her off. Went upstairs feeling good.

I meant to sleep.

Hell's Kitchen

by Chris Niles

Cyrus is a millionaire recluse – and a serial killer. His first victims are Gus and Susie, a young couple whose desperate search for a place to live in New York lead them fatefully to his door.

Tye is a beautiful young woman from Notting Hill who has come to New York to live off wealthy men. But when suddenly dumped by her lover she is forced to become more inventive to keep money in her pocket...

Quinn is a young man who has made a career out of being a writer who doesn't write. He's currently dossing at his brother's place, but when his brother seduces Quinn's girlfriend he realizes it's time to move on.

Marion is Gus's mother and she's come to NY to find her son and daughter-in-law who have disappeared into thin air.

All four are about to come together in a sparkling black comedy!

Published as a Pan Original in February 2001 at £5.99. Extracts from the opening scenes follow here.

Prologue

He hit thirty like a speed racer hits a brick wall.

It was like he woke up one day and found 'This Must Change!' tattooed on the inside of his head. The 'this' being his life.

Sometimes he even imagined he'd heard it out loud, but that couldn't have been. He didn't go in for mystic mumbo-jumbo. He was a modern man.

His revelation – he'd decided to call it that – was this: Here we are, stuck on a rock, light years from anyplace. Sure it's pretty and we're evolving as fast as we can and everything, but basically it's the dead ass-end of some minor probably-forgotten part of the universe – did anyone ever stop to think the reason nobody has visited from space is not because they didn't have the spaceships, but because they didn't give a damn?

So here we were, on Earth, talking amongst ourselves. And even if every single person, fish, tree and single-celled amoeba died, and the planet frizzled up into a congealed ball of carbon, who would even notice besides ourselves?

But even though we – that is Earth dwellers – are clearly unimportant we're still obeying the Big Plan of the universe. We've still got gravity and tides and we revolve around a star, just like every place else. We're part of the plan.

It's simple – everything follows a plan, no matter how big or small. It was like fractals – one millimetre of coastline looks exactly the same as one kilometre.

Once Cyrus came out of himself, looked at the big picture, it was easy and natural to see himself cutting a smooth swathe, like a planet's trajectory. Confident. In charge. Composed. Grooving right along with the cosmos. He did matter. He was part of the plan.

So things were going to be smooth from now on. He was going to make this happen. He was going to change the way he saw himself and the way he dealt with the world. He would know where he wanted to go and just go there. No messing around, everything smooth and nice.

He'd found the Master Motivator who'd begun showing him the way.

Chapter One

After three months in Manhattan, Tye Fisher had decided Upper West Siders didn't deserve New York.

It was a question of attitude. The city had everything one could want. Any perversion or passion could be catered to, at any time, in any place. Pleasure – or pain – could be ferreted out in a dungeon in the Lower East Side, in the foot-fetish bars of the Village, in the dance clubs of Harlem, in obscure ethnic restaurants in the garment district. New York was the cultural capital of the modern world, the most influential city in the most influential country on earth – the new Imperial Rome. And it was the beginning of a new century.

But this news had not reached the busy burghers west of Central Park, who thought they were living in the suburbs.

In the city that never slept, they dined early – in stodgy, over-priced chain restaurants with bad service and worse food. They stuffed their faces from plates piled high with the blandest of fare, drank Coke out of containers as big as buckets. Then they were home and tucked up by ten because one's personal trainer came at six.

It was a style desert. On the rare occasions when they could be prised away from the sweatshirts which advertised their colleges, the women looked as though their outfits had been pieced together in the aftermath of an explosion at a crafts fair. Matrons who clogged the pavements with triple jog-strollers and Golden Retrievers wore cutely embroidered jumpers, blouses with flouncy collars and chunky, woven overcoats in variegated shades of sludge brown. Men wore trainers with everything and talked incessantly about golf.

Tye had expected so much more. Americans had invented the twentieth century and everything that made it stylish, then turned their backs on it.

Not that she had tired of the city, far from it. It suited her just fine. She liked the way it made her feel. You could be anybody here; just jettison the old persona like a spent fuel chamber and speed off with a streamlined new one. As far as she was concerned, the booster rockets had dropped and stage two had begun.

Tye had had high hopes of Adrian, whom she'd met at a party in London and had followed across the Atlantic on a vaguely articulated whim. Adrian was an artist. He was good-looking in a Daniel Day-Lewis verging-on-a-nervous-breakdown sort of way and he liked to make barnyard noises during sex. This was no problem at all for Tye, who, possessing many faults of her own, considered they made her ill-qualified to judge others.

But there was no denying Adrian could be difficult. He was moody, over-bearing, pompous and ill-informed. He had only a spasmodic interest in personal hygiene and was, by most educated standards, a terrible artist. This, too, was perfectly fine by her. Tye could see past the surface and appreciate Adrian for an attribute more true and lasting – three-thousand square feet of Art Deco duplex on Riverside Drive.

It was a beautiful apartment, possessing all the right real estate buzzwords – spacious, sunny, south-facing balcony. It was obscenely, fatly large. People gasped with admiration and envy when they walked in. Tye, who'd initially only planned to stay for a few weeks, had known Adrian was the man for her the minute she had laid eyes on it.

But now, it appeared, Adrian was kicking her out.

'My wife is coming to visit,' he mumbled one morning over breakfast.

'Precious, you didn't tell me you were married,' she said sweetly. Not that it would have mattered one jot.

'I am.'

'Congratulations. And how long is your wife staying?' Tye was thinking she'd take a short holiday. Perhaps a little spa in the desert. On Adrian's money, of course. If he was going to inconvenience her, he'd have to pay. She'd act put out, just so he wouldn't get the idea she was a complete push-over, then skip off to Arizona and bury herself in expensive mud. Bliss.

'For good.'

'For good.' Tye repeated it calmly. It couldn't be as bad as it sounded. There had to be a way around this. Perhaps Adrian would set her up in her own apartment. She began mentally shopping for furniture. Fifties perhaps, or modern. She could never decide. Perhaps a classy mixture of both – yes, that was it. Eclectic. She didn't want to be pinned down. None of his art, of course. Not while she had eyes in her head.

'She has been living in France, but she is tired of France.'

'It can so easily happen, if one isn't careful,' Tye said sympathetically.

'Lyon is so provincial.'

'I'm very sorry to hear that.'

She pursed her lips as if to stop the question that was poised to emerge from them. No time for niceties. If Adrian was disinclined to give her an explanation for the wife-in-absentia, then she wasn't going to drag it out of him. Not her style at all.

'She comes here next week. You have to leave,' he said.

'But where will I go?'

Adrian shrugged. 'Wherever you like.'

Not back to London, that was for sure. Too many burned bridges in old London town. Besides, she liked New York. It was flash and brash and not nearly as important and sophisticated as it liked to think. She could admire that kind of attitude.

The problem was finding a place to stay. She had no real money of her own and no friends here. She needed a kind and preferably rich stranger to take her in – that would be the quickest, easiest way out of her problem.

She began a mental check-list of Adrian's friends.

Boring businessmen, mostly. Boring didn't matter, of course. Rich was the only qualification. But who was rich enough? Most of the people Tye had met through Adrian were either married, with their wives firmly in residence, or probably didn't have the kinds of funds needed to keep her separately in a style that made her feel relaxed.

But Lonzo Parker might be a possibility. A chunky guy who did something in mergers. He'd given her the eye at a cocktail party only last week. Poor old Lonzo. He played squash, never drank anything stronger than caffeine-free Diet Pepsi and thought his red braces the last word in sophistication. Still, he *had* mentioned the loft in Soho.

Tye had a weakness for lofts.

As she packed, she selected a pair of her tartiest knickers, crotchless black with purple bows, and put them at the back of a drawer in the walk-in closet. They'd been a gift from Adrian. She was sure Mrs Adrian laboured under no illusions about her husband, but the knickers would at least remove the agony of doubt. She sprayed some of her strongest perfume – one that she knew Adrian didn't like – onto the hanging fabric sweater-holders and tipped some more into the fabric conditioner compartment in the washing machine. It would linger long enough for wifey to get the message.

Three hours later she was done. Her life packed in two suitcases and ready to go. She smiled as she stepped out onto the street and inhaled deeply.

It was a brand new day.

Chapter Two

Gus and Susie Neidermeyer knew that finding an apartment in New York was going to be tough.

They'd read the articles in the *New York Times* about walk-in closets in the Village renting for two grand a month. Two grand! They'd heard the horror stories from people they knew who'd live there – the cockroaches, the sleazy landlords, the greedy doormen, the bribes. But they were mentally prepared. Gus and Susie had never done anything without careful research. That's what had made them honor students at school back in Michigan. And it was going to stand them in good stead for the rest of their well-thought-out lives. So when the Big World called, they answered gladly, but a little cautiously. Planning, research, groundwork. Their motto and their mantra.

Gus had a job at a respectable insurance company where he'd be starting in a couple of weeks. Susie had had a poem and two short stories published in a Michigan magazine. She planned to get a job in publishing. Her first job, though, was to look for an apartment. Gus had wanted to go to New York ahead of her and get everything lined up, but Susie said no.

HELL'S KITCHEN

In the three months they'd been married, they'd never been in separate towns, not even for a night. Even though she loved her husband, she doubted that he'd be able to pick out the kind of place she'd be happy living in. Gus's taste was basic dorm stuff. Besides, finding their first apartment in the city was going to be an adventure. Choosing the furniture, exploring the stores in the neighborhood. Setting up their home. She wanted to be part of it from the beginning.

Chapter Three

William Quinn had found himself abruptly homeless when the landlord of his place in Chinatown died. The fatality occurred after a dispute with a rival businessmen that left the landlord with parts of his body pierced in an unfashionable way. Quinn came home to find his building surrounded by cops and ambulances and blood sprayed up the walls of the take-out food bar that occupied the ground floor. After that he had had to leave. It wasn't the bloodshed that discouraged him; it would take more than murder to pry a New Yorker from a good, cheap apartment. But a couple of days after the landlord was zipped into his body bag, his son came by and let the tenants know that things were going to be different. He had found a convenient loophole through which to force a 200 per cent rent increase.

Quinn was more than a little irritated by this turn of events, but not as much as his brother Malcolm, to whom he'd immediately turned for succour and shelter.

'Two weeks, no more,' was brother's welcoming salutation.

'Nice to see you too, Mal,' Quinn said wearily,

having schlepped his two suitcases and a laptop computer several blocks. He dumped his bags in the living room.

'You're sleeping on the sofa.'

'You mean we're not having conjugal relations?'

'I mean don't get any ideas about the spare room. I've got all my computer gear in there and it's not moving. It's very delicate.'

'Unlike me,' Quinn said, stretching his shoulders. His bags had been heavy. 'Love a cup of coffee.'

'You know where it is. You're here often enough.' Malcolm crossed his arms to emphasize that he wouldn't be running around after his brother. He watched while Quinn found the coffee in the freezer and the plunger in the right-hand drawer above the sink, and put some water on to boil.

'Go easy with that, it's expensive,' he said as Quinn ladled several spoonfuls into the plunger. Quinn checked the packet: Dean and DeLuca – strained through the nose hair of a Mongolian goat, no doubt; that was the only way the outrageous price could have possibly been justified. Mal was such a yuppie. He would make the front page of the *Times* the day he bought something that didn't have a fancy-schmancy label.

'Strong is the whole point of coffee,' he said mildly, pouring the boiling water over the grounds. 'Besides, I've had a hard week.'

'Sure. Working your fingers to the bone. What's the occupation du jour? Busboy? Doorman?'

'I have a writing job, as a matter of fact.' It was true. Quinn sipped his coffee contentedly. Shelter, work and caffeine – what more did a guy need? The pay was crap, naturally. But it was worth it to be able to contradict his brother.

'I thought you were supposed to be blocked. Mom told me not to expect the Great American Novel this year.'

Quinn stifled his irritation. Deep down, his brother was a sweetheart. Trouble was, it'd take a diving bell to get deep enough. No point in expecting him to change. 'I never said that. I never said I was blocked. Anyway, the creative process is a mystery. It depends on the whims of the Muse,' he said airily.

'The goddamn Muse,' Mal snorted. 'You're a bum. And in ten years' time you're still going to be a bum.'

'Don't worry, it's not contagious.' There were times when he wondered how he and Mal could have come swimming out of the same gene pool. 'Hey, we'll have fun, eh? Go out, have a few brewskis?'

'This isn't college, Quinn. Some of us have grown up.'

Quinn sighed. 'Where should I put my stuff?'

CHRIS NILES

Spike It

Pan Books £5.99

City Radio reporter Sam Ridley is drunk. But not so drunk that he can't spot a good story when it's dead on the floor in front of him.

And as the first on the scene, Sam's ahead of the city's news pack – but not for long. Four hours and one wrong word later, he's demoted to a hard-drinking, hard-news reporter's definition of hell: *Female AM*, the station's daily women's programme.

Ridley's gone from crime and punishment to sex and shopping in one morning.

But now a man called Shark is on the phone, ready to tell what he knows about the murder. And when Ridley dives into the murky waters Shark calls home, he's going to find himself face-to-face with loss, love, and one monster of a car repair bill.

CHRIS NILES

Run Time

Pan Books £5.99

London radio reporter Sam Ridley has hardly been in Sydney long enough to slap on the sunblock, and already his holiday's out of control.

He's got a hangover wilder than a kangaroo on a trampoline. He's cut off from the son he's travelled halfway around the world to see. He's woken up to find his new female friend murdered in the next room. And now he's on the run, in a town that thinks he killed her.

Sam knows he's being framed. What he doesn't know is who set him up. Or why.

But he has to find the answers – before the police find him . . .